RIPPLES THROUGH TIME

Cassandra Jamison

Ripples Through Time By Cassandra Jamison
Copyright February 2020
Cover Artist: Rachel Leah Photography

*To Tommy, my sister's most beautiful love story.
If we could, we would travel a million worlds
and through a thousand lifetimes
just to find and hold you again*

*Original cover featuring Tommy & Naomi Pierro in 2003
when this book was first imagined*

CHAPTER ONE

June 2020

Tess navigated through another busy crosswalk, the phone in her purse incessantly buzzing. She dug irritably into her bag and answered without checking the number.

"This is Tess," she said, squinting at another road sign. There'd been a lot of modernizing since her last visit to the small touristy town, she was starting to worry she'd gotten herself lost.

"Hey, I'm so sorry to be calling."

Tess recognized her roommate's voice immediately and wilted.

"Hi, Devoney. Sorry I answered so abrupt, I'm just distracted."

"It's okay. I know you went home to relax for the summer and probably don't want to be hearing from me."

Tess scoffed. "You already know that being home is *never* relaxing."

She paused when she found the correct street and then peeked down the busy road, searching for her uber. What'd they say the driver's name was? Jeff or Jerry? All she knew for sure was that it was an UberBlack. She assumed that meant it was some sort of black vehicle.

"Oh please," Devoney jeered. "I'm sure the grand *Corbin estate* in that posh little mountain town is better than our ghetto Denver apartment."

Tess checked the app and found the uber on the map only a mile or two away.

"You still there?" her friend's voice chimed, and Tess threw the phone quickly back to her ear.

"Yeah, Dev, sorry."

"It's okay, I know you're busy. I'm sorry to call, I just didn't know what else to do."

"No, it's fine," Tess reiterated. "I'm just trying to find my way home and was getting sidetracked. What's the matter?"

"They gave me your schedule while you're away. I've never worked with Dr. Neiderer before."

"Ah." *Hence the panic.* "He's a little rough around the edges, but not too bad once you get used to him."

"I know. No big deal." She still sounded frantic. "I'm sure if you can handle him, I can too. We've been in residency training for the same amount of time. It's just that nobody went over the new system with me yet and I can't seem to get into our files. He's going to rip me a new one if I don't figure this out."

"It's simple, I have everything saved in my account. Just enter my pin. It's…"

A new incoming call disrupted, and Tess glanced down at her mother's number on the screen. The woman would throw a hissy fit if she let it go to voicemail.

"Dev, can you hold on just one second?"

"Okay."

She clicked over to answer. "Hey, mom."

"Where the hell are you? You said you'd be home by now!"

Tess sighed. "I said I'd be out for the afternoon and be back as soon as I was done. What's up?"

"I need you home, that's what's up."

Ugh. "I have somebody on the other line. I gotta go."

"Do not hang up on me!"

"Then hold on." She switched back over. "Dev, you still there?"

"I'm here."

"It's a capital T, underscore, Corbin. Then my birthday 0407."

"Thanks. Again, I'm so sorry to be calling!"

"It's fine, you can call any time. Just let me know when you get in."

"Yeah, it looks like I'm set. Thank you!"

"No problem. And I know Dr. Neiderer can sometimes seem condescending, especially to women, but don't let that stop you. Put on some thick-skin and show him what you're made of."

"You got it."

"Solidarity sister! Girl power and all that."

Dev laughed.

"And don't forget to water the plants while I'm gone."

"No promises on that. But enjoy your vacay!"

"I'm with my mom, so not exactly a vacay, but thanks. Oh, hey, looks like my uber just pulled up. I'll call you later." Tess hung up and opened the door to a stocky man in his mid-forties.

Don't take rides with strangers, they used to say. *Never meet up alone with people you found on the internet.* So much for that.

"Tess Corbin?" he asked.

"Sure am!" she said, slipping inside.

Her phone began to jingle again. "Oh, I'm sorry," she muttered to the driver, and clicked to answer the call. "Hello?"

"What do you mean, *hello*?!"

Tess rolled her eyes at her mother's histrionics. "Hey, mom. Sorry. Forgot you were holding. What's up?"

"Are you almost here? I've been waiting for hours!"

"Almost. Bye!"

She hung up and stuffed the phone into her purse, then glanced up at the driver who was eyeing her intensely through the rearview mirror.

"Overprotective mom," she uttered with an embarrassed shrug.

"I know the type."

She grinned and peered out the window as the car rolled out into traffic.

The driver only partly seemed to be watching the road and she found the heat of his eyes unnerving.

Tess shuffled her blond curls to cover her face, but when she heard him suck in a sharp breath, she knew that she'd already been recognized.

"Hold on a minute," he gasped. "Corbin? I didn't even make the connection until just now! That's you though, right? You're that Corbin girl! Holy crud, your dad was a rock *legend*! And you are his *spitting* image. What the hell – in *my* car? You live up here?"

Tess's heart sank. "Born and raised," she said with a well-bred smile.

"I would have bet you lived in some big city by now. Never would have pegged you for a country girl."

She forced another smile.

"Man, I barely recognized you."

"Oh, nobody does," Tess murmured, waving off his acknowledgment. "I'm not famous at all really..."

He yanked up a magazine from his dash. "I knew it!" he exclaimed, passing it into the backseat. "My wife makes me get her this magazine every week... she's a huge fan."

Tess took it and looked down at the thick celebrity tabloid.

"Could you sign it for her? She'd kill me if I didn't at least ask."

Tess was taken aback. "Really? She'd want *my* signature?"

"We're both huge fans of Asher Corbin."

"My dad *was* amazing, but I'm nobody important."

"We both would be honored to have the signature of the daughter of the greatest musician that ever lived."

Tess sucked in a sharp breath and then smiled softly at him. "Asher Corbin really was great, wasn't he?"

"Her name is Bernadette."

"Right," she said, pulling out a pen and flipping through the pages. Her heart sank when she found the page that the magazine cover had advertised. It took up the entire folio.

She was surprised as how happy she looked in the photograph.

Perhaps she should have pursued an acting career rather than an ER doctor since she was apparently very good at fooling the masses.

In the photos Killian Seymour stood beside her, radiant as ever. He was the most beautiful thing she'd ever seen, both in film and real life. America had been starstruck when the two found each other.

She and Killian had been holding hands in the photo, a happy couple walking swiftly down the L.A. Boulevard, ignoring the paparazzi.

They really were the most gorgeous and perfect duo imaginable – according to the tabloids, at least.

There had been a lot of photos taken of the two over the past year, but Tess remembered specifically the one in this magazine.

It was during her most recent trip out of Colorado. Killian had been pressuring her for months to move away from her home state permanently, but she told him that she'd only consider it when she was done with school.

He didn't see much merit in that.

Tess's father, after all, had been an American Rock Star. There wasn't a single person in this country who didn't know his music. Even high schoolers, who'd been born after his death, recognized his name.

It was only natural that the public would assume that his offspring would marry well and carry on the talent and riches. Tess may have had no desire to follow her father's legacy, but Killian was exactly what was expected for her.

The man had begun his first step toward acting at the tender age of seven, starring in commercials and sitcoms before taking on the theatrical role at nineteen-years-old that literally changed his life.

After grossing more than $1.92 billion in box-office receipts worldwide, the teen heartthrob had transformed seemingly overnight into a movie superstar.

Killian Seymour seemed to take well to being worshipped by teenage girls and young women everywhere.

Tess had been thirteen years old when she first saw Killian come on-screen. And like many others, she fell in love instantly. His combination of ease and youthful exuberance gained him many other movies and Oscars in the years that followed.

Tess almost couldn't believe it when years later she got the chance to meet him. No longer that doe-eyed thirteen-year-old girl who would hang his photos in her locker, but rather a twenty-five-year old emergency room resident who just felt foolish to be so star-struck while shaking his hand.

With her mother's pushing, Tess and the famous bachelor began dating soon after.

Nobody, including Tess herself, thought they'd last more than a month. Commitment wasn't exactly what the playboy was known for.

Their one-year anniversary last month was quite the topic of conversation among celebrity gossip.

The picture she was looking at now had been taken only about week ago when she'd flown in for one of his many functions. She remembered how Killian had scolded her for not dressing right for the photographers. The picture had been snapped by one of the paparazzi while Killian dragged her out of their luncheon to purchase more suitable footwear.

She glared down at the photo, at his unenthused expression and how his fingers possessively clutched her arm. Had it really been about the shoes, or had he pulled her away due to the meaningless conversation she'd been having with one of the up and coming actors in Killian's newest movie?

Pursing her lips, she scrawled out a sloppy note:
Bernadette,
Best Wishes. I'm sure my father would have loved to meet you
– Tess Corbin

She handed it back up to the driver and gazed out the window as he continued to gush about his favorite musician.

Sometimes it felt as though the entire world knew more about her father than she did. He'd died when she was only twelve, before she had the chance to see him through anything more than just a child's eyes.

"I heard there was a movie filmed up here in one of these mansions," the driver mused, staring in awe at the houses. Each one they passed seemed more gigantic than the last. "Was it your place?"

"Afraid not. Mine is that one over there," she said pointing. "You can drop me off at the gate."

"No way, I'll bring you in all the way. That's a heck of a long driveway you've got there."

He was already pulling onto the property before she could object. They made it to the house quickly and the car was still rolling when her door suddenly flew open. The driver slammed on his breaks and Tess leapt back in surprise. Then she saw her mother with the black door handle in her fist.

Tess sighed heavily. "I'm so sorry," she said to the driver. "Thank you for the ride. They didn't give me the option to tip you on the app."

"Oh, that autograph was plenty."

She pulled out a few bills from her pocket anyway and handed it over as she slid outside. Her mother slammed the door behind her and scowled as her fingers ran down her long platinum hair. She could barely keep her hands off it. It was probably the most beautiful thing about her, crowned with salon highlights, perfectly layered and brushed to the side.

Not that she didn't have a knockout figure too. The woman paid good money to be sure of that. Plastic was her badge of honor, and it was everywhere – in her lips, cheekbones, forehead, chin, and definitely boobs. Tess wondered idly what the former Miss Montana would have looked like today if she hadn't funded a fortune into turning back the hands of time. Maybe there'd be a few lip wrinkles, a dab of crow's feet, and a patch of sagging here or there. Perhaps there would have even been some faded smile lines from back before her face had lost flexibility.

Sometimes that stiffening in her features made it difficult to read her mother's emotions, but Tess was fairly certain that Mrs. Corbin wouldn't have been smiling today even if she could.

"So that's what took you so long. Waiting on an Uber car? Really? Do you know how many unwashed people have sat in that seat before you, Tesla?"

Tess sneered at both the snobbery and her full name. Her mother and father had considered themselves profound when they named their celebrity baby after the world-renowned Nikola Tesla. Luckily over the years the public had caught onto her nickname and her mother was now the only one to use it in its entirety.

"I left my car at an auto shop in Denver, you already know that," Tess groaned, climbing onto the wrap-around porch.

"Why you won't just upgrade is beyond me."

"I like my little Saturn."

"I can only imagine what people think when they see you driving around in that thing."

"That I must be a terrorist."

"You are the only one who thinks you are funny, young lady. Hold on," she said, grabbing Tess's arm to stop her. She urgently began clawing her nails through Tess's curls, tearing some strands of hair out in the process.

"What are you doing?"

"You're just such a mess!"

Tess ripped away from her and began back toward the door when the realization hit her. She stopped and turned around. "Wait a minute. Your earlier call rushing me home, and now fixing my hair? Killian's not here, is he?"

"He flew in this afternoon. Wanted it to be a surprise."

Tess chewed her lip. She had hoped this visit home would be an escape from that other world.

"Go on!" Mrs. Corbin chided, giving her a shove. "He's waiting in your bedroom. Act surprised!"

Tess rolled her eyes and stepped into the foyer. With a deep breath she headed up the stairs and pretended to do a doubletake when she finally opened the door and found him sitting on her bed.

"Hey, baby doll!" he said, flashing that Hollywood smile that made millions of women swoon.

"Killian! What are you doing here?"

"Whisking you away!"

"Huh?"

He climbed off the bed and scooped her up the way he liked her to hold onto him, arms around his neck and legs around his torso. She never cared for that; it was showy and clichéd. Luckily the Colorado winds had stopped her from wearing skirts ages ago.

"Tell the truth," he beamed. "Am I a good surprise or a bad one?"

She grinned. "Definitely good!"

She really *was* a good actress when she tried to be. Sometimes she even fooled herself.

Killian should have been a dream come true, but deep down she knew that it wasn't perfect. Her roommate Devoney had reasoned that it might have just been her insecurities holding her back. Of course, nobody would have an easy time with half of the civilized world wanting her man. But Tess didn't think that was it.

She had hoped to use this time away to figure it out. Did she honestly love the man enough to see a future with him, or was she just enjoying his fame while trying to please her mother?

She always thought falling in love would be such an easy, accidental thing. It was in the term itself. To fall, by definition, was to tumble freely without control. She never thought that it would take so much effort and convincing to love a person. At least not in the beginning when things should have still been exciting.

"I have a whole night planned for us," Killian said, setting her back on her feet. "It's going to rock your world."

"What's the occasion?"

"Showing my girl how much she means to me requires a special occasion?"

She forced a smile. "I guess not."

"Do you have suitable attire, or will you need to shop?"

"What's the dress code?"

"To impress. Always to impress."

"I think I have something."

"Then I'll be back in two hours to pick you up." He gave her a soft kiss and headed out the door.

Tess hurried for the shower as soon as he was gone. Luckily, she had stored a lot of her red-carpet gowns at the house rather than her apartment.

She checked the clock on her way down the staircase and was glad to see she made it with only a few minutes to spare.

"How do I look?" she asked her mom, doing a quick spin.

Mrs. Corbin grinned as well as her tight face would allow. "You clean up effectively when you make the effort!" Her approving smile then pressed into a hard line. "Haven't I already seen you in that?"

Tess's grin dropped. "Just once."

"But it was on the red carpet. Your picture has already been taken in it dozens of times."

"This dress cost more than my rent. I spent $5,000 on this dress. Trust me, you will see me in it again."

"I hope you at least remembered to Febreze it."

Tess scowled at her little joke and handed her the matching shoes to help her into.

Killian was of course punctual. Tess thought she noticed a slight furrow of his brow when he saw her dress, but he recovered quickly with a sweet kiss before he led her into the waiting car. She was glad he didn't spoil the night by asking her to change into something else. Since when could a girl buy her own dress and then not be allowed to wear it however many times she wanted?

The drive was shorter than expected, but Tess hadn't anticipated their destination to be a heliport.

"You ready for the ride of your life?" he asked, climbing out of the car.

Tess tripped a little on her dress, as she rushed to follow. "This is the surprise?"

"No, the surprise is where I'm taking you."

"Why in a helicopter?"

"Why not?"

Because this was over the top even for him.

It made her nervous what this big reveal was going to be.

"Good evening, Miss Corbin," the pilot said as they climbed inside.

"Good evening," she answered nervously as Killian began to strap her into the harness. When he was finished, he strapped himself in beside her and the helicopter rose smoothly into the air.

She held tensely onto Killian's arm, watching out the window as the bright lights of civilization became smaller and darker below them. Soon everything was pitch-black.

"How long of a flight is it?"

"Not long," Killian said. "Don't be nervous, Phillip is an excellent pilot."

Tess wasn't sure if it was really the flight that scared her, or just whatever he had in store for them. All of this was mindboggling and not at all how she expected her day to go when she woke up that morning.

After exchanging information with air traffic control, the pilot reached back to give Killian a bottle of champagne.

"Compliments from The Rocky's Aviation."

Tess hadn't noticed the wine glasses that sat in elegant holders near the helicopter door.

"Wow, Phillip, this thing must be a real babe magnet for you," she said, taking the glass Killian poured for her.

She thought she saw the pilot smile, but it was difficult to tell in the darkness.

"It's the company's helicopter, Miss Corbin," he smoothly replied. "Though I wish I could say it was mine."

"Still you should know for future reference. Babe magnet!"

This time he did laugh out loud, and Killian immediately took her hand. "Phillip used to be a pilot for pediatric medical emergencies," he explained, "So the aspiration behind obtaining a pilot's license was primarily for becoming a lifeline for terrified families, rather than for impressing women."

The chiding way he said it made her flush, and she was instantly embarrassed for making the joke.

Why did Killian's defense mechanism always lead to him scolding her like a child? Did he honestly think she was flirting with the man, or was his jealousy more directed at the pilot having a skill that he, himself, did not possess?

They rode in silence the rest of the flight, sipping their champagne and watching the black night until a small light beneath the aircraft slowly began to grow.

"Welcome to Breckenridge," the pilot said, slowing down the helicopter.

Tess gasped and leaned forward to stare out the window. She'd never been there before but knew the town. It sat at the base of the Rocky Mountains, known for its ski resort, year-round alpine activities, and their stunning scenery. Looking at it from the night sky was breathtaking as they flew among colorfully painted buildings from the 1880s, and past galleries and restaurants all nestled along a magically lit street that had the town seeming unearthly, almost dreamlike.

"Pretty, isn't it?" Killian purred.

Tess could only nod eagerly.

The helicopter landed just as smoothly as it had taken off, and moments later Killian was leading her into a candlelit foyer that must have been part of one of the ski lodges. A dark elegant piano sat in the dead center with a crystal vase on top filled with white roses.

Killian opened a large set of double doors where the candlelight theme continued into the restaurant. A dome-like ceiling that held a breathtaking chandelier enveloped the refined tables covered in white linen. *Beautiful* was too dull a word for it.

"Where is everybody?" she finally whispered. "Is this place even open?"

"They are. For us."

"Just us?"

This was new for Killian. He usually liked to show off. Nightly gossip that became morning headlines were his specialty. Such a romantic gesture done in privacy was baffling.

He took her hand and walked her through a glass door that led them to an outside balcony that overlooked the otherworldly town of Breckenridge with a backdrop of the Rockies beyond it.

Killian slid behind her, one hand wrapped around her waist while the other clipped her chin, turning her face around to kiss him.

"Ready for your surprise?"

"This isn't it?"

He smirked and nodded at the balcony door where several waiters walked in carrying heavy dishes with dome covers. Tess was completely mystified.

Killian waved to the servers, and they removed the fancy covers, but it wasn't food on the plates, it was engagement rings – every shape and size imaginable. The soft light of the moon and restaurant made the diamonds shimmer like a hundred fireflies. Her mouth dropped open.

"Pick one," he said. "Any ring you want, it's yours."

There were at least a dozen velvet lined boxes on each plate and thirteen servers.

He grinned again at her stunned silence and took her hand. She let him lead her down the length of the balcony, looking at each display.

When they reached the last one, he got onto his knee and that was when the photographer emerged.

Tess blinked wildly at the blinding bug like zap of his camera. Music began to drift from inside and she recognized the song.

"I had to call in a few favors," Killian said with a wide grin and she realized then that the artist must have been there singing it live for this insane proposal.

Now that he was done posing on his knee, he stood up and swept her into a dance that the photographer captured from every angle. This story would be all over the tabloids in no time.

She could only wonder what would happen if she didn't say yes...

CHAPTER TWO

Tess decided to call up some old friends, hoping it might distract her from the anxiety that had been building up since Killian's recent proposal. Catching up with these people were part of the reason she came home for the summer, after all.

Unfortunately, most of her old pack were either too busy working on their careers or away on vacation. Joel was the only one who could make himself available last minute.

Tess gave him a tight hug when he met her on the parking lot. They'd chosen to meet in the oddest place imaginable, where Joel had figured no paparazzi would find her – Half Hallow's historical museum. Even seventeen years later they could both still reminisce on their second-grade field trip to the place.

His son, Matthias, was almost the age they had been when they first met.

Tess gave the five-year-old a fist bump, then he ran away blushing.

"Matthias has got a bit of a crush on you," Joel admitted. "Ever since you drove out for his birthday and spent that week with us."

Tess laughed. "Well, I'm flattered, but you'll have to remind him how old I am. Half the time I have to do math just to figure out how old that is."

"Yeah, we were born during the dark ages when people barely took photographs and they actually believed the saying, *pictures don't lie.*"

Tess snorted at that one.

"Speaking of which," Joel said pulling up his phone. "I've seen some new ones of you recently."

"Oh God." She already knew what it would be, and her heart pummeled at the photos from that ridiculous over-the-top proposal. "How do they get these things done so quickly? That only happened the other day!"

"They manage to write an entire article on it, but you can't find a minute to shoot me a quick text with the happy news?"

"I haven't given him an answer yet."

"Not according to Mile-Higher.com."

"It's just gossip," she murmured, holding up her bare left hand. "I didn't even choose a ring yet. I never said yes."

"Did anybody tell Killian that?"

"It's complicated."

Joel sighed. "Most people would probably think you're nuts for saying that, but I get it. The dating world sucks. I just went on a first date last week and showed her a picture of Matthias. She asked me what I was going to do with him once *we* had kids."

"You're kidding."

He scoffed and clicked off the article, then glared at one of the popups. "You see this ad for that genealogy DNA testing? People are getting stupider and stupider."

"Why's it stupid?"

"Because it's not about your family tree, it's about them owning your DNA. Even after you die, they can still access and use it."

"I thought when you became a cop, you'd be stepping away from all that conspiracy theory stuff."

"It's a known fact that these companies make way more money from selling your DNA than they do off the kits."

"What would be the point?"

"Tess, you're training in the medical field! Obviously, DNA can be sold to test for diseases and to research new treatments."

"Well that doesn't sound bad to me."

"Fine. If you're good with your DNA floating around, then go for it. But as someone in law enforcement, I can guarantee that we have access to it as well."

"Once again, I don't see the problem. We want people who have committed crimes behind bars."

"Is it fair to everyone else though? That you send in your spit and activate your account online and suddenly they have your name, credit card number, and most importantly they have a perfectly collective clean sample of your DNA in a freezer forever?"

"You're starting to freak me out."

"Why? You didn't already do it, did you?"

Tess sucked in her lips. "Killian did a while ago, for the both of us. He wanted to know about our history and heritage."

Joel shook his head.

"Stop it! You're making me feel like we're in that stupid science fiction movie that Killian filmed last year. Sometimes I wish I could just go back to when the world was less complicated."

"You and me both," he groaned, following his son into an adjoining room.

Tess trailed slowly behind, admiring the antiques and old photos.

She paused halfway down the room and did a double take at one of the portraits.

The man in the photograph was weirdly familiar. Broad-shouldered with light brown hair and ice blue eyes... she was sure she'd seen him before.

"We're heading outside to the old buildings," Joel called, as Matthias dragged him through the double doors.

"Meet you there in a sec," she called and pulled out her phone to snap a picture of it.

Maybe this photo had been featured in an article or book cover. Or did this man just *resemble* somebody that she recognized? An old actor or someone she once knew...

"May I help?" a quiet voice asked behind her, and Tess jumped a little. She looked down at the plump woman standing behind her, gray hair in a bun just like her granny.

"I'm sorry," she whispered, shoving the phone back into her pocket. "Am I not allowed to take pictures in here?"

"Of course, you can," she said with a sweet smile. "I just noticed that your family left you behind while you seemed a little troubled over here."

"Oh, they're not my family. Just close friends."

"I see. I'm Ms. Tuttle. Is there something I could help with?"

Tess grinned awkwardly. "You're going to think I'm nuts, but this guy just seems so familiar. Has anybody else commented on it? That he resembles someone famous? Or has he been featured in a news spread or documentary?"

"Not that I'm aware of."

"Okay. Sorry again." Tess was about to walk off when the woman said,

"His name was Heywood Paxton. Lived from 1871 until 1900."

Tess stopped, intrigued. "Short life. Even back then, right? What was he, twenty-nine?"

"I guess nowadays we'd call his death a cold case. Nobody really knows how he died."

"You mean, he was murdered?"

"Body was never found. One day he just disappeared. Truth is that his case had always been an interesting one in this town. His father owned quite a large piece of land on what's now called Newberry Road. When he died, Heywood took over the Paxton farm. He was probably only twenty-five at the time. He had also lost his wife, Emeline, not long before this."

"That's awful. How is it you know so much about him?"

Ms. Tuttle grinned. "My grandfather, God rest his soul, owned the market in town. The Paxtons were all frequent customers of his. I've heard the stories firsthand and have been telling them for years."

"I'd love to hear more."

Her careworn face went soft. There probably weren't many who cared to hear these stories. Meanwhile Tess, herself, still wasn't even sure why she did.

"Emeline Delacourt and Heywood Paxton shared a forbidden love," Ms. Tuttle began quietly. "As it turns out, Emeline was already promised to a gentleman from a nearing town. Heywood as well had been expected to marry a family friend – a young lady by the name of Cavaliere. Although it's not known if his marriage was forced, I do believe that it was at the very least expected."

"I know the feeling," Tess heard herself whisper.

"Heywood and Emeline decided to marry in secret. Both of their families banished them when they found out and they eventually left Half Hallow."

"But I thought you said he took over the family farm."

"He did. I'm not sure why, but Heywood did eventually return with a two-year-old in his arms, but not with Emeline."

"What happened to her?"

"Her death has always been a mystery, much like his."

"Like some kind of curse?"

"I've never much believed in those." The old lady shrugged a little as she stared up into the portrait. "Some tales claim that Heywood had done it himself. Rumors of his insanity spread, that he'd gone mad and buried her body deep in a forest somewhere."

"But to kill the woman he loved? The mother of his child?"

"Well, the theory goes that maybe he was in over his head and got rid of her in order to get back into his family's good graces and take over the farm that he was promised. From what I've been told, the bulk of the town did believe it. To be honest, it wasn't all that farfetched. After his return, he devoted himself entirely to the farm.

Not to mention he was a hunter, and many knew he had a talent for a clean kill. There has been a lot of talk about his death in the years that followed. Some wonder if a vigilante had finally done away with him. Or if his guilt had led to suicide."

"Such a sad story."

"I always thought the suicide theory was more likely. His young daughter had passed only days or weeks before his disappearance, so one can only guess where his grief had steered him after experiencing such tragedies at such a young age."

Tess glanced again into the eyes in the portrait. So much heartbreak. It made her feel wrong to ever complain when her life wasn't nearly as grim.

There was a canvas displayed beside the portrait, but it was only covered in slashes of paint with no design or reason for them. It looked messy, just a bizarre tangle of angry strokes and colors.

"What's this?"

Ms. Tuttle walked over to the painting. "When Mr. Paxton disappeared, he left everything behind. This was just one of the artifacts pulled from the house."

"Did he paint it?"

"Well, he's no Picasso, but yes, I believe he did." Her soft smile fell as she perused it again. "If you ask me, it looks like the whole thing had been on the losing end of a fit of rage."

Tess frowned and moved in closer. Ms. Tuttle was right. It had a lot of angry depth and emotion to it. The man had a dark past, and this seemed such a small trace of his complexity.

Ms. Tuttle nodded toward the door. "It looks like your friends are back, uh... oh dear, I didn't catch your name."

"Tess Corbin."

Slight awareness arched Ms. Tuttle's features.

Of course, her name would spark recognition. Half Hallow had a welcoming sign at its entrance that introduced it as the home of former rock legend Asher Corbin. Everyone knew his family's name. It was one of the reasons she left.

People tended to view celebrities or even the *children* of celebrities as legendary creatures rather than average human beings, always judging them at a higher standard.

She still cringed when she thought back on the unflattering photograph taken of her when she was sixteen years old, and how people had begun to speculate that she was hiding a teen pregnancy.

It had destroyed her self-esteem back then when she'd been most vulnerable to the opinion of her peers.

Now that Killian had proposed, she was sure those pregnancy rumors were about to resume.

She wished she could live someplace where such cruel scrutiny under the facade of journalism and celebrity news did not exist. A third-world country was probably the only place where such ideals weren't part of human nature.

Saying goodbye to Ms. Tuttle, Tess hurried off to meet Joel on the other end of the room. "You boys ready for lunch?"

"Yes," Joel remarked, "But before that, Matthias had the most perplexing question."

Tess grinned at the playfulness in Joel's earnest statement. Somehow, he always had the ability to play with his son, while also talking to him like just another buddy at the bar.

"Matthias, go on and ask Tess what you just asked me."

Matthias blushed a little, but with a small smirk he peeked out from behind is dad and said, "I wanted to know what would happen if the whole world stopped farting... I mean, like, how long would it take for us all to realize it happened?"

"That's deep," Tess said, keeping a straight face, pondering this. "Maybe it's already happened though. When was the last time you farted, Matthias?"

He giggled. "I don't know."

"Oh God," Joel said with feigned panic. "What if all mankind has already simultaneously lost the ability to pass gas?" He grabbed his kid and began to tickle him, making a raspberry sound to feign flatulence. "Oh, never mind."

"That wasn't me!" Matthias howled in laughter.

Tess chuckled as she followed the duo out onto the parking lot.

She couldn't remember Joel ever being this goofy and fun before Matthias. Though Joel and Skylah were no longer in love with each other, it was good to see how much love they had for their son. It wasn't surprising that the high school sweethearts didn't work out, but if Joel *was* going to have to be linked to another person for the rest of his life, Skylah was a fine choice. The mutual respect they had for each other as parents was inspiring.

She wondered if her and Killian would ever be capable of that. She did want to be a mother someday but wasn't sure if she wanted to parent beside a man like Killian. She couldn't imagine raising a child in this world where other trolling mothers publicly bashed one another under the guise of the first amendment.

The way that Killian kept her in line in order to please his fans had her wondering how much worse he might be with his own offspring.

Vibrations from her phone made Tess jump as they reached the parking lot. She ripped it out of her pocket and opened the text.

Killian – On my way back to Colorado. Big surprise for you, Mrs. Seymour.

Her heart jolted at the surname, still so unsure.

Clicking out of the text message, she went instead to her pictures and pulled up the one she'd just taken in the museum. It was unnerving how drawn she felt to this stranger.

Heywood Paxton, she mused.

****

Killian was leaning casually against the wet bar, downing a glass of red wine when Tess got home from the gym the following afternoon.

He had been dressed in his customary button-down shirt open just enough with snug jeans and a thick belt. His hair was gelled to perfection.

Tess sighed. He never told her what time he'd be arriving, and she had hoped it wouldn't be right after her workout.

She stood for a few seconds admiring the view, embarrassed by her own tousled hair and sweaty body that wasn't anything like the sexy glistening goddesses that Hollywood portrayed. She was pretty sure she smelled too.

From the feet of space, he simply gave her that slow, lazy smile that rendered most girls speechless.

Tess instead felt incredibly insecure.

"Sorry that I'm gross," Tess said, combing her fingers through her hair. "I finished a mile on the elliptical right before I left the gym."

"Even sweaty, you look stunning," he purred, walking toward her. "Spandex form-fitting workout attire is something that I definitely approve of."

"No really, I have B.O. like you wouldn't believe." She backed up instinctually. "Let me shower and have a do-over."

He was close enough now to realize how right she was. He might have even grimaced.

"I'll pour you a drink," he said backtracking to the wet bar. "Meet me outside when you're decent."

Self-consciously, Tess backed out of the room. She had just made it up the stairs when Mrs. Corbin popped out of the master bedroom.

"The man can't stay away, can he?" Her face twisted suddenly, looking her over. "And you came home looking like that?"

"I was just getting in the shower."

"I suppose it doesn't really matter if he saw you like this. You already landed the whale. Congratulations!"

Tess grunted with surprise at her mom's startling hug. "What does that even mean?"

"You got the number one most famous bachelor to agree to marry you! You're Amal Clooney."

"I am not Amal Clooney, I haven't even said yes yet."

Mrs. Corbin followed at her heels into Tess's bedroom. "He told me that you just hadn't chosen the right ring yet, not that you said no."

"I didn't say no either. He never really asked. Just sort of assumed."

"Well, that's not wrong of him, is it? You've been exclusive for a year now. It only makes sense that this is the return he gets on his investment."

Tess scoffed and walked into her bathroom. "You make it sound so romantic."

"You know how hard it is for a woman to get a guy like Killian to commit. And you did it! If you're smart, you'll make sure to be pregnant by this time next year."

Tess snarled with disgust as she got the shower running. "You can't be serious."

"Every girl he's ever been with has hoped to bear his child. It ensures security for life… or at least eighteen years."

"Is that how you landed dad? Popped a few holes in his condoms? Fibbed a little about your birth control?"

"Your father and I were different."

Yeah, yeah. When Asher died, Mrs. Corbin wasted no time at all finding his replacement. Fourteen years later with six failed marriages and some bad financial investments, Tess had become the woman's new insurance plan. That wasn't love. Tess's mother knew nothing of the topic.

"Kids aren't meant to be some kind of bargaining chip," Tess grumbled, walking past her to her closet. She chose an outfit in a hurry and then walked back to the bathroom. "Killian's waiting for me."

Mrs. Corbin threw her hands up in surrender and Tess closed the door.

When she was clean and dressed, she found a glass of wine waiting for her on the wet bar. Grabbing it on her way outside, she was a little surprised to find that Killian had been waiting for her in the most secluded part of her backyard.

She knew the place well; it was her childhood playground. It felt as though she hadn't stepped foot on it in ages.

Killian's mouth quirked into a small smile when he spotted her.

She pursed her lips in response, unsure of how she felt to have found him there. "What are you doing all the way out here, babe?" Her voice sounded normal, though her fist clenched around her wine glass as she asked this.

He eyed her charismatically. "Looked like a nice spot."

It was. The place was beautiful, and from an entirely different lifetime.

"Why haven't you shown it to me yet?" he said, coming closer. He took her arm and waved at the scenery. "This is gorgeous, baby doll! That lake and this treehouse… though I can't imagine why *that* tree would be used to sustain it."

Her heart jolted. He didn't know the history here, there was no reason to be upset. She took a breath and smiled softly at him. "My dad built the treehouse for me. I picked the spot."

He didn't glance at her, instead he leaned back to look it over. "Good structure, I suppose. Nice view. But then again, if it was possible for a tree to catch herpes, this would be its posterchild."

She inwardly snarled at him.

Of course, the tree she'd chosen as a kid wasn't perfect. The damn thing had a gnarly bulge only about three feet from the ground. When she was a kid, she thought maybe a basketball had been growing beneath the bark.

"Its faults are what make it different," she murmured.

He snorted at that, clearly not understanding.

"Look at it, Killian! No other tree in the world looks like this one. It's special."

"Yeah, like a kid who eats the Christmas ornaments kind of special."

Her heart dropped. She never minded playful banter but didn't care for it when it came to something real. He never asked *why* the tree meant something to her. He didn't even pause to try and understand that it was one of the few good memories she had with her late father. Perhaps a man like Killian wasn't capable of understanding *real*.

She grimaced inwardly, but forced a smile when she said, "Things that don't mold into what society tells us is perfection are still beautiful."

He furrowed a brow at that. "You must've been an ugly duckling in your youth."

Tess physically winced. She couldn't even stop the disappointment that ran through her body.

Apparently, he didn't notice.

"You don't have to worry about that anymore, baby doll." He grabbed at the bottom of her shirt, pulling her into a kiss.

She knew that she was just being sensitive and gave him a kiss back before twisting around. She reached out to touch the knot on the trunk in front of her as she sipped her wine, patting it as though it would have been insulted by Killian's earlier criticism.

It was so silly. She hadn't seen the thing in years, but now it all came spiraling back. Like a child with an imaginary friend, or a little girl who truly believed her dolls lived – sometimes as a child Tess had played that the bump in the tree was a face and that it, too, was alive.

She must have been lonely back then.

It never was easy finding true friendship with her father being who he was. In truth, she was lonely even still.

"My dad wanted to tear the tree down," she finally admitted to Killian. "He tried endlessly to reason with me when I told him that I wanted it to hold my treehouse." She sucked in a deep breath at those last memories that she had of her father.

She hated to admit that things had changed since then. That beautiful man had died, and that little girl left with only the comfort of a tree's imaginary face had grown up. It was time to put childish things behind her.

Letting out a deep breath, Tess turned around to face Killian. If she was lucky, *he* would be her future. He was everything that her father would have wanted for her.

He gently took her hand and kissed it.

She wished it gave her the same butterflies that she'd read about in those beautiful romance novels. That kind of love probably didn't exist in anything other than fairytales.

"I have been good to you," he said softly, "haven't I, Tess?"

She was taken aback by that question. "Of course," she forced out.

"I've always felt that relationships such as ours should be built on honesty and trust."

"That goes without saying," she whispered, uncertain of where this was going.

Killian smirked and pulled a small velvet box from his pocket. "I want you exclusively for myself. Let's make it official then." He opened it and the diamond inside glowed multiple shades of light under the sun.

Her heart sped up. "I thought... wasn't I supposed to pick one out, myself?"

"I think this one suits you best." He twisted it around her left ring finger. "Let me care for you as a husband should."

She swallowed hard and stared into the gigantic and breathtaking diamond.

It was exactly what a girl of this generation would hope for. It was beautiful and expensive and perfect. Outwardly, Tess knew that this was everything she wanted and deserved; this was exactly what should have been expected for an all-American girl like her.

Inside, however, she reminded herself that an engagement meant so much more than a pretty piece of jewelry and a sensational proposal. There was more to marriage than a stunning spouse and financial coverage for her mother's building debts.

As for Killian, there was still so much she needed to learn about him. The man had always respected possessions more than he ever did people. She needed to know that he loved her as a partner and wife and not just as another of his exclusive belongings.

CHAPTER THREE

June 1900

Heywood stroked Saturn's mane before giving the horse a hard push out of the stall. Granting the stable floor with a quick glance, he tiredly grabbed the pitchfork.

He felt like he was roasting inside that barn house. It had only *just* become summer, and already a heavy wave of steam, too humid for Colorado, had taken over Half Hallow.

The soiled shirt was already clinging to his chest and arms. He poked his pitchfork into the array of compost, feeling the swarm of muck melt into his sweat.

His head ached, but he only pressed harder into his work. Thoughts of Emeline pulsed unwantedly through his mind, of what she would have thought had she seen him now, back at the dairy farm.

He balanced the pitchfork against a beam, then trampled outside.

This damned heat! He couldn't take it anymore!

Removing his sweaty hat, Heywood reached for the canteen he'd always kept on his side. Slanting his head back, he emptied what was left of the water over his face, washing away the grime.

God, he felt old. Days like these made him feel in his sixties rather than twenties.

He could still remember when he had first begun working with his father on the farm. He was only a skinny kid then who knew very little about the pride of real work. It wasn't until he became an adult that he realized how important agriculture was. By keeping his cattle, he was producing the milk that the town members lived on. Though he may never live to see the kind of money that men at the steamship companies were getting, he was proud of the success he'd made of the family business.

As his gaze swept the property, Heywood noticed his lackey, Gabriel Bruno, skittering from the house. Gabe had been fourteen years old when he started working at the Paxton Farm, an eager kid – maybe a little too eager to become a man.

It had been a year since then, and Heywood never regretted hiring Gabe. Though somewhat of a loner and perhaps a bit socially awkward, he was hard working and seemed to enjoy farm work much more than Heywood ever did.

"Mr. Paxton," Gabe called out as he drew closer. "Your brother just rode in. Says he's waiting for you in the front."

Heywood squinted at the boy. Theo was there? He unintentionally clenched his teeth, shoving the hat back onto his head.

"I s'pose you weren't expecting him?" Gabe asked.

"Don't reckon I am." Heywood gave his head a brusque shake. "The bedding needs to be replaced in the stalls."

"On top of it, boss."

Heywood strode toward the front door and wavered when he found the empty porch. There was movement coming from inside though, and he impatiently headed in where he found Theo helping himself to a drink from his stash in the kitchen.

"Well, go on right ahead!" Heywood jested. "Why don't you make yourself at home?"

Theo set the whisky bottle back on the wooden countertop. "Don't mind if I do." His eyebrows lifted as he held the cup out toward his brother. "Care for some?"

Heywood warily shuffled forward and put the cap back on his bottle. "What could possibly bring the Sheriff 'round these parts so late in the afternoon?"

"Just wanted to drop by. How are things?"

"Fine," he answered shortly, glancing out the window toward the barn. He began to wonder how Gabe was doing with the heat and the shoveling. "I'm just hoping we see a break in this heat wave. I don't know if I can take another week like this."

Theo nodded. "Didn't really come to talk about the weather. I meant how are *you*."

Heywood relented. "Alright," he muttered.

"It's been four years."

Heywood gritted his teeth. He didn't need reminding of his wife's death anniversary. "I know how long it's been."

Theo stilled, and Heywood wilted. It wasn't his intention to snap at his brother, but he also wasn't about to play dumb either.

"What are you *really* doing here?" he asked, though he had a good enough idea and wasn't in the mood for it.

This wasn't the day to come at him with another offer on the farm, but the man was tireless in his efforts. Heywood had no interest in selling his livelihood so that Theo could finally have his piece of the inheritance. He wished he'd give up pestering him.

"I already told you why I'm here," Theo said.

Heywood was apprehensive to believe him.

"I just know this day has been rough for you."

Heywood flicked off his hat and smacked it against his leg. "I know what day it is and I'm handling everything just fine. So, if there *is* another reason you came, let's just get it over with."

"It's okay to be angry."

That calming voice made Heywood fume.

Theo set down his cup. "Look, I didn't mean to step on your toes, kid! You've just been dealing with a lot lately, so I thought I'd come by to give you some company."

Heywood's eyes flicked up at him mistrustfully. "That all?"

"Well yeah." Theo combed his fingers through his thick dark hair. "Also, me and the missus decided that you should get away from the farm more often. It's high time you come over for another dinner."

Heywood snorted. "So, it was Grace who put you up to this visit."

"It was the both of us."

Heywood arched a brow.

"Well, *she* decided for the both of us."

Heywood scoffed and flicked back on his hat. "Well, I hate to wreck any plans, but it's not a good time."

"Why the hell not?"

"I'm just not up for any more games, is all," he said, beginning out of the room.

Theo reached out and took his arm. "What does that even mean?"

Heywood tugged his arm free. "You can't honestly believe I'm that ignorant. That every time Little Lotty and I pay a visit, Miss Antoinette Cavaliere just happens to be stopping by for flour or eggs or milk."

"What can I say? The woman likes to bake. Some of her breads are very big."

"Really? That's the excuse you're going with?"

Theo let out an embarrassed scoff. "Sorry, kid. We don't mean to be sneaky about it, but I guess we just want to see you settled down already."

Heywood's stomach sank. Deep down, he knew that was the least of Theo's concerns.

"It'll happen when it happens. In the meantime, I don't need you or your wife trying to marry me off."

Theo sighed loudly. "You know the situation, Heywood. Before dad died there was an agreement with Antoinette's father. I thought the same as you, that all would be abandoned when you went against it and started a life with Emeline, but clearly that's not the case."

Heywood bent his head, watching his feet as he started faster down the property. He could feel the broiling sweat moistening his cheeks and brow. Again, he thought of Emeline and how difficult the years had been without her. Agreement or no agreement, he could not marry another woman. Especially not Antoinette.

He busted open the barn door and allowed it to swing shut behind him, though he could hear Theo following inside.

"Hey, I'm only trying to help," he called out which made Gabe, who'd been working on the other side of the stables, perk up to watch the intrusion.

Heywood did not need Gabe telling stories in town about this argument. There were enough rumors already.

"I don't need your help," he hissed softly over his shoulder.

"You sure as hell do. In this family, our word is our bond. If Antoinette's father is still willing to hold up his end of the agreement, then so are we."

"Yeah, either that or I sell the land, right? No other option."

Theo shrugged.

Gabe was now standing outside the stable, his utensils abandoned at the stalls. "Uh, you guys want me to give yous a minute alone?"

Heywood clenched his jaw. The boy had already heard too much. *Dammit, Theo!*

"No," he said over his shoulder. "Go on about your business, Gabe." He sent his brother the evil eye on his way out of the barn. "Could you choose a worse day to lecture me?" he hissed as they made their way back out under the burning sun. "Get off my back!"

Theo drooped into an ashamed shrug. "You're right. I could have handled this better and I apologize for the god-awful timing." He put a hand on Heywood's shoulder. "There's still an open invitation for Sunday evening though. And please, for the love of God Almighty, do not make me go home and tell Grace that her preparations were for naught."

Heywood scoffed. "Lotty and I will be there."

"Thank you." He sighed and plopped down on a stump. "So, how's Charlotte handling it all this year? I know last year you told her more about her mother and her death..."

Heywood's heart sank at that. He hadn't even thought about it. For so many years he'd carried this anniversary on his own, but Theo was right. He'd told Charlotte about it on last year's anniversary. Did she remember that it was today? He'd been so distracted by his work but should have sat down and talked with her about it this morning. Maybe they should have done something special in tribute to Emeline.

Just another parenting failure on his end.

He never felt like he knew what he was doing when it came to fatherhood. It was only by God's grace that she was growing up as beautifully as she was. Emeline would have been better at this. It wasn't right that all his daughter got left with was him.

"I should go find her," he muttered turning for the house.

"You know she's not inside though, right?" Theo got up and followed him. "I looked for her when I first got here but couldn't find her anywhere. I assumed she was with you in the barn."

"She was eating a snack in the kitchen when I headed out an hour ago."

Theo swallowed. "Well, this wouldn't be the first time Lotty's wandered off. Maybe somewhere in the pastures..."

But Heywood was already shaking his head. Both he and Theo knew exactly where that daughter of his would have gone on the anniversary of her mother's death. It was stupid and dangerous, but she *was* Heywood's child, after all.

The sun was already getting low by the time the two brothers mounted their horses and headed off to the mountains.

The local main street of Half Hallow was placid during this time of day. Most wives were home cooking dinner, and most men were already there waiting for it.

The route was familiar to Heywood, but for all the wrong reasons. He hated the thought of his baby girl out there alone at this time of day.

It was hypocritical since he had run this same path when he was her age. It had always been with Emeline though. Always sneaking out after school to that stupid tree. It was a special landmark for them, where they'd sit and talk, and even kiss when they were old enough to want to. It was where Emeline had sliced his finger against the bark, and they made the blood pact to someday leave that town together.

He tried to fulfill that promise.

Heywood shook off the disturbing memories and focused on the trail ahead. It wasn't as safe as it used to be. The wolves had been detrimental this year to his livestock. Charlotte shouldn't have wandered out there. She should have known better, especially now that she understood how her mother had died.

He winced at that thought, wishing he could forget the pathway that had been sloshed with Emeline's blood, morsels of flesh, and bones.

Heywood could barely breathe, he needed to find Charlotte before...

"Over there," Theo said, rearing his stallion.

Heywood squinted into the dim light and found her. His heart wilted as he leapt off his saddle and ran over to scoop up his baby girl.

"Thank you, God," he whispered, wrapping his arms around his six-year-old's small body. "What the hell were you doing, Charlotte?" He choked back his hysteria and kissed her face again. "You made my life flash before my eyes, you know that? You already *know* you can't go out to these parts without me. You had me scared to death!"

"You were scared?" Lotty gasped, pulling back to look him over. She furrowed a tiny brow and wiped her little thumb against his left eye. "Were you crying, daddy?" She looked at her finger, wet with his tears. "I thought grown men didn't cry."

Heywood snickered. "I'm not crying, *you're* crying," he teased.

"I think you are, Pa."

"Well, sometimes adults cry too," he muttered, giving her another hug. "When they love somebody too damn much – and that somebody is in danger."

"But I wasn't in danger, I was just going to look at the tree."

He bit down on his lip. "I understand that, Little Lotty, but this isn't safe territory. I need you to understand that there are animals out here who can kill you, just like they killed your Ma. If you want to go out these ways you have to ask me to take you."

"You would have said no."

"No, I wouldn't have."

Her eyes lit up. "Then can we go?"

He leaned back. *Well played, little lady. Well played.*

Theo shrugged. "You kinda walked yourself right into that one, kid."

Heywood glared back at his brother.

He was right though. He'd told Charlotte about the tree many times, but he hadn't taken her out there to see it since the first anniversary of Emeline's death when she was three.

Even *he* hadn't been back since. There were just too many memories…

"Please, Pa!"

"Okay," he whispered shortly. "We'll look at the tree. As long as *you* promise not to ever run off again without telling me."

"I promise," Lotty said, and grinned as he put her onto the saddle before he climbed up behind her.

His heart felt heavy as the path opened. He could still see himself running through these beaten paths as a boy, Emeline's glossy black hair flowing behind her. In his mind he saw the crimson smears they'd left on the tree with their blood pact when they were only thirteen years old.

When he closed his eyes, he also saw the blood trail in a similar looking forest that he'd followed years later to her broken body.

Emeline had been the most beautiful woman he'd ever known. His last image of her was nothing like the girl he'd fallen in love with. The grounds had been forcefully torn up from at least three or four wolves that had fought over her body, struggling in opposite directions. It was the grisliest sight he'd ever witnessed.

He couldn't breathe. He was wheezing. This wasn't right.

Theo's hand was suddenly on his shoulder. "Nobody ever said that walking through memory lane would be a pleasant outing."

Heywood glared at him and his cheesy remark, but Theo was already on full alert with something else. The man had gone from big brother to Sheriff, instantly wielding his gun.

What had just happened?

Then Heywood saw it too.

A figure swept past the trees in the corner of his eye, followed by a few howls that made Saturn rear back onto his hind legs, nearly knocking Heywood and Lotty both off his back. Heywood gripped the reins, getting the horse steady. He was close enough to grab onto Theo's reigns.

"Take Lotty," he said, passing her gently over to his brother. "Stay behind me," he added, hopping more comfortably onto his saddle and bolting forward.

Whatever it was he was chasing, surely the wolves were following it as well. He instinctively reached for his rifle as he moved down the trail.

It was difficult to tell what it was with such little light, but his gut told him this wasn't a gazelle or doe.

The path seemed to be leading away from Emeline's tree and to an opening. In the moonlight, Heywood spotted the prey immediately, but when it stood up, his mouth dropped open.

Not an animal.

It was a woman!

She looked as though she could have been his age, maybe even younger – with soft features and long legs exposed from the thighs down. What the hell could she have just come from and how had she managed to get lost here? It was easy to tell by her physical state that she'd been running hard and was exhausted.

Heywood scanned the woods and spotted one of the wolves creeping out from behind the trees. As he lifted his gun, he saw another half dozen join it.

The woman had fallen onto her side, gasping to catch her breath as she choked into the dirt. The nearest wolf bared its teeth, its hackles raised. Heywood cocked his gun as the wolf leapt. He fired quick, hitting it in the side and sending it to the ground hard.

He fired off three more shots into the pack and watched them disperse before he dismounted and stalked toward the dying animal. He supposed he could have done the humane thing and put the mongrel out of its misery, but he figured the creature wasn't worth anymore of his bullets. Instead he flipped the rifle over and slammed the stock into the thing's head, fracturing its skull with a loud crunch.

Then he turned to the stunned girl.

He stared at her, completely mystified. He'd never seen hair that was such a deep buttery gold, yet there were sections that didn't seem blonde at all. It was like looking into the swirling light and dark shades of a honeycomb.

Meanwhile she was dressed in a costly nightdress that clinched to every lush curve. Even torn and shredded, he could tell that it was just as expensive as the diamond glowing from her finger. There was no doubt that this one came from money.

"Oh my God, what happened to her?" Theo asked, approaching.

"Keep Lotty back there," Heywood ordered, then knelt to the girl. "Are you okay, Miss?"

Desperate and frightened green eyes met his just before she wilted.

"Is she responding, Heywood?"

His heart shriveled. "No, she looks severely dehydrated. Maybe lost some blood."

She must have just barely escaped the pack. How? She couldn't have possibly outrun them. Just the wrong place at the wrong time maybe? He couldn't let her die.

Instinctively he scooped her up, not sure if he should have been moving her at all. He had no idea of her injuries. All he knew was that he had to get her somewhere safe where the doctor could see to her.

His heart hammered at the thought.

No matter how much he hated the town doctor... no matter how much he wanted to run from this and only focus on his own affairs... this was right.

It was right to transfer her onto his horse and carry her down from the mountain. Even if it meant... *ugh*...

Heywood really did not want to have to call upon Emeline's father... especially not on a stranger's behalf.

CHAPTER FOUR

Heywood and Theo watched the loft where Dr. Delacourt had been treating the unconscious mystery woman. Theo squeezed Heywood's shoulder reassuringly and then moved to the open window to puff his cigar as the doctor began his descent.

The wooden stairs squeaked awkwardly under the old man's feet. They weren't used to the weight of anyone other than Lotty. He seemed tired, as if maybe their call had woken him. Though, to be fair he almost always looked tired. Heywood couldn't blame him. He'd aged tremendously since his only child's death. It was probably only his daughter's daughter that still kept him going at all.

Dr. Delacourt stroked Charlotte's hair when he made it to the ground floor, then glanced around, finding Heywood by the fireplace and walking toward Theo instead.

"I've got good news and bad news, Sheriff. Which do you want first?"

Theo folded his arms over his chest thoughtfully. "Good news."

"Does it matter?" Heywood grumbled, but neither men acknowledged him.

"She's begun coming around," Dr. Delacourt said with a sigh. "I think she'll be okay. There were a couple of scrapes and a hard bump on the head, but she doesn't seem to have lost too much blood and will more than likely recover just fine in a few days."

"And the bad news?" Theo murmured.

"She's utterly confused. I've never seen anything like it."

"How do you mean?"

"I asked her for some basic information – colors, how many fingers am I holding up – that sort of thing. And she got all of them right."

"Yeah?" Theo pressed.

"But then I asked her the date." Dr. Delacourt shook his head. "She claims to have been climbing into a tree house built on a two-hundred-year-old oak in her backyard. She claims she slipped and hit her head on the rounded outgrowth underneath… in June, 2020."

Theo kept his cool, the sheriff in him coming out full force as he nodded patiently. "So, she believes it's a hundred and twenty years later than it actually is."

Dr. Delacourt shrugged a little. "I think it's safe to say that she'll need some time to recover before I'd trust her to be on her own." He glanced half-heartedly at Heywood and then back at the Sheriff. "I'd suggest finding out if any ladies from the church have an extra room for her to stay in."

Heywood looked away. He already knew how little the man thought of him, it was no use commenting on it.

"You know where to find me if you need anything," the doctor said on his way to the door. "Charlotte, sweetheart, come give your grandpa a kiss, then you head to bed. It's much too late for you to still be up."

Heywood's lip curled at the underlying jab at his parenting.

When the old man was in his wagon, Heywood turned back around to his brother. "That girl can't stay here."

"Come on," Theo snapped. "It's only a couple days. She can't be on her own, I wouldn't feel right about it."

"What's this going to look like? It's obvious what Dr. Delacourt thought of the idea, and the town's talking enough as is."

"Since when do you care about small town gossip?" Theo grumbled. "You know I'd take her in myself if I had the room. You've got a house meant for a family. She can stay up there in your old bedroom until we find something better."

Heywood clenched his teeth.

"You're a good man, Heywood! I've got to get home, but I'll see ya Sunday for dinner."

Heywood let out a slow exhale as his brother departed, completely defeated.

He glared up into the darkness of the loft and then made his way into Charlotte's room on the ground floor where she had just begun climbing into bed.

"Hey, Lotty, why don't you come sleep in my room for tonight."

"Why?"

"I'd just feel better about it with a stranger in the house."

She scowled thoughtfully and then shrugged, following him into his room where he could be sure she was safe.

****

It was quiet when Tess opened her eyes. The bed had a musty smell but was warm and comfortable. There was a moment between that tranquility of sleep and awake that she found herself enjoying this rest despite the strange and unfamiliar atmosphere.

She stretched and squinted up into the muted light, letting her surroundings sink in. She glanced at the wooden rafters overhead, the plain cedar headboard behind her, and then at the bedding which wasn't a mattress, but rather a cushioning of wool.

She realized then that she had no idea where she was, she'd never seen any of this before.

Panic immediately set in. She'd always been afraid of something like this, of some creep seeing her as a goldmine and stealing her away for a ransom. She didn't think this would happen in her twenties though.

She instinctively threw the blankets off in a hurry. There were no ropes or chains underneath. In fact, she was still in the nighty she remembered putting on after Killian had left her house. It was very torn and dirtied though. What had she just woken up from?

Her befuddled brain struggled through its last visual memories.

She remembered walking Killian to the door and then eventually moseying on her own back to the treehouse. She wanted to climb inside of it and feel like a kid just one last time before she became someone's wife. Then the broken ladder... *Oh God!*

She remembered falling quick and then slamming hard into the protruding bark on her way down. That was it. When she awoke there were howling wolves.

Wolves!

Fractured memories of running from their shadows slowly came back. And a man. He saved her life... he must have brought her here.

She fumbled out of the strange bed and sprinted toward the attic window where the sun was rising just barely over the treetops. She could see the familiar mountains to the west, but it wasn't the Colorado she knew at all. This was all farmland and ranches, not a business or vehicle in sight.

Down below, the barn door suddenly swung open and Tess leaned forward to watch the man walking out of it. He was the one who brought her here, she was sure of it.

She recognized his face even from the distance. She thought she could still hear his voice in her head; that deep, yet comforting tone vowing to get her to safety. Who was he? She'd heard his name, but now couldn't remember.

The man's bright blue eyes darted up toward the house and Tess jumped away from the attic window. She scurried back to the bed, just as the stairs began to creak outside the entryway.

She whirled onto the bed and then yelped at the feel of somebody else now under the blanket.

She tore the comforter off but wasn't prepared to find a raven haired six-year-old underneath. Tess froze at the blue-eyed little girl.

"Good, you're awake," someone said, materializing from the stairs.

Tess leapt back again as a woman approached. She was probably only around thirty-years-old with long dark hair braided down the back of her pretty face.

"Lotty!" the woman said, swiping the stray wisps from her eyes.

"No, I'm Tess."

The woman looked at her, startled. "No, I apologize, I was talking to Charlotte."

"Sorry," the little girl said, climbing off the bed. "I just wanted to look at her. She's so pretty."

The woman smiled softly. "That she is, but you know your father said not to come up here."

"Don't tell him, kay, Aunt Grace?"

"Lotty," she chastised. But Tess could see the affection in her eyes.

"Please!" the little girl begged.

As expected, the woman gave in immediately. "Fine, you can stay, but don't you go getting me into trouble for this!"

She giggled as her Aunt turned back to Tess. "Again, I apologize. I didn't mean for such a rude welcoming to Half Hallow."

Tess sucked in a startled breath. "Half Hallow?"

"Yes. Did you not know where you were? You poor dear. I can only imagine what you've been through." She moved closer and held out her hand. "I'm Grace. This nosey little booger is Charlotte."

The little girl giggled again. It was infectious.

"And you said your name is Tess?" Grace went on. "I never heard that name before. It's lovely. Is it short for something?"

"Tesla," Tess murmured. "Named after Nikola Tesla."

"Who?"

"The inventor."

Grace furrowed a brow thoughtfully.

That was strange. She never met anyone who hadn't at least heard of him. "I've only ever gone by Tess."

"Well both names are pretty," Grace said kindly. "I wonder if you met my husband yet. He helped bring you here. The sheriff, Theodore Paxton?"

Tess froze.

Paxton?

That was it. That was exactly why she recognized the man in the barn... it was why the name she heard last night had sounded so familiar.

Heywood Paxton. The man from the portrait at the museum.

Was this some kind of joke?

"I brought some stuff for you," Grace went on, walking back to the stairs.

If this *was* a joke, it was an elaborate one.

Who in their right mind would set something like this up just for a laugh or a scare? Finding the right farm and an old enough house, not to mention these people – including a *kid* actress at that would be quite the effort. For what purpose?

Tess eyed the pretty little girl suspiciously.

"You said your name is Charlotte?"

"Lotty," she corrected, and Tess smirked at that.

"I like the shorter version of my name too," she said, sitting down on the bed beside her. "What year is it, Lotty?"

Kids didn't easily lie, did they?

"1900," she said with a furrowed brow. "You're silly."

The breath whooshed out of her.

Lotty scuttled across the bed and touched the nighty Tess had been wearing. "I've never seen anything like this. It's so delicate. Like a flower pedal."

Tess froze a little, catching her breath before she tried again to analyze this amazing little actress. "Thank you."

Lotty stared up at her and smiled. "I want you to teach me to do my hair like yours."

"Okay," Tess whispered uncertainly.

Grace suddenly returned, tugging a suitcase behind her. Tess leapt up to help drag it onto the bed.

"What is all of this?"

She didn't need an answer once Grace hauled it open. The thing was clearly full of dresses. Grace began to pull them out one by one, laying them gently out on the bed.

Each one was awfully long, and some had sloping shoulders with very close-fitting bodices.

Tess lifted one to examine. She'd been dressed up to the nines hundreds of times for many glamorous events by the most prestigious designers. But these were something from another world. These were things she'd only seen in dated movies, and even those were mostly costumes. Finding vintage dresses in such good condition wasn't easy. So, how the hell did she...

"That's one of my favorites," Grace said, touching the fabric in Tess's hand. "It even matches your eyes."

Tess set it down, examining her closely. "How'd you get these?"

"Oh, all over," Grace mused. "We travel a lot, but I've decided a long time ago that I collect more garments than a body should own. And when Theodore told me about you and your predicament, I thought you'd benefit from them more than I would. We do look about the same size."

Tess shook her head, completely thrown by this. "And that's the truth. This isn't some highly structured, phenomenal prank?"

Grace's brow furrowed. "Prank?"

It was as though the word was foreign to her.

"This can't be real," Tess stammered. "This place, that man, these clothes."

Grace clenched her teeth. "Theodore told me what the doctor said. He told us about the hit to your head and your confusion. I can only imagine how scary this is for you."

Her childhood backyard that had once held her treehouse was now infested by carnivorous wolves, and the man she had seen from a hundred-year-old portrait in some stupid small-town museum was the owner of the house she now stood in. Yeah, Grace hit it right on the nose – scary and unreal and freaking ridiculous!

"Would you like me to help you into it?" Grace asked, taking the dress from where Tess had set it.

"Yes, let her!" Lotty said, "And maybe I could brush your hair? It looks like sunflowers."

"Forgive her," Grace murmured with a gentle grin. "She's never seen hair like yours. I can't honestly say that I have either."

"Oh," Tess said, touching the layers. Yes, people from this era never would have seen a cut or dye quite like this. She examined Grace for another moment, then smiled weakly at Lotty. "Yes, sweetheart, you can brush it after I'm dressed."

Grace stared at the nighty Tess already had on. "What an interesting style and material. Do you remember anything before that night my husband and Heywood found you? I'm so curious where it came from."

Tess looked her over again, still trying to read into this obvious hoax, but there wasn't anything. "No," she whispered. "I don't remember anything before."

"That must be horrible for you."

Grace pulled Tess close to her and took off the nighty, immediately replacing it with what Tess could only compare to an undershirt with a slip attached. No support whatsoever. And the underwear seemed to have legs attached.

"Have you never seen these?" Grace asked, helping her into the ensemble. "Maybe you're used to something better. This is an all-in-one, it has split drawers with a slip panel across the back to make the trip to the bathroom quicker and easier."

Tess forced a smile.

Holy freaking crap. Did they even have toilets?

Grace slipped on the corset next, and it was something that Tess had only ever seen in movies but never imagined herself in. It was interesting how it shaped her body, forcing her chest and backside out.

She shook her head thinking of the underwire bra and three-inch heels she always hated that did the same job at home. It seemed women *always* suffered for the perfect form no matter what era.

It was clear the corset had been made of bones as Grace began lacing up the back. The thing was uncomfortably tight, but she didn't dare complain.

It made her regret all the times she loathed her far superior pushup bra. How spoiled she'd been before she'd fallen into this otherworld blackhole.

Grace buttoned a cover over her corset next and then added a slip before she finally reached for the waiting garment.

Good God, such a show for a simple everyday dress. She wondered if Grace considered this a special occasion or if it really was the norm to waste this much time every morning, time that could have been spent on more important things. No wonder it took so long to put a man on the moon and assemble wheels on luggage.

To be fair, women may have worn less layers in her era, but they still spent an elaborate amount of time on hair and makeup. Maybe people from other generations weren't all that different.

The skirt came on next and it was just as beautiful as the blouse with stitched embroidery and a belt made of leather.

Grace turned her around to a mirror on the wall and Tess gasped at the unexpected sight of herself.

How was it even possible that something which covered her so well actually looked more appealing than the backless mini dresses she wore at home?

Lotty was waiting anxiously behind an antique mahogany chair. Though it wasn't exactly an antique yet.

"I'll prepare us some breakfast," Grace said as Tess sat down. "Lord knows Heywood can do many things, but a cook he is not."

Lotty laughed.

"Don't tell him I said that," Grace whispered with a wink on her way down the stairs.

As soon as they were alone, the young girl's featherlike fingers immediately began to shape and comb Tess's blonde layers. She was sure Lotty wasn't exactly styling it and rather just enjoyed playing dress up but didn't mind.

"I was there when my pa found you," she finally said, folding her hair into a barrette. "We thought you were a gazelle at first. Didn't expect a lady. My pa was worried. He said you'd be fine, but I could tell he was scared. He's no good at fibbing."

"And your father is Heywood Paxton?"

"Mhmm, he runs this dairy farm. We both do."

"You must be a lot of help."

"Sometimes. Other times he says I'm too mischievous for my own good."

"Sometimes my dad told me that too," Tess said. "He'd tell me it took a lot of work to keep me alive."

"Were you bad?"

"No, I was mischievous like you. Climbing, exploring, picking up animals I shouldn't."

"Wow, that *is* me!" Lotty said, coming around to look at her. She was wide-eyed. "Where's your pa now? He must be worried about you."

"He died when I was little."

Lotty's forehead creased. "How little?"

"When I was twelve."

She seemed to be mulling over that. "Did your ma die when you were a baby?"

Tess was taken aback by that strange question. "No." Then her heart softened. "Did yours?"

Lotty nodded.

"I'm sorry you lost her," Tess whispered gently. "It's hard to lose someone we love. But you don't have to worry about your dad. Just because mine died when I was twelve doesn't mean that yours will. I bet he lives to be old and gray."

Lotty giggled at that mental image of him, but Tess felt a dull pain in the pit of her stomach. If this truly was the Heywood Paxton that she had learned about from Ms. Tuttle then in fact he *would* die. And very soon.

****

Heywood was riding Saturn toward the pastures when he noticed the ladies materializing from the house. They must have already finished breakfast.

He squinted past the sunlight at the stranger walking beside Grace. She looked like an entirely different person than the one he met on the mountain. Gone was the frightened and muddied girl, and in its place stood a sophisticated woman.

Though her features were quite lovely, he was surprised she hadn't sought after the same "pale complexion" as most other women who tried desperately to hold onto their youth.

Lotty was lingering behind them and he snarled a little at that. He'd told her to stay away from the visitor and yet there she was holding the woman's hand like they had already become great pals. The last thing he needed was his daughter getting attached to someone who wouldn't be around for long.

He nudged Saturn in that direction and dismounted in front of the women. "Morning," he said. "Theo didn't say anything about you coming by today."

"I'm not sure if he even knows," Grace said with a smile, then turned toward the newcomer. "I need to get back. It was nice meeting you, Tess."

"You too," the lady said in a whisper. "Thanks again for the dresses."

"Of course! Please keep and enjoy them."

Heywood gave Grace a hand as she climbed up into her wagon.

"I'll see you tomorrow at church," she said with a wink and Heywood arched the corner of his mouth at her subtle persuasion.

"We'll see."

Grace didn't need explaining of what a bad idea that would be. With the town still inquiring on whether or not he'd murdered his wife, he knew that bringing another woman around would only be trouble. As though Antoinette Cavaliere wasn't enough of a headache for him already.

Grace waved goodbye and a sense of dread fell over him when her wagon dematerialized around the corner.

He forced himself around to look at the woman. Again, he grimaced at Lotty's hand inside hers. She was practically beaming. The girl was much too friendly for her own good.

"Lotty, why don't you go get the horses some oats for me."

"Okay," she said, moving toward the barn.

"I appreciate it, sweetheart." A thick silence hung when she was gone. "Your head feeling any better this morning?" he asked dryly, giving Saturn's reins a pull.

The question seemed to catch the woman off-guard.

"Yes, thank you." She followed him toward the pastures, lightly stroking the horse's mane between them. "I appreciate your hospitality."

"Well, we certainly couldn't have just left you out there, Miss…"

"Corbin. Tess Corbin."

She blinked expectantly at him, as though she anticipated some sort of recognition. She must've been somebody of importance where she came from. Here she was nothing more than trouble for him.

It wasn't her fault though. He was the one who brought her home, but never would have if he'd known he'd have to keep her. He had just assumed the good old doctor would bring her back with him to be cared for.

Damn you, Theo for making her my responsibility!

"How long do you think you'll need before you can head home?" he grunted. "Watch that mud there."

She lifted her skirt awkwardly and hopped over the section he'd warned her about. Getting back her balance, she sighed and stared ahead uncertainly at the pastures.

"You do know how to find your way home, right?"

"I wish I did."

He glanced again at Miss Corbin, and then at Saturn who trotted between them. Her small and delicate hand lay upon the horse's neck, but her eyes were glaring at the scenery.

He watched them move from the open fields, to the grazing cattle, then the barn and quaint log cabin. He figured he already knew what those raspy breaths meant. When women gave that sort of look and made those kinds of sounds it usually meant displeasure. She'd probably come from much better than this.

Well, nobody's making her stay, he thought, fighting the urge to say it out loud.

He could only imagine the kind of life she'd fled from. She'd probably left home dead in the night without even making real plans. Perhaps it was just simply to escape a life she dreaded, or possibly even the giver of that diamond on her left ring finger. Reasons didn't matter, it was careless of her and she shouldn't have headed this direction if Half Hallow was below her standards.

There was a time that he despised the thought of living there as well. He had worked his ass off though to keep it running and to give Lotty a suitable home, and he was proud of what he'd accomplished. At least until someone like Tess Corbin came by to sniff at it.

Scowling at that, he jerked on Saturn's reins, picking up their pace toward the pastures. Tess's hand slipped from the horse and she jerked back in response.

He glared at her, her fern green eye staring back widely. Until that moment, he hadn't noticed the color of pure honey around the iris. In the sunlight that small bit almost looked amber. It wasn't just the color he was seeing for the first time. He began to question if it really was dissatisfaction that he thought he'd seen in her expression as well. Maybe it was just fear.

Before he could even think to apologize for jerking the reins on her, Gabe came sweeping down the property in their direction.

"Morning, Mr. Paxton," he called. "Sorry I'm late. Won't happen again."

"Isn't that what you said yesterday?"

"This time I mean it," Gabe said with a sly smirk, but it dropped the instant he saw that they weren't alone. The boy was instantly mesmerized by the golden-haired beauty who stood slunk back behind the horse's tail. His face was practically red with obvious fascination. "Sorry to disrupt," he said at last.

"You didn't. This is Miss Corbin. She'll be visiting with us for a couple days."

Gabe didn't say anything, just stood there eyeing her as if she were naked.

The kid's ill-manners forced Heywood to step in. Putting a hand on his shoulder, he said, "This here is Gabe Bruno. He works on the farm, milking and tending the cows with me. Though maybe not for long if he continues sleeping in like a house cat."

Gabe snorted awkwardly, never taking his eyes off Miss Corbin. "I think maybe for the next couple of days I'll find reason to come to work early."

His boldness gave Heywood pause, then he scooped off the boy's hat and teasingly whacked the back of his head with it. "Get on outta here, Casanova. There's work to be done."

"It was nice meeting you, Miss Corbin," Gabe called out clumsily as he began to tread toward the barn.

She gave the boy a small wave. "You too, Gabe," she said following Heywood the rest of the way to the pastures.

He had to admit, he was surprised that she hadn't been more bothered by the boy's blatant disrespect. Most other women turned up their noses to that and even scolded him, though his awkward flirtation was only ever meant innocently.

She must have been used to her fair share of admirers. Or maybe she was just different from other women in this town.

CHAPTER FIVE

"How the hell did Grace get this thing on?" Tess moaned, squeezing herself into another dress.

She hoped this new one was good enough for Sunday services. She hadn't been to church since her father died. If she wasn't even sure how to behave herself in a twenty-first century church, how would she blend in a 1900's one?

"Do you need help with the buckle?" Lotty asked, creeping up the stairway.

Tess spun around and then smiled softly at the snooping little girl. "You scared me, Lotty. How long have you been hiding there?" She hoped she hadn't heard her swearing earlier while struggling into the ridiculous dress. "Come on up here and help me out."

Lotty finished crawling up the stairs in a hurry and hopped into the room. "It's easy, you've just got to loop it," she explained, finishing the belt on Tess's dress. "That's a really pretty ring. Can I try it on? What's it made of?"

"It's a diamond," Tess said, twisting it off her finger and sliding it onto Lotty's. "You've got to be careful with it."

"Is it special?"

"Well, that depends," Tess said plopping down onto the bed beside her. "Do you like it?"

"Very much!"

"Then, it's special. Beauty is in the eye of the beholder"

"This is a marriage ring though, isn't it?" Lotty asked. "Does that mean you're married?"

"No. The ring only symbolizes a promise to do so."

"So, you've promised somebody to marry them?"

"Well, no, not yet. I'm not sure if I should. It's complicated."

Lotty twisted her mouth as she examined the diamond this way and that. "Everyone always tells me grown-up stuff is complicated, but I think it's simple. If you don't want to promise to marry him then don't." She handed the ring back and Tess stared quietly at it before slipping it onto her finger.

"Sometimes there are obligations that are difficult to understand when you're not in the situation yourself. Killian is a good man. I have no reason to turn him down."

"Is this Mr. Killian handsome and strong?"

Tess scoffed. "He is."

"And you love each other?"

She chewed her lip. "I think so."

"Sorry, Miss Corbin, but I think that's something you should know for sure," Lotty said bluntly. She got up and stroked the sloppy French Braid Tess had thrown into her hair that morning. "Where'd you learn to do that?"

Tess self-consciously touched it. She hadn't a clue about hairstyles in this era but noticed Grace had worn a braid when they met. "It's just something one of my cousins taught me."

"Can you teach me how to do it? My hair's not as pretty as yours though."

"Yours is *very* pretty. It reminds me of a raven."

"It's not as soft."

"Well, I have to do a lot to make my hair feel soft. Lots of products. It doesn't come naturally."

"What are products?"

Tess caught herself. "Well, shampoo and conditioner."

Lotty's forehead creased.

"What do you use to wash your hair?"

"What everybody uses," Lotty answered, "beaten egg mixed with water."

Yikes. "How often?"

Lotty shrugged.

"Okay, come with me." Tess got up and walked swiftly down the stairs to the small kitchen. She remembered learning how to make her own shampoo while on a girl scout camping trip. Even here, they had to have the ingredients. It was only one tablespoon of baking soda and a cup of water.

"Aha! Come on, Lotty." She gathered the ingredients and then led her to the pump outside. Dipping her hair into the water, Tess gently massaged the concoction into Lotty's scalp and hair for a minute or two before rinsing it.

"That feels nice," Lotty mused.

"Does anybody ever wash your hair for you?"

"No. Pa helps sometimes, I suppose."

"Well, I'm sure you can handle it, but I'd be happy to do your hair while I'm around."

"You remind me of a Ma."

Tess snorted. "Any mom in particular or just all moms in general?"

"What I imagine a Ma would be like."

Tess's heart sank. Lotty never knew a life with a mother. In some ways neither did Tess. Mrs. Corbin wasn't exactly the nurturing type.

Though she was sure that she hadn't been tossed into this strange place in order to mother the sweet child, Tess couldn't help giving her a tight squeeze. "You still want me to French braid your hair for church?"

Lotty's grin was all teeth. "Yes, please!"

"Let's go!"

****

Heywood had just finished linking the horses to the carriage when he saw Miss Corbin step onto the front porch. She was wearing a yellow frilled skirt that pinched her narrow waist with a tight white blouse. It was the kind of dress that thrust her bosom forward and hips back, creating an S-shape to her body. She looked beautiful, though he remembered her in practically nothing and knew her body didn't need the reinforcement.

He squinted past the sunlight at the dainty braid that interweaved her golden hair. She reminded him of how mystic nymphs were described in many folklores.

A pinch of crimson warmed Miss Corbin's cheeks, and Heywood realized suddenly he'd been staring at her.

Setting his jaw, he finished linking the horses in silence.

This wasn't going to be good. Parading a woman who looked like that around town would only get him into trouble. Tess Corbin wasn't family or even a friend, he didn't owe her anything more than basic human decency. He shouldn't have been allowing her to stay another hour let alone another night.

51

Then he saw Lotty coming out of the house behind her, grinning ear-to-ear. She looked different. He knew immediately that it was her hair. He'd never mastered how to style those sweet locks. They always seemed to need a good detangling no matter how hard he tried. This morning, however, it had been combed back into the same pretty braid that Miss Corbin wore.

Heywood felt a tightness in his belly as he stared at his daughter who positioned herself to stand exactly like the mysterious heiress. Lotty had certainly been lacking feminine guidance thus far and seemed to thrive with it. She'd be a woman soon too, after all. He'd always wondered what this sweet six-year-old would be like when she grew up. Seeing how she attached herself to this exciting stranger frightened him. She had her mother's blood in her, blood that sought adventure, to never settle in any one place.

He couldn't say he loved Half Hallow, but it was home. The place would be worthless without Lotty.

He gave his head a shake. No point in upsetting himself about a far future that may never exist.

"Well, aren't I a lucky man to be escorting such a fine beauty this morning," he said with a wink at his daughter.

Lotty giggled and took his hand, hoisting herself up into the carriage. "*Two* fine beauties," she corrected, eyeing her new companion.

Heywood forced a nod and held out his hand to Miss Corbin. She accepted his assistance onto the carriage, showing him a delicate smile as she sat down beside his daughter.

The large bell swaying in the steeple of the small white church had gone silent by the time they pulled onto the property. It wasn't surprising that the service had already begun when they entered.

Heywood nodded Lotty and Tess to their customary seats in back. He sat quickly, scowling at Theo and Grace for craning their necks and causing others to follow suit. His brother just smiled before turning back to that morning's service.

Heywood slipped off his hat and listened silently as Micah preached from the pulpit.

He hated to admit how much of a struggle it had become to show up to these weekly services. When he was a kid, it had gone without saying that he would not miss a Sunday. When he returned to Half Hallow without Emeline, however, it just became a new home base for cruel gossip. The old busybodies of the congregation had called him many hurtful things, with the full knowledge that he was of range to hear. After a while he stopped coming altogether. It wasn't worth the headache.

That only lasted a few months before Micah Gibson paid him a visit. As encouraging as the young pastor's words were, it hadn't been easy for Heywood to rejoin the congregation. All these years later, his visits were still sporadic and difficult.

Lotty tugged Heywood's hand suddenly. He hadn't realized that Micah's opening benediction had already completed, and the congregation had risen for a song of worship.

"Thank you, sweetheart," he said, getting onto his feet. The congregation was just finishing the first hymn and getting into the second when he heard a voice singing above the others. It wasn't loud or overbearing, yet it seemed to stand out over anyone else's. It was beautiful and yet coarse. He couldn't help but silence himself to listen, already knowing that it was Miss Corbin.

When the congregation sat for the service, Micah took the opportunity to welcome their new guest. Heywood could only assume that either his brother or Grace had clued the minister in. He glared in their general direction when Miss Corbin was forced to stand as the minister introduced her to the other churchgoers.

An unwelcome jolt coursed through him when he saw the other men in the congregation eyeing her with friendly attention.

He knew that Miss Corbin wasn't his to protect, so he couldn't pinpoint what exactly he was feeling in that moment. Certainly not jealousy or possessiveness. Those would require some level of attraction and he'd already learned his lesson about the dangers of that.

As the sermon ended, Heywood stood from the pew and took Lotty's hand. He'd hoped to make a clean getaway but was stopped by Micah Gibson who offered an open hand with a wide grin.

"I'm glad you came," he said enthusiastically. "It's been a while."

"Yeah I know," Heywood muttered. "It's just work."

"You work yourself too hard, Paxton." He punched his arm neighborly and then held his hand out to Miss Corbin who immediately took it. "I do hope you're finding your visit to Half Hallow a pleasant one. I'm sure Mr. Paxton has been a good host, but if you need anything at all please let me know."

Heywood watched as the tiniest of smiles arched her full strawberry lips. "Thank you," she said gently.

"I hope I didn't embarrass you with my earlier introduction. I was just so glad to have a newcomer."

"Oh no, not at all."

Heywood actually believed her. How could it *not* have embarrassed her though? Either she was a good liar or was simply unbothered by unwanted attention.

A hand was suddenly on his shoulder and Heywood jerked back to look at his brother.

"I knew you'd make it," Theo said with a toothy grin. "Perfect day for an outside dinner, huh? What do you say about you, Lotty, and Miss Corbin joining us around five o'clock?"

Heywood had nearly forgotten about the dinner invitation. He glanced over at Miss Corbin who'd instantly become the center of attention to the small community. Again, that pang of he-didn't-know-what touched his chest.

"We'll have pork and potatoes," Theo went on, "But if you want to bring fish like you did last time, we can cook that up too."

"Yes, fish!" Lotty shouted with a leap. "Can we go fishing, Pa? Can we?"

Heywood jerked his attention back to his brother and daughter, inwardly berating himself for having allowed himself to be distracted by the pretty stranger. "Yeah, yeah, fish," he muttered under his breath as he began toward the carriage. "Lotty, why don't you go on and collect Miss Corbin so we can get out of here."

He had just managed to reach the carriage when a woman slipped between him and the horse, placing her hand in the crook of his arm. The only woman he knew who could move so lithely was Miss Antoinette Cavaliere.

"Good morning, Mr. Paxton," she said softly. "I must say, I was quite pleased to hear from your brother that you'd be attending services this week. Do you like the dress?"

Heywood glanced down at it, a little confused. "It's lovely."

She gave him a satisfied smile. "I thought I saw you notice it at the horse show last month."

He didn't recall.

"I had a space saved for you on my pew. I'd hoped you'd sit beside me this morning."

It occurred to Heywood what a fool he was not to be drooling over this rare beauty who stood before him. She was petite and delicate with lovely coloring and auburn hair that reminded him of a sunset. But he only ever felt anxiety in her presence.

She might have been a sure thing, which would tempt most men, but the woman showed no real depth and zero interest in Lotty. It made her attraction for him even less appealing than it was comprehensible. After all, he *had* humiliated Antoinette when he went against their fathers' agreement and chose Emeline. She should have hated him, but instead her desire had surged to greater heights upon his return. Maybe she simply viewed him as the one who got away.

"I apologize for wrecking any plans," he said politely. "Had I known you were saving a spot for us we'd have joined you."

"Well, you could easily make it up to me by coming over for lunch. I have a pot roast already cooking. I put potatoes and onions in it just how you like it."

"But we're going fishing with Miss Corbin!" Lotty interjected quickly as she joined them.

Antoinette forced a sharp grin at the approaching little girl. It always felt as though she didn't know what to do with children, as if they were some foreign beings she couldn't comprehend.

"Miss Corbin? Really?" Although she was responding to Lotty, her questioning gaze was for Heywood.

"Yeah!" Lotty said, looking back as Miss Corbin made her way over. "She's been staying in Pa's room."

"In my *old* room!" Heywood corrected. "My childhood room up in the loft."

Antoinette shook her head, somewhat flustered. "I don't understand why this new visitor to our congregation is staying in your home at all."

Of course. Nobody would.

"She got hurt and needed some looking after," he murmured.

Antoinette pressed her lips together, hands clenched at her small waist.

He saw Miss Corbin joining them and hoped Antoinette wouldn't make a scene.

He spotted the bitterness flash before Miss Cavaliere's eyes just seconds before she recovered with a stilted smile. She managed those farce emotions so well.

"Pleased to meet you, Miss Corbin. I'm Antoinette Cavaliere."

He felt momentary guilt for not having warned Miss Corbin about this fire-breathing vixen. But then again it wasn't really his concern, was it?

Miss Corbin took Antoinette's outstretched hand and shook it gently. "It's nice to meet you too." There was something in her eyes that made it seem as though maybe they *had* met before. Or she'd at least heard of her. Maybe Grace said something.

Antoinette on the other hand only looked at Miss Corbin how one would a rattlesnake that needed to be put down quickly. "How is it that you and Mr. Paxton became acquainted?"

Miss Corbin's breath visibly haltered. "Mr. Paxton was of some assistance to me the other night."

"Then I'm to assume you are family?"

"She's my friend," Lotty said, taking the woman's hand, which Antoinette turned her nose at.

"Well, family friend or no, certainly you can both see how improper it is for Miss Corbin to remain at the Paxton farm." She eyed the stranger with a cold smile. "Mr. Paxton lives alone, after all. I'm sure even where you're from it is improper for an unmarried man and woman to share a home unchaperoned."

Lotty scowled. "Pa doesn't live alone. He's with me."

Antoinette scoffed and looked at Heywood as if he were a child. "What would people say?"

Her condescending tone made him snarl. She knew what she was doing bringing the town gossips into this. His character had already been destroyed due to those busybodies, and no doubt she meant to use them now to control him.

"I have no intention of wearing out my welcome," Miss Corbin interrupted, surprising him. "My hope is to be heading home soon."

"No!" Lotty gasped. "You need to stay, Miss Corbin!"

"Just Tess, Lotty. You can call me Tess."

Antoinette sniffed at that.

Heywood had had enough. "Miss Corbin is welcome to stay until she finds residence elsewhere. As for the town members, let them talk till they're blue in the face."

He offered his hand to his daughter.

"Come now," he said, assisting Lotty into the carriage. He didn't want any more talk that would upset her. Yes, Tess Corbin would leave soon enough, but no need distressing Lotty on the inevitable.

He aided Miss Corbin up into the carriage next and then bid farewell to Antoinette.

****

Tess hadn't expected to attend a picnic after Sunday services. When Lotty had mentioned fishing, and Heywood went inside to pack a lunch, she'd merely assumed it was a father/daughter outing and made herself scarce. She'd been utterly shocked, however, to find Lotty climbing up to the loft to tell her that they were waiting.

Given how silent Heywood had been the entire trip to the lake, Tess had to wonder if it was more Lotty's invitation than his.

The man was a mystery to her with many layers she couldn't even begin to pull back. The moment she met him, she found only kindness, but all sympathy had been long gone by the following morning. It was clear that he didn't trust her, but she wasn't sure why. Perhaps it had something to do with his wife, whom Tess remembered had inexplicably died. Or that lady, Antoinette Cavaliere. She had a hold on him that Tess didn't understand. The name had been familiar, Ms. Tuttle had mentioned it. An old flame of his, perhaps? She couldn't remember.

Though Heywood wasn't exactly easy to read and may have been a little rough around the edges, one thing that was evidently clear was how much he cherished his daughter.

Tess grinned as she watched the two splashing in the shallow water. Several times Heywood had scooped her up and threatened to throw her in headfirst. Lotty's high-pitched screams of delight made birds flock away and the horses whinny.

Tess tore a few grapes from the bunch stem and was chowing down on them when she suddenly felt the picnic blanket shift. Assuming it was Lotty who'd plopped down beside her, she tossed a grape playfully in that direction. Rather than the young girl, however, she found Heywood catching it instead.

For some asinine reason it made her flush.

"Sorry," she murmured.

She wasn't sure why being alone with him made her nervous. Even her palms felt sweaty.

Maybe it was just human nature to react that way to a man that looked like him. He really *was* a sight. His unshaven jawline, towering height, and black hair made him dangerously attractive. Heywood Paxton could have carried the nickname Ol Blue Eyes himself for the color and boldness in them.

Surely, he must have captured women's attention regularly. The fact that he never remarried must have been by choice.

He smiled at her, and a small dimple folded into his lean cheek.

Far too handsome, Tess muttered inwardly, and forced herself to look away past his shoulder to where Lotty had begun digging into the wet dirt near the lake.

She had been grateful for Lotty's presence ever since she'd woken up in this strange place. Her time with Heywood would have been much more daunting without the child's light and comfortable jabbering. Sitting now on that blanket, just the two of them, she didn't know what to say. His presence felt suffocating.

Heywood seemed just as uncomfortable and glanced away as well. He watched the water for a moment until he said in a deep resonant voice, "Lotty tells me you made her some soap and helped wash her hair this morning."

Tess's shoulders squared. She wondered if that was wrong to have done. He'd probably come over to scold her for it.

She had a feeling that her presence upset him. It wasn't as though she hadn't noticed him flinch nearly every time Lotty took her hand or stood too close.

"I appreciate you being so kind to her," he went on softly.

Tess blinked with surprise.

"Oh," she whispered. She hadn't expected that. Maybe she'd just gotten too used to Killian's nonsensical berating.

Her shoulders relaxed a little as she squinted past the sunlight at him.

"Lotty hasn't had much female influence in her life," Heywood went on gently. "And I know it's something she craves more and more as she ages."

She saw him struggling and stopped it. "No need to thank me. It doesn't take any effort at all with Lotty. She's a sweet girl."

"That she is. Losing her Ma at such a young age..." he sighed tiredly and rubbed a hand across his face. "I guess I'm learning as I go."

"It seems like you're doing fine."

He looked at her again, this time with deep inquisitive eyes.

She curled the wisps of hair that had escaped her braid back behind her ear, cheeks already flushing from the intense examination. Why did he stare at her like that?

"Miss Corbin," he finally said. "What is it you're running from?"

Tess sucked in a startled breath. "I'm not running from anything," she whispered sharply.

He frowned thoughtfully. "If you say so."

"Why would you even assume that?"

"I just can't think of a single other reason that you would have been in the forest in the state you were in when we found you."

Tess looked down.

"The story you told the doctor isn't true, is it? About the tree in your yard and the year you came from. You made it up because you didn't want to be sent home."

She shook her head. "That would be stupid."

"Or very smart." He leaned slightly forward, his voice dropping when he said, "It's okay. I've done my share of running too. But sometimes it's better just to face your problems head-on. If you're in trouble –"

"I am not in trouble."

"If you *are* though... "

Oh God, here it comes. He didn't want any of her drama near his family. He was sending her packing.

She looked back at him with agitated anticipation.

"If you are, please tell me," he went on. "Because I might be able to help."

Oh.

So many layers to this man.

Her eyes met his gaze and held it for a long moment. "I'm not in trouble," she murmured sternly. "I just can't remember."

"Huh."

She scowled as his eyes continued to dissect her. "What does *huh* mean?"

He shrugged and popped a square of cheese into his mouth. It was too casual for the conversation they were having.

"You think I'm lying," she finally blurted.

"I just find it interesting that you don't recall how you got here or where you came from, but have no problem remembering who gave you that ring."

With surprise, she moved her hand over to glance down at it. Her heart wilted. "Lotty told you."

"She did. About a man named Killian. If he's the one you're running from..."

She rolled her eyes. "I am not–"

"In trouble, yeah I heard you. Fair enough. If you don't want to talk about it then we won't. I just want you to know that we *can*."

She drew in a deep breath, then looked away from Heywood and back to Lotty who came scampering over, her clothes wet and muddied but wearing the biggest grin.

"Come on, Pa, let's fish already! I see some big ones in there!"

"Alright, fishing gear is over by the tree." He looked at Tess. "We'll be back soon."

Tess shook her head. "I'm not invited?"

"Little Lotty has a habit of scaring the fish away by trampling in the water. Wouldn't want you to get wet."

"I don't mind. Fishing sounds fun."

Lotty and Heywood eyed each other, though for obvious different reasons. While Heywood's was a look of concern, Lotty's was full of anticipation.

"You think you could handle reeling in a big one?" Heywood asked.

"If Lotty can then I'm sure I could as well."

"What do ya think?" he asked his daughter playfully. "Should we let her muddy herself in that trout-infested water?"

"Yes!" Lotty hollered, running up and pulling Tess to her feet. She gasped as she fixed the skirt that had bunched up beneath her, but then saw Heywood's amused grin and straightened up. Lifting her chin to meet his gaze, she took the fishing rod that Lotty handed to her.

"Where to, Mr. Paxton?"

He stared into her eyes for a long moment before saying, "Found a good spot over there. Let's go."

In all truth she didn't know what the hell she was doing. There was just something about the way he smirked at the idea of her coming along that had her convinced that she had something to prove. She wasn't just another flimsy female like the sort he was probably used to and wouldn't be treated as one.

With determination, Tess kicked off her shoes, hoisted up the skirt, and stepped into the cold creek water behind them.

Though it was shallow, she still felt the weight of the dress shifting her balance. She gave it a hard yank which only caused her to stumble.

She hadn't even noticed Heywood coming back for her until she'd completely lost her balance and felt him catching her at the arm.

As he stood her back up, Tess found herself face-to-face with the man, their hands locked and bodies only inches apart. She could see the dark stubble of his beard up close and wondered what it would have felt like to touch. Killian had always been cleanshaven, in fact most men she'd dated had been beta males with soft features and baby smooth skin. Suddenly all she could think of was what it would feel like were he to kiss her and rub his roughened cheek against hers.

Tess's pulse quickened and her mouth went dry. The thought was ludicrous and overwhelming.

"You're not used to fishing in church dresses, are you Miss Corbin?"

Tess huffed with amusement as she glanced down at the pretty yellow skirt swimming around her. It had been soaked all the way up to her hips. She'd never worn a church dress let alone fished in one. "I suppose there's a first time for everything. But I *have* fished before. It may not seem it right now, but I did a few times back when I was a Girl Scout."

"Girl Scout? What's that?"

Her heart spiked. "Oh, it's just something we have where I come from, teaching outdoor skills and good citizenship to young girls."

"The place you come from that you can't remember."

She stared blankly at him, realizing she'd messed up once again. If she didn't want them thinking she was nuts for claiming time travel, then amnesia was the only solution.

Heywood just smiled and looked down at Lotty. "Can either of you tell me what the one crucial factor is that Miss Corbin is missing when it comes to fishing?"

Tess furrowed a brow, but Lotty jumped on the game fast. "Bait!" she squealed.

"Guess I should have known that," Tess said, embarrassed. "I'll have to find some."

"Nah, don't worry about it. You can just use mine," he said, switching over her fishing rod for his where bait had already been attached on the end. It wasn't anything like the rods she remembered, built from an entirely different era with strips of bamboo and horsehair lines.

Maybe sensing her unfamiliarity with it, he held her arms and helped guide the pole's release into the water. She hadn't expected that, and her breath hitched when he steadied her footing once again, leaning her back against his front.

Lotty began to plod around them and Heywood shushed her. "Be still, baby, we're trying to sneak up on them, remember?"

"I'm not a baby, Pa!"

Tess felt the vibration of his chuckling ribs against her back. "My mistake. Be still either way."

A tugging motion jerked the hook within a moment or two, and Heywood gripped the rod from around Tess's slim body. He had the arms of a man who spent most of his life doing hard manual labor and this close he smelled of the earth after a rainstorm.

She breathed him in.

"Help me reel this in," he said, close to her ear.

Tess felt an odd flutter in her stomach as his scratchy cheek rested gently against hers. She couldn't understand her reaction to this man. She didn't know him at all, but she couldn't remember the last time her heart skipped a beat this way.

Together they yanked hard on the rod and brought the fish to surface. Lotty screamed delightfully and Heywood let go of Tess to get a grip on it. It flailed in his hand, spraying them all and making them laugh.

He finally passed the fish to his daughter, who surprised Tess by taking it in her bare hands without a squeal.

Heywood was smiling broadly when he looked from Lotty to Tess, but his lips fell a little as he wiped the water from his face. He seemed oddly uncomfortable suddenly and glanced away.

"We should probably head back."

"Aw, Pa, we only caught one though!"

"If I'm gonna be gone most of tonight, I'd better see to my chores while I have time."

Lotty pouted.

"Any longer anyway and folks would get to talking."

"About what?" Tess asked, following him toward land.

Heywood paused to take her arm as she stumbled in the mud. "About this," he said quietly. "You. Me. Unchaperoned."

"But nothing happened worth any gossip at all."

He scoffed. "I've learned long ago that nothing has to happen in order to get folks talking about you."

Tess glanced again at Heywood, her breathing becoming shallow and quick as his ice blue eyes briefly met hers.

With Lotty between them, they left the lake and walked back to the carriage. Tess didn't look at Heywood again, but she was conscious of his close proximity in a way she'd never been conscious of anyone before.

CHAPTER SIX

Heywood thrust his pitchfork into the compilation of manure and hay that buried the floor of the stalls. There was still so much to do before dinner at Theo's, he shouldn't have been wasting so much time thinking about Tess Corbin.

He couldn't help it. He'd tried just about everything to rid his mind of her. It hardly even mattered that she was a liar and clearly hiding something. He still regrettably admitted that he liked her.

Maybe he just liked the way she was with Lotty.

It had made his chest swell up when he saw the way Tess had sat listening intently to the child's cheerful banters on the ride home from the lake. There weren't many people besides himself who doted on Lotty like that. Most grew weary of her silly chatter too quickly.

His mind wandered then to the water, and how pretty she looked that afternoon in that elegant dress soaked up to her hips and the wet wisps of hair that stuck to her cheek.

But he also remembered the diamond marriage band she wore.

He shouldn't have been thinking of a taken woman like this, shouldn't have been thinking of her at all. Even if she was running from this man, like he suspected, she would not be running toward *Heywood*. A ring like that was more costly than anything he could even dream of providing. A woman who was used to such finery would never take well to being forced to do without it. It wasn't even worth allowing himself to admit attraction to her.

The barn doors opened behind him. He expected it to be Lotty coming to hurry him for dinner and didn't immediately turn around. At least not until he felt the heavy footfalls that could never belong to his daughter.

He froze when he heard the deep raspy breathing and already knew that it was Mr. Delacourt.

"Coming by to check up on Miss Corbin?" he asked, shoving the pitchfork back into the grime to continue his work.

"Somebody's got to."

"Well, you *are* the doctor in town."

"Cut the bullshit."

Heywood paused and looked over his shoulder.

"I know what's going on here."

Heywood turned around to face him, taking note of the horse whip in his fist. He eyed Emeline's dad, and set the pitchfork down. "Why are you here, Mr. Delacourt?"

"I saw what you did. Bringing that girl to church and then what happened at the lake…" He sniffed. "Didn't take you long to sink your teeth into another one, huh."

"Whatever you say," Heywood muttered, but was suddenly struck by the whip in the doc's hand and the pain in his bicep was nearly blinding. He caught himself against the wall, perplexed as another came at lightning speed, tearing flesh from his hip.

"The whole town knows what you did to my daughter, whether you admit it or not." Mr. Delacourt threw the whip hard at him a third time and it ripped open his shoulder and neck with a loud crack.

Heywood fell to his knee. "I did not hurt Emeline!"

"Don't you dare say her name!" The whip struck him a fourth time and then a fifth.

The agony of his torn flesh was too strong to focus. He could barely get his feet back under him. He held up both hands in a defensive position. "Stop!" he grunted. "Put it down, old man, and let's talk like civilized adults."

He heard the next snap of the whip before he felt it lacerate his back. He groaned, trying again to stand and get to the dropped pitchfork.

"You're not a civilized human being!" Mr. Delacourt growled. "I can only treat you like the animal you are." He threw back his arm. "I won't stop reminding this town of what you are until justice is served. And I will not stand by while you replace Emeline. How dare you allow that woman near Emeline's child!"

Again, he hit him; tearing flesh, hitting bone. The hay underneath him was already wet with his blood, the entire barn reeked of it. Pain was hardly even the word to describe it. It was like a wolf's teeth and the claws of a grizzly all at once.

"Say it now that you will leave Lotty with me and then get the hell out of this town."

Heywood grunted under the blood and pain. He would never leave his baby with this monster. He was insane to suggest it. Doc already knew there wasn't a chance.

Then the pain was unlike anything he'd ever felt. Not the whip, this was like a knife through his side and he shouted in agony.

"Consider this a warning. Next time I'll aim somewhere vital."

The only thing that made it all the more frightening was the sound of the barn door opening. Heywood knew it would be Lotty coming to get him, and he knew this bastard would take her if he didn't stop him.

Heywood glimpsed past the sweat dripping in his eyes at his little girl, standing wide-eyed and frightened. She was still stunned frozen when Miss Corbin walked up behind her and gasped, grabbing Lotty by the shoulders and pulling her back toward her body in a protective hold.

He breathed a sigh of relief that Miss Corbin had been with her, that she would never hand Lotty over to the insane doctor.

Mr. Delacourt stared back at them, his apologetic eyes toward Lotty turning to hate when he glimpsed at Tess. He curled his lip as he pulled a handkerchief from his pocket and wrapped it around the whip. With one quick pull he cleaned it off, spraying Heywood with his own blood.

"I pray that we won't need another visit," he muttered down at Heywood.

He turned then and trudged toward the barn door. Miss Corbin still had Lotty close against her body, forearms over the little girl's chest and she shifted back a few steps as the doctor stalked past them.

Then Heywood saw nothing at all as the darkness consumed him.

****

Tess could see where every lash of the whip landed on Heywood's body, including a particularly deep one on his left ribcage. But the worst was the puncture in his upper thigh where an arrow had sunk several inches in. It hadn't pierced any vital organs, obviously, but he wouldn't survive an infection from its removal if done wrong.

A white-faced Lotty ran back into the barn with a damp cloth, but Tess knew it wasn't any use simply cleansing the open wounds. She needed to somehow get him inside the house and stitch him up.

"Is he going to die?" Lotty choked out.

"No," Tess rasped, stroking Lotty's hair. "But we need to get help fast. Do you know how to get to your Uncle Theo's house?"

Lotty looked up and let out a small cry. "I think so."

"Okay, let me just stop the bleeding where I can, and you show me the way." Tearing off pieces of her dress, Tess went to work making them into bandages to tie around the gushing wounds. Then with a hand on Lotty's back, she steered her to one of the horses in the corral.

Tess froze at the two-thousand-pound animal, fully intimidated. With a deep breath, she glanced down at the little girl. "You're going to help me, right? It's been a while since I've ridden a horse."

Lotty looked at her with fear-filled eyes and nodded shakily.

Within minutes they had the horse cinched up and ready to go. Lifting the child up first, Tess hiked up her skirt, slipped her foot into the stirrup, and mounted behind her.

Clinging onto Lotty with one hand and the pommel with the other, she jabbed her heels into the horse's sides and held tight as he set off in a flat-out run past the half-moon shaped pond at the end of their property and beyond it.

The distance between the Paxton farm and town was closer than it had seemed that morning. They passed the church, and Lotty pointed out a small road ahead that Tess led the horse down.

"That's it," Lotty said in a voice still choked with tears. Tess veered the horse in that direction and found a small white house with a table already set up outside for their upcoming dinner date.

"Tell Theo and Grace what happened," she said, hoisting Lotty off the saddle. "Tell them to take you back to the farm and to get him into bed. Tell them *not* to touch the arrow until I get there. I have one more stop to make."

"But Grandpa's the only doctor in town and he's the one... he... he won't help."

"I know, Lotty, you've just got to trust me and do as I say so we can help your daddy."

Lotty nodded, trying to look brave. Behind her, the front door opened, and she could see Grace squeezing onto the porch with a puzzled stare.

Lotty went racing in her direction as Tess steered the horse back toward town. Her heart was pounding so hard it was almost painful by the time she found the sign for the doctor.

She half hurdled, half fell from the saddle, barely managing to stay vertical when her feet landed on the ground.

She stumbled to the door and began to bang on it. A curtain shuffled in the second story window and then stilled.

"I know you're in there!" she yelled. "Open the door, or I'm letting myself in!"

She only gave him till the count of three then hoisted up her skirt and catapulted the hardest kick she could into the door. Again, and again she struck the thing with full force until it swung off the hinges.

Stalking inside, she went straight for the shelf of supplies.

"What in Christ do you think you're doing?" a deep baritone growled from the stairs.

Tess scraped away the hair that was sticking to her cheek and glared at the man trampling down from the apartment upstairs. She sneered at him. "You might be okay with leaving a man for dead, *doctor*, but I am not. These supplies belong to the town, so I'll help myself."

"He's a murderer. Anybody tell you about that?"

"I know you believe him to be one, but that makes no difference right now."

He visibly grimaced. "You'd side with a man who you know to be a dangerous criminal?"

"When I meet a new patient, I don't usually ask for their history of penitents before I attend to them, do you?" She found the eyed needles and grabbed them, snatching the carbolic acid for sterilization as well.

He watched her warily. "What do you know of any of this? Is your father a physician?"

"No," she muttered, searching for the stitching. "I am."

He scoffed. "You're an amusing woman, but my patience for your histrionics is up. I *will* have you arrested for any stolen supplies."

"Arrested by the Sheriff whose brother you're trying to kill? Good luck with that." She paused when she reached his wooden desk, reading the name carved there. "Dr. Delacourt," she mused. She'd heard it said before but seeing it in writing was a whole other thing. "Augustus Delacourt."

He furrowed a brow. "I don't believe I gave you my first name."

No, he didn't, but she knew him. Or at least *of* him. There was a wing in the hospital where she did her residency that had been named after someone with that title. Was he a well-known medical genius of some sort? Or an inventor of some kind? She couldn't remember.

None of that even mattered now.

"Where is your suture material?" she blurted. "What do you use to close open wounds?"

Dr. Delacourt pursed his lips at her.

"He'll bleed to death. Either you give me the supplies and I stitch him up myself, or you face murder charges in the morning."

He ground his teeth.

She imagined he'd never been spoken to with such force by the likes of her, so she arched a brow impatiently. "What'll it be, Doc?"

He flicked his chin and she followed the motion to what had been labeled as resorbable catgut. She vaguely remembered mention of that in her history books.

Grabbing everything she needed, she hurtled herself back onto the waiting horse and prayed she could remember the way home. She wasn't used to having to focus on her bearings rather than a GPS. She concentrated hard on the familiar landmarks – the church, the fat rock by the tree, the half-moon shaped lake that led to the farm.

After what felt like a lifetime, but couldn't have been longer than a few minutes, the horse stopped in front of the house. Thank God this was a stallion who wasn't easily spooked by a panicked and inexperienced rider. She slid off the saddle and bolted inside.

She expected just his family, but there were several men standing in the living room. Theo must've called for reinforcement. She hurried on, not caring for the way the men were staring at her, pushing open the closed bedroom door.

Heywood had been laid on the bed just as she requested, stripped down to the waist and still as death. Theo stood over him, cleansing the ugly gashes, but the arrow remained. That was good.

Lotty saw her immediately and bolted forward with a loud cry, burying her face in Tess's torn skirt.

"I did what you said," she choked out, hugging her around the waist, "I brought them here, but Pa's really hurt!"

Tess stroked her hair and met Theo's gaze, seeing his concern. "You did good, Lotty. He'll be alright. Why don't you and your Uncle go outside for a few minutes."

Lotty looked back at Theo and then clung to Tess. "I'm scared," she sobbed again. "I want to stay with Pa!"

"Oh, baby you can't."

"But what if..."

"Shhh," Tess crooned, waving Theo over. "It's all right. I'm gonna take care of daddy. I give you my word."

Theo walked over, but he didn't take Lotty like Tess had expected. Instead he grabbed onto Tess's arm, tearing her away from the clinging girl. She gasped as he yanked her toward a dark corner of the room.

"What the hell are you doing?" he hissed in a quiet grunt. "I thought you were bringing back the doctor."

She tore her arm out of his grasp. "The good ol' doc is the one who left your brother for dead. Needless to say, he wasn't very keen on coming back to save him."

"Dr. Delacourt wouldn't do something like this. He's not a violent man."

"Tell that to Heywood."

"I'll go back into town... I'll force him to come."

"You'd be wasting your time."

"Dammit woman, even you must realize that prayers and false hope given to his daughter aren't going to save him. He needs a doctor!"

"And I'm the closest you have to one! Get the hell out of my way, Sheriff, and let me do this."

Theo arched back with astonishment and then shifted toward her. Tess's heart thumped at a fearful pace, suddenly unsure of what this man would do.

Theo, however, stopped himself short in front of her and raked both trembling hands through his hair. "I can't lose him," he let out. "Everything he's been through... and Lotty. She needs him."

"Let me help."

"But if what you say is true... if the doc really is responsible..."

"He is," Tess whispered, then glanced through the open doorway at the men still standing around the living room. "I can do this. But these spectators need to leave. It's as though they're waiting to announce a death and it's scaring Lotty." She put a hand on his arm. "Trust me, okay? I won't let him die." Even as she said it, she couldn't stop the involuntary shudder.

Nonetheless, Theo nodded and half-heartedly shepherded the men out of the house, then brought Lotty to the porch where he and Grace sat with her on the step.

Tess went straight for the kitchen, grabbing all of the alcohol she could find and the sharpest knife before tumbling into the bedroom.

She closed the door behind her and took a deep breath at the unconscious man. Her lack of confidence was silly. She'd dealt with numerous disruptions to vital organs as well as infections and gunshot wounds. It seemed to reason she could deal with this as well.

She stopped at his bedside and was startled when his eyelids began to twitch.

"Lotty," he whispered. He awoke with sudden panic and then growled in pain from his jolt forward.

"Don't move," Tess said, hurrying over. "Lotty is fine. But I'm going to need to stitch you up."

He blinked his eyes open, struggling to focus as he stared wildly at her. "Do you know how?"

"Yes."

"Everything hurts."

"You're pretty torn up."

"He's never..." Heywood grunted with pain. "Emeline's dad. He's threatened me before, but he's never been physical."

"He must be getting desperate."

"Seeing you with us probably set him off."

"Oh, now I can't take *all* the credit for this madness."

He smirked at her teasing tone and then winced again.

"No more talking," she said, straightening up. "I need you to roll onto your side, I'll help."

Heywood groaned as she shifted him over, then stood back to observe the deep six-inch cut starting on his left side and running to his back. She pulled the whiskey bottle out and Heywood seemed to do a doubletake.

"It's for my hands and your wound," she whispered, cleansing her fingers with it and then pouring it over the laceration. He grimaced. She knew it would sting and regretted doing that before she'd sterilized the needle.

"I'm sorry," she whispered.

"You'll at least save some for me to drink too, right?"

Off his look, she smiled softly. "I'll try."

Moving quick to sterilize the needle in the carbolic acid, she began threading the suture.

"You have a few lacerations," she said gently. "The one I'm working on now is your deepest, and the only one that I believe needs to be stitched. The others we'll clean and bandage and will likely heal on their own." She caught his eyes lingering on the needle. "I've done this dozens of times, I'll be finished in a few minutes."

"I believe you," he whispered back.

"Just try to relax."

He gritted his teeth and she stitched him up as quickly and efficiently as she could.

"You *have* done this before," he gasped when she finished. "I'll admit it now – I didn't believe you."

He laughed brokenly and then cringed at the pain that came with it. Tess forced a smile and handed him the bottle of whiskey. "Drink up."

"Really?"

"It's anesthetic," she whispered. "It's time to remove the arrow."

He grunted. "I thought it was a knife."

"I'm sure it felt like one."

"Jesus. He really wanted me dead, didn't he?"

"If so, he'd have aimed somewhere more critical. Drink up, cause this is going to hurt." She grabbed the knife she'd carried in from the kitchen and he shrank back automatically.

"What are you doing?"

"Removing the material around the wound," she explained, digging the blade into his pant leg and tearing it open.

She gazed at his upper left thigh where she could see a plum size bruise inking out from the arrow. She touched the long spine and he lurched, a quiet sharp gasp of pain escaping him with the jolt.

"Relax," she whispered. "I know what I'm doing."

His clear blue eyes drove firmly into hers, undoubtedly *wanting* to trust her. He had good reason not to. Truth was, she'd never dealt with this kind of injury before. That didn't mean she hadn't been taught how to get it done though. The biggest problem with arrows were their removal. Not just the destruction of vital organs on their way out, but the ensuing infections were what made them worse than a gunshot wound. Nonetheless, this arrow looked simple, and she could see that it was a clean front-to-back hit. The feathered fletching was fully visible, followed by an inch or two of shaft that dissolved somewhere around the quadricep tendon. She felt around for the metal part of the arrowhead, finding it an inch inside the back of his leg.

Heywood choked down a long hard swallow of the whiskey. "What's the plan?"

"I'm going to push the arrowhead further into your leg so that it will come out the other side and I can snap it off."

He chugged again.

She took a deep breath, crouching down for a better angle.

"You know you're the first woman since Lotty's mom to see me without clothes on," he said teasingly.

"I'm honored," she scoffed, trying and failing not to eyeball the man. The new wounds were literally his only imperfections. "On three," she murmured quietly. "One, two, three!"

He gripped the bedpost as Tess pushed.

Reflex tears of pain formed tracks down the grime and soot on his cheeks. She could only manage one hard shove before she had to stop due to the ghastly sounds coming out of him. She knew he didn't mean for them and could plainly see that he was trying not to let Lotty hear it.

Feeling around, she was sure the metal head was at the surface of his skin.

"Just one more push and it should be out," she told him.

Heywood gulped another mouthful, then shoved his pillow between his teeth. It didn't muffle his grunts as much as he'd probably hoped. Tess gave it all she had, putting her entire weight into the arrow until she felt the release of it tearing through flesh. His shredded, stifled cry of pain and horror forced her back.

"I'm so sorry!"

He fell sideways onto the bed, sweat caking his skin, face matted in feathers from the torn pillow.

Tess didn't let him see the knife back in her hand. She sliced off the metal arrowhead as discretely as possible and he winced at the spasm to his fresh wound.

"Sorry again."

"You're a sadist," he heaved, and she was surprised at the small arch of his lip; that he could be witty at a time like this.

"I just need to pull it out now."

He tipped the bottle in his weakened grip, getting another mouthful. When he swallowed, he looked at her. "Thank you, Miss Corbin."

"For torturing you?"

He shook his head. No more humor. "Just let me say it now in case I don't get a chance later. I appreciate you doing this." He smiled weakly at her, almost apologetic, as though he knew how hard this was for her.

Tess forced a shaky grin, then he closed his eyes and breathed carefully from his nose. She felt the blood trickling from both sides of his wounds and knew that she had to finish this fast and stitch him up before he lost too much.

She braced herself. "Maybe I should take a swig of that alcohol."

He yanked the bottle back. "You just focus on what you need to do."

She gritted her teeth. "On three again." He downed his last helping, practically sucking the residual moisture out of the empty bottle.

Ready or not, it had to be now. Tess grabbed the end of the arrow, and on three gave it an enormous yank that ripped the shaft out of his leg. She expected a garbled moan, but instead he fell back quietly.

She didn't waste time, moving fast to treat and dress the wounds.

He had fallen into a shallow sleep by the time she finished. Standing back to look over him, she knew that she'd done all she could. She closed her eyes and tried to salvage what was left of her equilibrium.

It wasn't worth it. She was just as drained as he was.

She laid down on the small bed beside him.

It was the deepest she'd ever slept. That must have been why she nearly jumped a mile out of her skin when something touching her face forced her awake.

It was his knuckles grazing her cheek.

Heywood's eyes were soft and unfocused, but they reached her in the sunlight, watching her closely. She couldn't believe it was already morning.

"Thank you, Tess Corbin." He leaned back and scoffed tiredly to himself. "I didn't think someone who looked like you could manage it, but you proved me wrong."

"Someone like me?" she whispered tiredly.

"You're like one of those mythical fairies or nymphs. Pristine, delicate, perfect." He closed his eyes and shook his head. "Fairies and nymphs shouldn't touch blood."

Tess couldn't help chuckling. "I'm sure that's the alcohol talking."

"It's me. You're made of porcelain... but somehow unbreakable."

"You, sir, are drunk." *Lucky bastard.*

"You're beyond human."

She scoffed and forced herself up. He was already asleep when she leaned over to check his bandages. Squeezing out of the bedroom, she closed her eyes when she made it to the front door, welcoming the fresh cathartic breeze.

Nobody was out there though.

Hurrying back inside, Tess found Lotty fast asleep on the sofa with Grace. Theo was passed out on the floor in front of them.

There would be little point in waking them.

After fetching water to keep Heywood hydrated, she finally collapsed, once again falling into a deep sleep at Heywood's bedside.

CHAPTER SEVEN

The sun was fully up by the time Tess awakened. For a long moment she laid on her back, staring up at the bedroom ceiling which seemed to have been bright for hours. Then it all hit her, everything that had happened last night, and she sprung up to search for Heywood.

She found him still asleep beside her and went to checking his bandages and wounds.

"You did good," a voice grunted from the other side of the bedroom. Tess jerked at the unexpected voice, then took a deep breath when she spotted Theo sitting on a chair in the corner. "Where did you learn how to stitch like that?"

She chewed her lip and shrugged. "Same as stitching curtains and dresses, right?"

He scoffed. "I imagine not."

Through the bedroom door, Tess thought she heard Lotty's voice and was sure she must have been wondering about her dad.

"I should let her know that Heywood is okay."

Theo was beginning toward her, but she didn't want to have to answer any more questions. Instead, she swung the door open fast and catapulted out. Only it wasn't just Lotty and Grace in the living room.

The sound of Antoinette's horrified gasp froze her in place. The woman's eyes were wide circles as she took in Tess's disheveled look while still halfway inside Heywood's bedroom.

"Good gracious," Grace said, stepping into the line of fire. "This isn't at all as it appears, Miss Cavaliere."

"That's very good," Antoinette gasped wretchedly, "Since it appears a whore spent the night in Mr. Paxton's bed." Then she glared at Lotty. "While a young child is in the house, no less!"

"Don't you call Miss Corbin that foul name!" Lotty yelped in a harsh voice. "She saved my pa! Don't you dare…"

Grace pulled her back, stroking her hair. "Heywood had an accident last night," she explained.

"And apparently Miss Corbin used her feminine wiles to ease his pain," Antoinette said, adjusting her hat.

"Settle down," Theo murmured, as he made his way out of the bedroom. "The accident Heywood had was a serious one and Miss Corbin mended the critical wounds. She deserves a hell of a lot more respect than you're giving her, Miss Cavaliere."

Antoinette sniffed. "I demand to speak with Mr. Paxton and hear it from him."

"Another time. He needs his rest."

"If you're lying, and he and this woman are sneaking around..." she curled a lip at him. "The wrath of God will consume you. You know that, don't you? If you allow such unholiness you *will* live to regret it."

"That is not the case," Theo said softly, "But even if it is, let that be my burden to carry, not yours."

She snarled at him. "I'll make sure to follow up on this."

"Please, do."

"If this woman remains in Heywood's home *and* bedroom, the town will be informed."

"The spread of false gossip can only do more damage than good, Miss Cavalier. Surely you can see that."

"The people have a right to know," she said, shoving open the front door and plodding to her waiting carriage.

When she was gone, Theo closed the door again and walked toward Tess, putting a hand on her shoulder.

"Last night has made it clear that you are not in the poor mental condition that you claim to be in," he whispered. "You *do* remember your past, and it makes no sense for you to hide it since your education surpasses us."

Tess didn't say anything. Instead she held her breath, waiting.

He sighed. "It doesn't even matter. Even if this is some elaborate affair between you and my brother, you saved his life. And for that I will be indebted to you until the day I die."

She forced herself to breathe. "That's very comforting, Sheriff. But all I want now is to get this blood off me."

He took his hand off her shoulder and stepped back. "Grace has already filled the tub for you. All I ask now is that you rest."

In the bathroom, Tess found a deep brass tub and reached in, testing the lukewarm temperature. Though she'd much rather an actual shower, it was a godsend.

She bathed slowly, trying not to think about how she had cleaned off Heywood's skin similarly last night after she'd finished stitching him.

She clothed herself in the nightgown Grace had left for her and then went to her loft to lie down. She couldn't sleep though, couldn't shut her mind off for even a minute. Staring up at the wooden rafters and the walls around her, she suddenly spotted a few boxes stacked up in the corner and was curious about them.

Pulling a few open, she found old baby clothes and random artifacts. None of it was as interesting as the large wooden crate shoved in the very back filled with canvases.

She did recall Ms. Tuttle mentioning his art. Some had even been saved in the museum. She rifled slowly through them. Most were abstract and colorful though there were a few landscapes as well.

She continued to pull each out one by one until she reached the last in the pile. She froze when she saw it, her blood instantly running cold.

It was as though time itself had frozen and she could not think or breathe.

****

Heywood hadn't felt this useless since he was a little kid. He didn't know what he would have done without Gabe there to keep the farm running.

The place had seen more visitors these past couple of days than ever before. He was surprised at how many people from the church had come by with food and good wishes. He had a feeling Micah had had something to do with encouraging that. It certainly helped. Not to mention it gave Tess the chance to meet more members of the town.

He didn't honestly think she'd choose to stick around now that he could manage to move around the house. So, it was a relief every time he woke to the sound of Tess talking or playing with Lotty outside his bedroom.

"Pa?"

Startled, Heywood opened his eyes to the feel of his daughter's hand on his arm. "Hey sweetheart."

"How are you feeling?"

"Will be good as new soon enough."

"Tess made lunch. Are you hungry?"

"Sure am," he said, pushing himself upright. Then he paused at the sound of somebody else's voice outside the bedroom. "Do we have another visitor?"

"Pastor Micah came by an hour ago."

"Again? Did he at least bring me some of his sacramental wine this time?"

His quip was rewarded with a smile. "I think he comes to visit Tess more than he comes to visit you, Pa."

Heywood furrowed a brow, oddly disturbed by Lotty's teasing statement because he was sure it was true enough. The pastor was already hitting thirty-four after all and had only briefly dated in his past. It made sense that he would pursue a newcomer, especially one who looked like Tess. A man would have to be a saint not to find himself physically attracted to every piece of her. And though Micah was a holy man, a saint he was not. Neither was Heywood.

Sliding to the edge of the bed, Heywood groaned as pain shot through him.

"Maybe you should stay in bed and let us bring lunch to you," Lotty said.

He could tell she was still afraid that she might lose her father just as she had her mother, and he wished he could disperse those worries. "Just flesh wounds," he said, touching her face and smoothing out the worry lines. He pushed himself up onto his feet, a hand on Lotty's shoulder as he limped out of the bedroom beside her.

Micah and Tess were sitting on the couch sipping tea, but both stood when he approached.

Somehow Miss Corbin looked even more beautiful than before, in an emerald dress that accentuated not only her lovely feminine curves, but her warm green eyes. Strands of her golden locks curled around the nape of her neck.

Even as a man of the cloth, Micah was also clearly enjoying the pretty image of this lady. He walked over to Heywood now and shook his hand.

"Heywood, it's good to see you up and about!"

"Getting a little better every day," Heywood grunted. "What brings you by, pastor?"

"Just checking in. I make it a point to look in on my church members throughout the week so that I might provide care and counseling where necessary. I'm always willing to lend my assistance in crisis situations."

"Luckily for you the crisis seems to be over for the most part."

"Oh, I also don't mind visiting just to visit," Micah said with a toothy smile.

I'm sure you don't, Heywood thought darkly as he eyed Tess's returned smile. He wondered if she was just being courteous or if she had an interest in the man.

It wasn't his business either way.

Heywood hadn't had any need to add another woman to his and Lotty's life. Another wife, another mother. To give himself one more thing to love too hard and risk losing wasn't worth it. Things were good the way they were, and he had no intention of changing that.

If that were true, then why'd he feel such deep jealousy toward anyone else taking an interest in her? He should have been happy and encouraging to his friend's pursuit. Instead he turned to wobble himself over to the kitchen.

"Smells great in here! Are you staying for lunch, Pastor?" Even he could hear the dismissiveness in his own tone, but Micah didn't seem to notice or care.

Although he answered Heywood, his smile was clearly for Tess. "Thank you. I would like that very much. And I second Mr. Paxton's sentiment. It does smell amazing."

Tess grinned politely as they took their seats around the wooden table. "I can't take the credit. This is a casserole one of the ladies from the congregation brought over. I had a hard enough time just trying to figure out how the oven works."

"You're modest."

Heywood snorted. Of all the things that made Tess a pleasure to share a home with, cooking was not one of them. The kitchen seemed like something from another world to her. But she at least made the effort and was no worse than his own culinary attempts.

After Micah said a prayer over their meal, he gave himself a helping of food and then passed the casserole dish to Heywood. "I was just telling Miss Corbin about our Independence Day picnic," he said.

"Oh," Heywood answered, filling his plate and then Lotty's before offering to scoop Tess's helping as well. She accepted with quiet gratitude. "Do you suppose you'll still be in town by then?"

"I couldn't say for sure."

Micah seemed disappointed. "I do hope you'll at least visit if you do leave before then. It's loads of fun for adults and children alike."

"It's true," Lotty said, scooping a spoonful of food into her mouth. "Me and Pa always love going. It's where my Ma and Pa first met. Isn't that right, Pa? When you were like me?"

"That's right, Little Lotty. We were about your age."

"You thought she was super pretty," Lotty interrupted with new eagerness, then looked at Tess. "He said she was like a princess."

Tess grinned warmly. "Probably just as pretty as you are."

"Nah, she was prettier."

Heywood stroked his little girl's hair. "You're her spitting image."

"Tell Tess about the tree, Pa!"

"Maybe another time," he replied halfheartedly.

"It's a super special tree," Lotty insisted. "Nothing like any others. And it's theirs."

Tess's attention immediately reshuffled toward Heywood and he shifted his glance to his plate, troubled over the way that looking into Tess's eyes made him feel.

"Nobody wants to hear about that," he murmured.

Micah seemed to take that as an opportunity to get the focus back on himself, but he'd only managed to lean forward and open his mouth before Tess interrupted with,

"Actually, I would be very interested in hearing about it, Mr. Paxton."

He couldn't help a smile. "I think you and I are on a first name basis by now."

"I agree," she said, then leaned forward giving him the same encouraging smile she often gave to Lotty when listening to her stories.

Astoundingly, he found himself talking without more urging. "We used to sneak off into the mountains when we were growing up. Would always meet at the same tree."

"Tell her how you knew which tree it was," Lotty implored.

"I bet I can guess," Tess said. "Did it have a knot in it?"

What?

Lotty's jaw dropped wide open. "How'd you know?"

"I found a painting of it up in the loft. I'm sorry for snooping, I just kind of stumbled into it and have been wanting to ask ever since."

Micah took a sip of his water. "I didn't know you painted, old boy."

Heywood shrugged, feeling embarrassed and uncomfortable.

"But back to the tree," Tess urged. It surprised Heywood how interested she was in this.

Lotty touched his hand. "Tell her about the blood pact."

Heywood shook his head, giving his daughter an irritated grin. *Come on, kid!* "We made a blood pact," he said at last. "Emeline and I made a promise to marry each other, so we sealed it with a blood pact on the tree."

"On the knot?" Tess asked.

He leaned back thoughtfully. "Yes."

"Where is this tree?"

"Not far from where we found you," Lotty said.

Tess was silent for a moment or two, then said, "That's quite romantic."

Heywood just shrugged again, then allowed Micah to fill in the rest of the conversation. The pastor was an easy talker, but Heywood found Tess's end of the conversation to be distracted and somewhat indifferent. Her mind was clearly elsewhere. He hated to admit that he'd hoped it was with him.

He was an idiot to feel that way. And was even more of an idiot for allowing himself to obsess over that night she'd saved his life and fell asleep beside him. He kept remembering the velvetiness of her hair and the heat of her body. And when that sweet shape of her mouth would smile.

He shook his head, forcing out those thoughts.

****

Tess couldn't think of anything other than that tree. She'd known it was the one from her backyard the moment she saw the painting. She recognized the thick trunk that held her treehouse.

It was the same crazy knot three feet up from the ground that she'd fallen over and knocked her head on. There was no other like it in the world.

She laid awake all night thinking about it. It had to have been the trigger. Maybe it had something to do with the blood.

Could it have really been that easy? It was unlikely that this sort of phenomenon could happen all because of one ridiculously perfect accident! It was unheard of... though technically so was *all* of this.

People spent their entire lives researching time travel. Was there even the slightest possibility that there could have been triggers lying all over the place, just waiting to be found?

It sounded crazy but was at the very least worth a try. If what threw her back was her blood spilling in the same place as theirs once had, then doing so again would have to also carry her forward.... logically.

She awoke the following morning and dressed in a hurry. This was the day she would find that tree. Heywood was fully capable of functioning without her by now. In fact, she had a feeling she'd done all that she could for this era. Those wounds were probably what had caused Heywood's death in the first place and she fixed that. This little girl would now grow up with her father.

You're welcome.

She scrambled down the stairs and opened the door, suddenly freezing at the warm rain slashing down onto the farm, making it hard to see.

"Pa and I already collected eggs before the storm," Lotty said, taking Tess's hand.

Oh no. They were going to be quarantined until the rain ended.

"Can I help make breakfast?" Lotty went on, oblivious to Tess's disappointment.

Tess blinked, reminding herself that there would be another time to search for the tree.

Swallowing her anger, she turned around gently and scooped up the child.

"Of course!" she said, setting her down on a stepping stool in the kitchen. Together they scrambled, seasoned, and flipped the eggs.

"When your daddy tries them, you let him know that *you* made these!"

"With help," Lotty said with a childish roll of her eyes.

Heywood joined them soon after and they all ate quietly while Tess outwaited the rain.

It finally stopped around noon.

Tess put on the warmest coating she could find in Grace's box and headed back downstairs, completely unaware of Heywood in the living room. She paused when she reached the front door and noticed him awkwardly bent over the arm of the couch.

"Are you okay?" she asked, inching into the room.

Heywood jolted upright and then cringed a little at the fast movement. "Yes," he said, laughing at himself. "Lotty and I are just playing a little game of hide and seek, but I can't seem to find her."

"Oh," she said with a small chuckle. "Have you tried the Marco Polo technique? Kids can't help giving themselves away with that."

"Marco Polo?"

Too early for that game? "Hot and cold then maybe?"

He arched a brow at her.

Not that either? "So, you guys just literally hide on immense property and there's no end to the game until you find each other?"

"That's the game," he said with a shrug.

"How long has she been hiding?"

"Well, that's my concern. I've been looking over thirty minutes. The house isn't that large."

"No, it's not and I've just come from upstairs."

"That only leaves..." he glanced outside and sighed.

"I'll check the barn," she said. "But you need to better regulate the rules of this game."

"Yes, Ma'am."

She glanced at the sky as she made her way to the barn. She'd never seen it so dark this early. The strange mix of hot and cold wind was very familiar to her. It was definitely tornado weather. Colorado was famous for them. In her world, there would be sirens to warn of any tornados touching ground, but she knew that there wouldn't be any such forewarnings here.

"Lotty!" she screamed, then stared up where the dark clouds formed ominous cyclones. This was serious. Again, she screamed her name till her throat was raw. "Game's over, you win! Come out now!"

She trampled to the barn, but Lotty wasn't in there. Where the hell could this girl be hiding?

She forced the door back open as a crackle of thunder roared in the distance.

Lotty was suddenly visible far out in the pastures, running between haystacks as though unaware of the thunderstorm.

"Lotty!"

The child couldn't hear her screaming and Tess's heart did a somersault when the little girl climbed under a metal feeding tank.

Dammit, Lotty, NO!

The thunder rolled again, closer this time. There was a tingling sensation in Tess's entire body. Lightning was about to strike again, and she crouched down immediately.

No, no, no!

Lightning lit up the sky and Tess watched the bolt zigzag horizontally, hitting its target perfectly. The sparks were blinding when it touched the metal box, forcing Tess back into the mud.

She lunged forward as soon as she had the power, running hard and fast through the slick grass.

"Lotty, no!" she screeched. "Please, baby. Oh, God please."

When she made it to the feeding tank, she pried it open and let out a howl when she saw the still small body laying inside.

She gave her a small shake, but Lotty was unresponsive. The rain had begun to cascade once again over the farm, making it impossible to tell if she was breathing. Tess scooped her up and made a run for the house.

Heywood met her on the porch and grabbed his little girl, hurling her to the couch where his trembling fingers fumbled across her lips, searching for warm breath. He pressed his head against her chest and then wailed in pain for her.

Tess winced at the wretched, brokenhearted sound.

He kept shaking and hugging her, but it was no use. He was holding emptiness.

And that's when Tess remembered Heywood's death. It wasn't the doctor's wounds that had killed him like she thought. Mr. Delacourt only went after him because he saw them together. If Tess hadn't been there, he wouldn't have attacked him.

No, what Ms. Tuttle had clearly told her was that he'd disappeared soon after his daughter's untimely death.

CHAPTER EIGHT

Tess was not about to accept this. This little girl was not going to die like that!

"Let me," she said, pushing Heywood out of her way and crawling to Lotty on the couch. She pressed her fingers into her neck where a pulse should have been found, then immediately began to pump the heels of her hands over Lotty's tiny chest, praying her ribs wouldn't break.

"What are you doing?" Heywood gasped, hurling himself forward.

With enormous strength he ripped her off his daughter and threw her down hard onto the floor.

Tess was stunned by the wind being knocked out of her. Despite that, she was not at all surprised by his reaction. Heywood's world was a completely different one. What Tess was trying to do had clearly frightened him.

Now that she'd gotten over the shock of being catapulted to the ground, however, Tess got her feet back under her and tried to shove Heywood off again, even resorting to slapping his face.

Heywood shoved her squarely in the chest, this time holding her down on the hardwood. "Have you gone mad?" he growled into her face.

"Dammit, Heywood, what the hell does it take to gain your trust?"

He blinked, suddenly understanding. This wasn't the first time she'd done things he couldn't comprehend, and he reluctantly climbed off her, sinking back on his heels.

Tess bolted upright and went straight to pumping Lotty's heart to the rhythm of "Saturday Night Fever" just like she'd been taught ages ago. She tilted Lotty's mouth open next and blew air into her lungs.

"Her chest is rising," Heywood gasped, crawling closer.

She breathed into the little girl's lungs again and then went back to the chest compressions.

Heywood leaned forward, watching desperately for some sign of success.

Tess didn't know how long she should give him hope when the girl had clearly passed. She continued to try though.

She almost couldn't believe it when Lotty miraculously let out a small cough.

"Charlotte?" Heywood gasped, sweeping the damp black strands of hair from her face. Tess felt around her neck again and breathed a sigh of relief when she found a strong pulse beating against her fingers.

Lotty's lashes finally fluttered open and her eyes met her father's.

"You found me," she said weakly. "It's your turn to hide, Pa."

Heywood laughed, despite the tears pouring down his cheeks. He scooped her up and cradled her small body against his as he stared back at Tess.

She expected only desperate gratitude on his face, but his look was strangely puzzled. He panted hoarsely, staring at her as though she were a mythical creature come to life. He finally gave his head a slight shake, too much of a mess to even question what had just happened.

He rocked his baby girl on the floor of their living room, his awful choking sobs the only sound in the house.

Tess got up and brought him a handkerchief. He blew his nose loudly and mopped the tears off his face.

"She was dead," he gasped at last. "Her heart stopped."

"She was electrocuted by the lightning."

"You brought her back. You have no idea what you've done for me today."

Tess was sure that she did.

She'd just changed the entire course of his life, hopefully for the better.

She sank back onto the carpet, wiping away the rain and sweat with her skirt.

It was strange how little people knew then and how far human beings had come throughout this century and into the one after.

She decided to stay the night, but by sunrise was gone.

She'd taken Saturn and a kitchen knife and found the tree before anyone at the Paxton Farm had woken.

Cutting her arm open wasn't nearly as painful as letting that horse flee. She prayed he would find home, that they both would.

****

It was blinding light that met her when she opened her eyes again. Tess squeezed them shut quickly. It was as though they hadn't been used for days.

She forced herself to try again, this time spotting the tree through her lashes. Her eyes slowly widened at the bright sunlight cascading over it. She recognized the knot, the tree house, and yard – but it felt different.

She didn't know why.

Climbing onto her feet, it was abruptly clear that she wasn't in the same pajamas she'd been wearing that night that she originally fell. This was one of Grace's laced and bowed nighttime garments.

But that shouldn't have been possible!

Everything she experienced with Heywood and Lotty and that whole other world had to have been a hallucination from the bump on her head.

Clearly it couldn't have been a delusion though if she still wore the clothes! Figments of imagination did not leave behind physical proof like *this*.

She couldn't catch her breath, the ground seemed to be rocking beneath her feet. Grabbing the tree for balance, she forced in a deep breath. Her head throbbed.

When the dizziness finally weakened, Tess moved as quick as she could toward the house.

The distant rumbling of the train was a pleasant, safe sound. It whistled loudly to warn the town below of its journey through, and she breathed easily listening to that. Any bit of familiarity was comforting after the inexplicable days she'd just come from.

The front door to her house was locked, so she punched the code into the keypad and then deactivated the alarm.

"Mom!" she called when she made it into the foyer. "Ma!"

She wasn't home. That was probably good.

Tess stripped off her clothes as she bolted up the stairs. After stuffing the old-fashioned nighty into her closet, she hurried to the bathroom and got the shower running.

She studied herself in the mirror while waiting for the water to reach a good temperature. She could see no wound except a few scratches at her elbows. Whatever knock on the head she'd gotten when she originally fell from the tree was gone by now.

The shower was hot and steamy by the time she climbed inside. She held her face under the cleansing stream, and as the grime washed away, she swore that she would never again take a shower for granted.

When she climbed back out, however, she felt just as uneasy and sick as she had when she had first woken up. She didn't know why her body was reacting this way. Something was off about the world she returned to. Very, very wrong.

Finally heading to her closet, she dressed quickly in one of her pretty new white romps and heels before towel drying her hair. Once she had her appearance under control, she went for the phone that she kept hidden from her mother behind the dresser. Mrs. Corbin had been caught snooping many times and had a knack for breaking into even password protected devices. She clearly hadn't found this new hiding place yet.

The clock surprised her. It was already late afternoon. She must have been knocked out for hours. Taking a deep breath, she scrolled through her contacts and dialed Joel. If she had to face reality again and pray to God that she wouldn't be dubbed insane, Joel was the one to contact.

"Hello?" Joel said on the second ring, except it didn't sound like an answer. More like a man who'd never expected his phone to chime.

"Hey, it's Tess."

There was silence on the other end, until he blurted, "Is this for real? Tess, is this actually you?"

"Of course."

"Are you okay? I mean, you're calling from a safe place, right?"

"What are you talking about?"

"Did anybody hurt you?"

"No," she said, irritated. "You're scaring me!"

"Let's meet. Where are you?"

"Home."

"I'll be there in a few minutes."

He hung up fast and Tess went outside, her heart racing as she scrolled through all the unopen texts.

Joel had sent a few, asking if she was okay and there was another handful from her mother, demanding that she come home.

Killian had sent far more than anyone else. They'd started off gentle and then swiftly morphed into something else.

She rapidly began scrolling through them one by one…

"Babe, why haven't you called me back? Shoot me a text when you see this."

"Still waiting. Where are you, baby doll?"

"Why are my calls going straight to voicemail?"

"Your mom said you haven't been home. Where the hell are you? Call me NOW!"

"Really? A whole day with no word. Nice, Tess."

"I wasn't supposed to make another trip to Colorado this week, but I guess I have no other choice. Where are you?? You better be home when I get there."

"Are you serious? I got into Half Hallow over an hour ago and have been calling and waiting ever since!"

"Your mom says you still haven't come home since Friday night. You're starting to scare everyone. ANSWER YOUR DAMN PHONE!"

"I'm afraid to ask. Starting to get an idea of what this might be. Never expected that from you. At least have the decency to talk to me."

"Really? Are you seriously trying to run out on me? You know how many other girls would kill to be you, and you're just gonna bolt?"

"So I guess you turned your phone off so you wouldn't have to deal with me while making your runaway. LMAO. I hope this other man you apparently found is worth it. Can't wait to meet him."

"This is getting ridiculous. I'd be scared to face me too after what you put me through. Let me make it easier – I will not come chasing after you with my tail between my legs. Chicks like you are a dime a dozen."

"WHERE ARE YOU?!"

"Sooner or later you'll have to face me again. The longer you stay away, the worse it's going to be."

"I deserve more than this."

"Just get your ass home."

"I already talked to a private investigator. I'll find out soon enough if you've been hooking up with another man behind my back. Would be better for you if you just come clean now."

Tess stared again at that last message.

Killian claimed that he didn't need her, that he wouldn't come chasing after her. Yet he seemed increasingly desperate in the texts that followed.

Rejection must have been terrifying to the man.

She shivered and shut down her phone, even more happy now that she'd chosen to call Joel first.

His car arrived within minutes and he sprung out of it the instant it was parked.

"Tess, oh my God, this is insane!" He was nearly panting on his way up the porch, pulling her into a bear hug. "Do you have any idea what your family's been through?"

"I'm starting to. Just got done scrolling through Killian's insane texts."

"Can you blame the guy? You've been gone for a week! You better be able to explain that! You were almost a missing person. For real, your mom came into the station while I was on duty, but Killian convinced her not to make it a missing person's case. Guess he didn't want the attention. He convinced her that you were just taking a break but come on. I know you better than that. You wouldn't just run out. So, what the hell is going on?"

"You wouldn't believe me if I told you."

"Try me."

She sucked in a breath, then noticed he was alone.

"You didn't bring Matthias?"

"Who?"

Tess scowled at that, and then smirked with amusement. "Funny. Your son?"

"My son? What the hell are you talking about? Jesus, Tess, you're freaking me out. Tell me you're joking, *please*."

"Now you're freaking *me* out," she gasped. "You honestly don't know who Matthias is?"

He shrugged, and Tess's heart sank. This was all wrong! How could Joel not remember his own son?

"You and Skylah had Matthias five years ago," she said softly. "Skylah Pasfield."

Joel shook his head. "The hell are you talking about?"

He made it seem as though it never even happened. But...

"Why would something like that change?" she murmured, hurrying inside and up the stairs to her laptop. Joel followed at her heels.

"What else is different?" she muttered. "Does Cora Corbin even still live here?"

"Your mother? What'd you think she moved out when you disappeared? The woman's been out there searching along with everyone else. Your fiancé's done a good job of keeping this out of the press, but she hasn't given up. Search parties, posters."

"Why'd Killian keep it secret?"

"To keep his name out of the tabloids?" He sighed loudly. "It pissed me off, truth be told. I figured you'd been human trafficked and needed the public to keep their eye out for you. Seriously, where the hell have you been?"

"I couldn't even explain it if I wanted to."

"Amnesia?"

"Sure, let's go with that," she muttered, bouncing onto the bed and turning on the laptop. Skylah Pasfield's facebook and Instagram were both gone. There wasn't a Skylah Pasfield even listed as ever having gone to their high school. "What was Skylah's parents' names?"

"Again with this Skylah person. You're talking nutty!"

"Edna and Richard Pasfield," she reminded herself, typing in their names.

She filed through pages of documents before she finally found an obituary for a Richard Pasfield from forty-eight years ago. That couldn't have been the same one. This boy was only nine years old and had died in a hospital from asphyxiation.

How odd to die of that. Why didn't the hospital use the forced respirator to keep pumping air into his lungs? They used those all the time at her hospital as a way of consistently breathing for a person who couldn't on their own. To die of asphyxia in that setting was unheard of.

It wasn't a new idea either; the thing had been around since the early 1900's.

Her breath stopped. "The Delacourt," she let out in a squawky whisper. "The forced respirator was called The Delacourt."

Joel sat down beside her, but she was in such shock she barely noticed him.

"Augustus Delacourt! That's why my hospital had an entire wing named after the man, because he had invented the tool used to save millions of lives! But *I* didn't change that! He was still alive when I left."

"You're losing me, Tess."

"Listen to me," she gasped, turning around to face him on the mattress. "This is going to sound crazy, but when I disappeared, I was still here, just in another time."

"Your alibi for this missing timeframe is a parallel universe?"

"No, I just went back. I met that man from the museum portrait. I must have changed something while there. Something that stopped Augustus from inventing that device that would have saved Richard Pasfield. Because he wasn't born, neither was Skylah and that's why you never met her. That's why you never had Matthias!"

She could only wonder how many other lives were lost or changed due to this, and what those people could have contributed that the world was now left without.

Joel's expression changed as he appraised her. "It'll be okay, Tess. We'll see a doctor. You must've been through a lot." His tone sounded vaguely threatening to her, and Tess shifted away from him toward the closet.

"I can prove it, I still have the dress," she said, pulling out the garment.

Joel got up and met her across the room, taking the nightgown in his hand and examining it. "Where'd you get this? It's barely worn."

"That's what I'm trying to explain to you. The year 1900. Brand new."

He shook his head. "Well, this is definitely cool, but I'm sure you could have found it at some antique shop."

"Dammit, Joel, when have I ever been a liar – or insane?"

He shrugged a little. It was infuriating.

The doorbell rang, and she noticed Joel shrink back to the bed automatically. It was such a strange reaction. Then she clicked the doorbell app on her phone and saw who was standing on her porch.

"You told Killian I was here?"

Joel shrugged a little. "He asked me to tell him the minute I heard from you."

"Since when have you two been bro's?"

"It's not like that. I mean, it's freaking Killian Seymour. Said he'd get me on the guest list for his next premier party if I kept him in the know. How could I turn him down?"

"Wow. Et tu, Brute? You got your thirty pieces of silver, now what?"

"Don't be dramatic. It's your fiancé."

The doorbell chimed again, and Tess winced. Giving Joel the evil eye, she slammed the bedroom door behind her, moving slowly down the staircase.

She reluctantly opened the door to a much more casual Killian than she was used to. He wore a white linen shirt and chino trousers, his feet in sandals and hair still wet from a shower.

"Well, well," he murmured, gazing down at her.

All she could manage to squeak out was a timid, "Hi."

"I guess I could ask the obvious question."

"I don't even know what to say," she murmured. "I fell off that damn tree house and everything after is blank."

"Joel mentioned you seemed out of sorts." He studied her a moment. "Sounds a little like something that happened with my Uncle a few years back. He went missing and then showed up out of nowhere at a gas station buck naked. Had been in a Fugue State apparently."

"Fugue state?"

"The psychiatrist diagnosis was reversible amnesia for identity and memories... for him it lasted months, but you seem to be back to normal."

"I am."

"Good." He walked inside the foyer, forcing her back a step. "Wouldn't want to have to call another psychiatrist and have you committed." He scoffed a little at that, but Tess just ground her teeth, heart racing.

"I'm okay, I swear," she whispered. "I'm sorry I scared you."

"You did! You scared all of us!"

"I didn't mean to."

"You really can't remember anything? You're that screwed up?"

She glanced down, but he clipped his fingers under her chin forcing her to look at him.

He studied her closely, those beautiful hard eyes digging deep into hers. "You seem different," he finally murmured. "Tell me the truth."

"I am," she whispered hoarsely.

His fingers tightened a little on her chin, and she inhaled sharply.

"I swear, Killian. I wouldn't lie to you."

Except she would. Of course, she would! If this man knew how insane she actually was, he'd have her locked up and hidden away from the media in a second flat. Anything to salvage his own reputation.

"Tell me everything you do remember," he urged, still holding her face, still gaping into her eyes.

"After you and I spent time at the tree house, I was feeling nostalgic and went back outside to climb inside. Stupid idea, it was rotted. I remember falling and hitting my head. I woke up today."

"Bullshit. We searched your property."

"I must have wandered around. That fugue state you mentioned."

He scowled at her, his handsome perfect features creasing with mistrust.

"You know me," she urged softly. "I wouldn't have taken off without letting someone know. I only just found my phone this afternoon."

He let go of her finally. "I hate to admit it, but I'm a little hurt that I wasn't the first one you called." Taking her hand, he gazed at the magnificent diamond. "I'm glad to see that this didn't leave your finger. I won't lie, I did wonder."

She sighed, remembering the hurtful accusations he'd made when he believed she'd run off with another man.

He let her hand drop and they stood in an awkward silence until he turned around and began toward the wet bar. He poured them each a glass of red wine.

"I suppose now that you have access to your phone, I should explain myself."

Tess took the glass he offered her and sipped slowly, listening.

"When I thought you ran out on me, I sent you a few texts that I kind of went off on. It's of moot point now, so probably best if you just delete them without reading."

She forced down her mouthful of wine, nearly choking. Was that supposed to be an apology? "You mean the one where you demeaned me and said chicks like me were a dime a dozen? Yeah I read those."

He scoffed. "I don't even know what to say."

"That you're sorry would be nice."

"Well I don't entirely know if I am."

Her jaw dropped.

"Come on, Tess, you disappeared right after I handed you a $250,000 engagement ring! What was I supposed to do?"

"Not be a dick for starters."

"Don't say that," he said dryly. "It's not witty enough and belittles *you* more than it does me. You should know better than to talk to me like that."

"Like how you spoke to me in those texts?"

"I mean it, Tess. Speak to me with respect or don't speak at all."

She chewed her lip.

"Thatta girl." He gave her a wink and downed his wine.

She fumed as she watched him turn his back to her, setting down the glass to pour himself another.

"I'm not just some groupie in your entourage, Killian."

He set down the bottle and straightened but didn't turn to look at her.

She took a deep breath. "I demand respect too. Putting this ring on my finger doesn't mean that you own me. I can come and go as I please, and I should not have to prove that I'm being faithful."

"I have no reason to assume otherwise."

"You have my word."

He sniffed at that.

"What does that sound mean?"

He turned around now and looked her over thoroughly. "You seem to forget that I am never outside of the public eye. When have I ever allowed anyone in my life to make me appear weak or foolish?"

"That's not what I was trying to do."

He held up a hand to quiet her. "With or without a marriage license, you are still my fiancé. That ring shows the world that you are my soon-to-be wife. According to social order, yes that does make you mine and any side fling *is* in fact infidelity and will not be tolerated."

"I wasn't doing that..."

"Well, as far as you can remember, right?" He curled his lip at her and took another sip.

"You should know me better."

"Oh, I plan to make certain that I do."

He glanced over her shoulder, noticing Joel in the doorway.

Killian finger combed his hair back and then walked toward him with his hand out.

"Joel," he said softly, shaking his hand. "Can I pour you a drink?"

"I'd love one," Joel said, clearly curious of what he'd walked in on. "A scotch on ice if they have it."

"Mrs. Corbin has everything," Killian said charismatically, pouring him a glass. "Your friend was of great service to me today," he said to Tess. "Helped me out a great deal."

Yes, she'd already been made aware of this traitor. Tess didn't answer, but she saw Joel inhale his scotch in one swallow and then nod for another.

This wasn't like him. Joel was always warm and fun and comfortable. This new desire to please a celebrity for the hope of landing an invitation to some playboy house wasn't her best friend.

The two talked briefly as they drank until Killian set his glass down.

"I guess we ought to be going," he said suddenly. "I wish we could stay, but I've already lost a great deal of work due to this impromptu stay in Colorado."

Tess furrowed a brow. "What do you mean – *we* ought to be going?"

Killian snickered. "You're joking, right? Obviously, you're coming back with me."

Tess shook her head, but Killian interrupted before she could object. "You're going to need to be watched over after that ordeal you put us all through. Now go on upstairs and pack. We're leaving in fifteen minutes."

"I don't need a babysitter."

"Tesla, please don't argue," Killian groaned. "You've already put me through quite enough. Help me out, Joel. You agree that part of my husbandly duties is to care for her, right?"

Joel must have seen the anxiety in her eyes, because the Judas in him wilted, and in its place came Tess's childhood friend.

"Her mom's been worried sick," he murmured, setting down his drink beside Killian's. "Mrs. Corbin was all but ready to report her as a missing person. She still might if she doesn't get to see her daughter face-to-face."

Killian offered one of his charming grins. "You're right. Of course. I wouldn't dare keep Tess from her mother."

He looked at her. "Indeed, we'll make sure you see your mom before we leave." He pulled his phone up from his pocket and began to type. After several back and forth messages, he nodded and put the phone back. "She's hurrying home now. Should be here in twenty minutes. Now go on and pack some stuff. We're going straight to the airport after we're through here."

Tess began reluctantly toward the door while Killian poured himself another glass of wine.

"This is going to be quite a shock for her," he uttered over his shoulder, stopping her in the doorway. "Her life stopped when you disappeared. I hope you're happy with yourself." He turned around and watched her as he sipped. "You understand the affect your decisions have on others, don't you?"

She lowered her head, but felt his eyes on her, clearly not buying the amnesia tale.

"Not just your mother, but the people around her," he went on. "All of her charity work got put on hold, the projects she was running for the town. Those people who would have benefited from her work were let down too. A whole ripple effect because of one person."

Tess felt a tightening in her gut. That was it. *A whole ripple effect...*

"It was Little Lotty," she whispered.

Killian furrowed a brow. "What'd you say?"

Ignoring him, she turned toward Joel. "It was the kid! Charlotte's death was what made Augustus Delacourt discover his medical phenomenon that saved so many lives. It's because I saved her that he never pursued it."

Joel gave a small huff of amusement. "So, because you saved some kid, I have a son that was never born?"

"It sounds ridiculous, but yes! She was hit by lightning. His forced respirator would have kept her lungs filled and saved her, that must have been why he created it. But I used CPR instead and he never invented it."

He and Killian eyed each other.

Joel finally smirked, and with a shrug said. "Well, hell, unsave her then."

She was taken aback. "What?"

"Yeah, if all this is true, then fix it. Go back and electrocute the kid."

"You're not serious."

"Is it really murder if she is technically already dead? Sounds to me like she was never meant to be, so everything she touches from the day she should have died, changes history."

"You're right."

He snickered. "Jesus, Tess, you really believe this don't you?"

She stared up at him, wide-eyed. He was only toying with her. She should have detected the sarcasm in his voice.

"What in the hell are you two babbling about?" Killian asked.

"Just make-believe stuff," Joel answered, cocking his brow uncertainly at Tess. "Theories and speculations on what could have happened."

She snarled. "You want me to prove it, I'll prove it." Spinning on her heel, she grabbed a knife from the kitchen and made a run for the backyard.

She could hear Joel's feet pounding into the earth behind her and Killian's shouts from somewhere behind him, but she didn't look back or stop until she made it to the tree house.

Stopping there, she pressed the point of her knife against the flesh on her forearm, cringing at the tearing sensation as the warmth of blood ran down to her hand.

"Tess!" Joel gasped, stopping short. The cop in him froze, hands up as if to steady her. "Easy now. Put down the knife."

"I'll fix this, Joel. I'll make everything right," she said swiping a hand down on her arm and coating the knot of the tree with her blood.

"Tess!" he exclaimed, and she could see the shape of Killian racing down the yard behind him. Except there shouldn't have been so many trees in her yard. The two men faded in and out, halfway between a forest and her backyard.

She shut her eyes, blocking out the inconsistent world, trying to make sense of it.

CHAPTER NINE

Tess had no idea how long she'd been wandering the woods. She felt deliriously weary, cringing at every howl. It was a far journey down the mountain without a horse, especially in heels.

She only knew that hours were passing by the darkening sky.

There was a moment where she considered heading back to the tree, away from the danger of wolves, but then there was music.

It was so strange to find that in the middle of nature. She recognized it as the soft plucking of guitar strings. Then slowly a voice joined its melody.

Tess reared toward that sound, padding down the path where an orange glow showed beyond the trees. When she made it to the clearing, she saw that it was a bonfire, and two sat beside it. She crouched behind a tree to better eye the tent and its occupants.

There was a pleasant harmony drifting softly between a young female voice and a deep baritone. It reminded her of the few summer nights that her father was not on tour, when they'd look at the stars in his telescope and sing his music.

Coming out of her memory, she'd noticed that the smaller figure had stood up and was facing the tree that she hid behind.

"Tess?" the kid gasped, and the music froze.

Lotty?

Was this for real?

Tess emerged reluctantly.

"You came back!" Lotty burst. She pulled up her nightgown and bolted toward her.

Tess let out her arms just an instant before the small body slammed against her, knocking them both over.

She chuckled as she landed on her back, bear hugging this little girl. She actually made it. Somehow she'd managed to travel through decades a second time! She couldn't believe it, she'd not only found the portal, but understood how to use it. How many other doorways might there have been in this world, still yet to be discovered?

A larger shadow fell abruptly over them, and Heywood immediately bent down to pull them apart. He pushed his daughter against his broad body, studying this stranger in the darkness.

"Tess Corbin?" he asked doubtfully. "Is that really you?"

Tess chewed the inside of her lip, suddenly curious of how different she looked. Straightened hair, makeup. Not to mention what must seem a ridiculous ensemble to them.

Tess forced her feet back under her and stared at Heywood Paxton. His eyes were indeed as blue as periwinkles just like she remembered.

"We thought you left," he said at last, setting an arm around his daughter.

Lotty was already shaking her head over and over, completely distraught. "You didn't even say goodbye," she gushed. "You were just gone!"

Tess wilted. "I'm so sorry," she whispered. "I thought it would be easier that way."

Lotty gritted her teeth, surely angry, but then she grinned and ran back to her.

Tess barely caught her this time. Lotty landed hard against her middle forcing Tess back a step.

"You say goodbye next time," Lotty ordered against Tess's stomach. "Promise me you'll say a proper goodbye before you leave."

Tess touched her back gently. "Okay."

"Come on now, Little Lotty, ease up on the lady," Heywood said. "You trying to crush her to death?" He looked Tess over. "You seem to enjoy traveling in your undergarments, Miss Corbin."

Tess flushed a little at that. Certainly, underwear was exactly what an eyelet lace romper would look like to them.

"I didn't have time to change," she squawked.

He smirked at that and then went into the tent, returning seconds later with a blanket that he shook out and flung over her shoulders. He eyed her curiously as he closed the material under her chin. "Are you okay? I know you told me before that you're not running from anything…"

"I'm not, I'm fine," she said, clutching the blanket he'd wrapped around her.

"In that case, would you like to join us? We've got food cooking and plenty of room in the tent."

"Oh, please?" Lotty begged. "You can sleep on my end with me."

Tess stroked her hair. "Of course, I will."

She thought she saw the ghost of a smile on Heywood's face, but he had turned back to the fire before she could be sure. Both Tess and Lotty joined him as he flipped the meat over the flames.

Tess watched him, curious if he really did care to have her back or if he was just being polite since she saved his daughter's life. And ruined so many others in the aftermath.

She cringed thinking back on the altered world she'd returned to and what it would take to fix it.

Heywood grabbed his guitar again and the music wasn't anything like what she'd heard earlier in the forest. This had a fun beat to it, something you could dance to. He began to sing, and Tess grinned at the silly lyrics.

Lotty clapped with joy and attempted several times to keep up with the fast-paced tongue-twisters in the song but broke down in hysterical laughter each time she distorted a word. Heywood had clearly sung this one before, making faces at his daughter as he wittily finished each verse about this endearing pony who by the song's end had a jumble of tongue-twister characteristics that Tess couldn't even attempt enunciating.

They sang a few more absurd and lovable songs together until dinner was ready. After they ate, Heywood opened the tent for Lotty and Tess to climb inside.

"You coming, Pa?" Lotty asked, poking her head out.

"Naw, I'll leave you ladies some privacy. I'll be just fine out here."

"Oh, that wouldn't be right," Tess said, attempting to climb back out, but he stopped her.

"What *would* be right? Leaving you outside? Better it be me, I've slept under the stars plenty of times."

"There's enough room in here for all of us."

"I reckon my mother would turn over in her grave," he teased.

She snorted at that, having forgotten the rules of his time. "I suppose you're right. It would be a little inappropriate."

"The busybodies can probably already sense a disturbance in the town just at the very thought of it."

Tess smirked.

"It's not very comfortable on the dirt though, Pa. You want a pillow and blanket?"

"Wouldn't say no to that. You're very thoughtful," he said, giving his daughter a kiss as she handed him the bedding.

Lotty secured the opening of the tent and watched as he set himself up against one of the logs.

"Can you sing me a bedtime song?"

Heywood grunted. "Haven't you heard enough of my terrible voice by now?"

"You sing great, Pa. Doesn't he, Tess?"

"I wouldn't boo him off stage."

"What a compliment," Heywood muttered teasingly, and picked up his guitar. He began to strum softly, the soulful notes whispering through the evening breeze, a forlorn, gentle lament. Tess thought she recognized it, a song her father used to sing to her when she was younger, but she wasn't sure.

His expression was bleak, just like the music, but his playing was exquisite.

Tess scooted down beside Lotty, listening, entranced. He was such a gifted instrumentalist. She wondered what else she didn't know about this man.

By now she recognized the beautiful piece and began to sing softly to the despondent melody.

"Through many dangers,

Toils and snares.

We have already come.

T'was grace that brought us

Safe thus far.

And grace will lead us home."

His expression was unreadable when he glanced back at her, and she flushed.

"I'm surprised I still remember the words," she murmured, embarrassed.

His lips quirked up into a half smile as he rolled the music into the next verse of "Amazing Grace". This time he joined her in a soft harmony.

Tess knew she had sung this hymn as a lullaby with her father, but it felt entirely different singing it now with Heywood.

Maybe there was some truth to music being a universal language, a way of connecting even distant generations.

Heywood finished the song and set the guitar down on his legs. Tess couldn't read his mood. He seemed a little downcast, but she wasn't sure if it was just the nature of the piece he was playing.

"I was worried about you," he finally said. "You shouldn't have gone out on your own like that. If you had somewhere to be, I could have taken you."

She nodded softly. "It was just something I had to do on my own."

"Theo and I went out searching. I was afraid you'd gotten hurt."

Tess's heart sank. Apparently, she was worrying everyone. She only imagined what Joel, Killian, and her mother were feeling back at home. "I'm sorry I took Saturn. Did he get back okay?"

"It was his whinnying that woke us up this morning and had us realizing you were gone."

She chewed the inside of her cheek. "I didn't think I should stay."

"Then what brought you back?" Heywood met her gaze in the firelight, an abundance of meaning in his simple question.

Uncertainty flickered across her features before she managed to hide it. The notion that it could have been for him put her stomach in knots.

He gave her a crooked smile. "Goodnight, Tess."

"G'night, Heywood," she murmured slipping back inside the tent.

She curled up close to the dozing child but couldn't sleep. Why *did* she come back? She couldn't possibly ever take Joel's suggestion and hurt this child. She cared too much for her, it didn't even matter how many other lives it would spare in the long run. Her only option was to visit the doctor and convince him to create the respirator without her death.

She sighed and closed her eyes, seeing Heywood's small slanted grin again in her mind.

She didn't come back for him. That would have been ludicrous.

It couldn't have been possible to fall for somebody like him, somebody who did not even exist in her time.

****

Thick storm clouds darkened the sky, throwing long shadows across the town. Heywood leaned on the wall outside the mercantile, mopping the sweat with the back of his sleeve. Theo and Callum had been watching the sky, equally complaining about the brewing storm and the threat of a tornado while Callum swept the wide porch.

Heywood's mind was still stuck on last night. Tess had come back. He couldn't help but wonder if it had anything to do with him. Deep down he had wanted to share the tent with her and be able to wake up together. Admitting that to himself did something strange to the pit of his stomach. Luckily, he'd known better than to give into temptation. Even with the innocence of Lotty sleeping between them, Antoinette or any other meddler was apt to barge onto his property unannounced and assume the worst.

"Hiya, Mr. Paxton," a voice called from the street. Heywood jerked from his thoughts at Gabe strolling up the porch steps. "Couldn't find you at the farm, so figured I'd look here."

"Well, of course you wouldn't. I'm not expecting you to work for another hour."

Callum brushed the long broomstick left to right, polluting the porch with its filth. "Wish I had some workers like you in the store."

"He aint always this accountable," Heywood snickered. "Why you really out here?"

Gabe stared into the array of shoppers on the street, a smile lifting the folds of his mouth. "Personal reasons."

Callum suddenly stopped his sweeping and went to open the door for some approaching customers. The light from inside the grocery store brightened the murky porch. Or maybe it was the beautiful person walking up the rickety stairs with Heywood's daughter.

Lotty had wanted to show Tess the candy shop before joining him, but he hadn't noticed until then how radiant Miss Corbin was in that lemon-yellow dress that contrasted the downcast morning.

Gabe's pursuit into town now made sense. The boy was grinning ear-to-ear but was too red-faced to speak.

Tess hadn't noticed him, as Lotty was speaking a mile a minute to her. She managed a warm smile at Heywood though, and the eagerness that surged through him in response took his breath away.

Theo tilted his sheriff's hat in greeting. "Well, this is a surprise! I'm glad to see you came back," he told Tess.

"You left?" Gabe interceded with shock, but Theo disregarded the boy.

"Grace was sure praying for this, I'll have to tell her you're safe and sound."

"Thank you," Tess said softly. "I apologize for causing alarm."

"No need."

Realizing his impoliteness, Heywood kicked off the wall and motioned toward the man still holding her door.

"I don't believe you've met Mr. Tuttle, the owner of the market."

Callum held out a hand and enthusiastically shook hers. "Good to meet you, Miss Corbin."

Heywood hadn't realized he already knew of her.

"Mr. Tuttle," she repeated thoughtfully. Then a soft smile of recognition arched her pretty mouth. "Yes, I've heard of you."

Heywood wondered how.

"Good things I hope!" Callum teased.

"Of course."

He nodded at that. "If you need any help inside, my wife will be happy to assist you."

"Thank you," she said, taking Lotty's hand and walking through the door. He closed it behind her and gave Heywood a look of astonishment.

"She sure cleans up nice."

"You've already seen her?"

"Well yeah. That evening you got your injuries I was here when she rode into town and broke into the doc's office. She had been really torn up. I mean physically, her dress in shreds, hair flying around her, riding that horse like a real cowboy at full speed. I thought there might have been a fire!"

Heywood crossed his arms and huffed a small grunt of appreciation. The image of Tess with her dress' long beautiful fabric blanketing Saturn on both sides made him smile. He knew she cared an awful deal for Lotty, and even proved its depth the night she'd brought her back to life. But she really did give a damn about him too, didn't she?

Who would have expected that?

"Heads up," Callum murmured and Heywood followed his squint, then groaned when he saw Axel Cavaliere headed their way. "Maybe he's just doing some shopping," Callum offered, but Heywood knew by the man's heavy footfalls that he was on a mission.

He squared his shoulders as the blacksmith approached the porch. From the corner of his eye he noticed Theo readying himself as well. They both had good reason to be on their toes. Antoinette's older brother was a beast. Well over six foot and built like an ox.

"Paxton," he said, stopping on the top stair of the porch. He stood straight; feet planted wide apart with his weight equally distributed between them. "We need to talk."

"Just a friendly conversation, I hope," Theo said, exposing the badge on his left chest pocket.

Axel grinned a mouth full of crooked teeth. "All's well, Sheriff. Your brother and I just need to have words in private."

Heywood clapped his brother on the back to let him know he could handle the guy, then followed Axel down to the road, walking with him out of earshot of the others.

"You got any idea how much grief you're making my life, Paxton?"

Heywood shook his head, following him to the other side of the street. "Sorry to hear that, but I've got my own problems to deal with."

Axel shot his hand out to catch Heywood's chest, forcing him into a hard stop. "*I'm* your only problem right now, Paxton. And you know why, don't you?"

"I've got a good guess."

"Antoinette won't stop yammering at me. To put it in my own words, it was something like *'Axel, Heywood's been brushing me off again.' 'Axel, Heywood is humping some whore behind my back.' 'Axel, I'm going to drive you mad unless you straighten this out and tell him what's what.'* So that's what I'm here to do."

"To straighten me out and tell me what's what?"

"I'm just trying to get my little sister off my back."

"I sympathize, but I can't marry the woman simply because she's hassling you."

"I don't think you understand," Axel said, moving too close, forcing Heywood back a step. "Our families had an arrangement and I've come to collect on that. Her tantrums aren't going to stop until she gets her way."

"That arrangement is long over. When I came back four years ago, I had no intention on reinstating it and Antoinette knows that."

"Listen, I'm being nice about this. I have to live with my family's grievances, but not yours. So, I only want to say this once."

"Listen–"

Axel held up a beefy hand to stop him. "Do what you want with the whore. That's none of my business. I hear she's got an attractive and usable body, so go at it till you're both sore. But when you're through, toss her back and make things right with Antoinette."

Heywood shook his head, disgusted.

"What is it about her that's got you willing to take the beating of your life rather than be with my beautiful sister? She got whiskey laced ta-ta's?"

The man was repulsive. "Stop."

"Cause if so, I think you're awfully selfish for not sharing," he mocked, licking his lips.

His vulgarity shot a spear of protective rage through Heywood's gut and his fist went soaring, cracking the large blacksmith square in the jaw.

Axel fell back a step, touched his chin, then came at him like a boomerang. The blast of Theo's pistol overhead was the only reason more damage hadn't been done, as both men immediately withdrew and crouched to take cover.

When he got his bearings back, Heywood could see Lotty and Tess emerging from the mercantile along with all the other patrons.

It was humiliating to be looked at like that, as though he were some loose cannon who needed his brother to control him.

Shamefaced, he moved away from Axel and back across the road to the market. He felt all eyes on him until a small commotion took their attention. Glancing down the road, he was surprised by several men charging into town, thick clouds of dirt kicking up behind them.

They halted in front of the market and Theo immediately trudged down the porch stairs. "What's wrong?" he demanded.

"We've got some trouble at the edge of town," one of the men huffed. "The Frye kid got attacked by a wolf."

"Is he okay?" Heywood asked, jogging over.

"Mr. Frye shot at it and scared the thing off. Maimed the kid's leg though. The doc is there now."

"He's lucky to be alive," Heywood murmured.

"That's not all. It also killed a lot of Frye's sheep and goats. If we don't move fast there's going to be some real trouble to deal with."

"Then let's move," Heywood demanded, unhitching Saturn from the carriage.

"Be careful, Pa!" Lotty yelled, and Heywood's heart sank. He'd just gotten back to normal and knew this was the last thing his daughter needed. Hurrying back over to the porch he scooped her up and gave her a kiss on the nose.

"I promise I will. You stay with Miss Corbin and I'll be back home tonight." He glanced at Tess. The worry lines on her face made her look so young and vulnerable. Unable to leave this way, he nudged her playfully with his elbow. "Don't look so glum. I'll be back to annoying ya in a few hours."

She scoffed and took Lotty's hand as he set her back down.

Heywood mounted the horse, giving his fingers a snap toward Gabe. "Accompany the ladies back to the house. You're in charge of the farm for the day. You know what to do."

Gabe nodded. "No problem, Boss!"

"And kid. Behave yourself."

Gabe rolled his eyes shyly, but Heywood reared the horse after Theo and the other men before he had a chance to respond.

****

By late afternoon, Heywood had taken the lead, following a rocky trail up a steep incline. He reined in his horse at the top, waiting for the others to reach him.

Wiping the grime and sweat off his face, he glared at the brewing storm. They would get soaked if they went much further. He knew Theo would suggest heading back and feared what that would mean for the safety of his cattle and the people in town.

Pushing himself further up the trail, Heywood's horse suddenly reared at a pack of wolves cryptically emerging from the trees around him. Their fur bristled as growls rumbled up their throats. He pulled up his rifle, hesitating in order to weigh his options. The rest of the hunting party was still twenty feet back. If he fired now and set the pack into attack mode, he'd be helpless to protect himself.

One of the wolves suddenly leapt at Saturn and Heywood moved on instinct.

He felt the crack of his rifle just seconds before it all went to hell.

CHAPTER TEN

Tess bit down on her bottom lip to keep from expressing how frightened she was now that the storm clouds thickened. She'd put on a brave face for Lotty ever since they made it back to the farm, but as the wind picked up, she couldn't hide it anymore.

Ms. Tuttle had told her that Heywood disappeared soon after his daughter's death. She never said that the two events were directly related. There was a good chance that this was it.

Disappearing on a hunting voyage seemed quite plausible. It would have been easy to fall over a cliff, drown, or get dragged off by an animal and demolished.

She'd finally convinced Lotty to change into her nightgown, and Tess used this opportunity to step outside, shivering at the rising wind. It was oddly warm though, reminding her too much of that afternoon that Lotty had hid under the metal feeding trough.

Gabe ran up from the barn, panting and fanning himself with his hat as he made it onto the porch beside her.

"Finished at last," he said. "This weather is insane."

Tess smiled weakly. "I know Heywood will appreciate you taking care of the farm while he was gone."

He gave her a broad grin. It reminded her of how a child might respond after receiving a golden star or line leader duty.

Tess pondered that. She had originally thought the lad just enjoyed responsibility, but maybe Gabe just thrived on praise, like most elementary children. Except he was almost a man, somewhere between fifteen and sixteen years old. And though he didn't carry much weight, he was still thicker than she was, and stood at least a few inches taller.

She became more aware of this when she felt his hand wrap around her waistline.

"Don't worry about the storm," he said. "It'll come and go, and I'll be here to watch out for ya."

Tess scoffed. "I was worried more about Mr. Paxton."

He snorted at that. "He'll be fine. Greatest hunter this town has got."

She looked back at the sky and shivered again.

"You cold?" he said, moving his hands to her shoulders.

It was too much touching. She didn't like it. She offered what she hoped was at least a friendly smile when she said, "I better get dinner started," then headed inside.

"I'll help you," he said, following her into the kitchen.

She didn't stop him from trailing behind her but at least made sure to give him a job.

Slicing potatoes shouldn't have been difficult but somehow he managed to lag behind.

"Like this," Tess said, leaning over to grab another potato from his bowl.

Gabe noticeably peeked down her blouse as she did this without the slightest hint of indignity.

She straightened, barely believing that even happened. He just grinned.

"Outward," she said coldly, demonstrating how to peel the potato. She was still completely thrown by what happened. "Only take off the skin, don't waste the potato."

"Yes, ma'am."

She turned away from him to get the water boiling but could still feel the heat of his eyes on her back. This boy was starting to make her uncomfortable.

She went to work on the rest of the meat and vegetables, finally reigning in Gabe's potatoes to complete the stew.

The steam hit her face as she stirred the pot, frizzing her hair and filling the kitchen with a hardy smell.

Gabe took a long whiff from the pot. "Smells delicious," he said. "We work well together, Miss Corbin."

Out of nowhere he lurched forward, pressing his skinny lips against hers and she jerked back immediately. Falling against the counter, she gasped and stared wide-eyed at him. But he was still only smiling, just as he had when he'd gazed down her shirt.

Easy girl. You're the adult here.

She knew he was just a kid with a crush, and she shouldn't have been glaring daggers at him but couldn't help it. He'd caught her off guard and she wasn't about to be taken advantage of.

"It's okay to be nervous, I am too," he murmured, walking toward her. "But you don't have to worry, I won't tell anyone."

She scooted back and swallowed hard, willing herself to be mature about this.

"You know better than that," she said, pulling out that bedside manner she'd learned during residency. "We don't do that. We don't kiss a girl unless it's invited, right?"

Gabe paused. He furrowed a brow, seeming confused. "But you *were* inviting me, weren't you? I mean I heard what the town's been saying about you – about the kind of woman who would stay with an unmarried man. And just now you leaned over like that and smiled at me…"

Tess was sure she'd paled a full shade, her mouth dropping. She could either beat the boy like an escaped convict or address him as one might a kindergartner. She chose the latter.

"Believing cruel rumors is a dangerous thing. And just because you steal a peek or a kiss or a hug, it doesn't mean she was inviting it," she explained softly. "Though I am flattered, I think it's best that you head home and cool yourself down."

Gabe leaned back, eyeing her uncertainly. "Mr. Paxton told me to care for you."

"He told you to get us home and care for the farm. You've done a fine job of both, but your duties are finished. I think it's best that you get back to your mother before the rain gets worse."

He huffed. Tess was sure being stormed in with her was exactly what he'd hoped for.

The fact that he resented being treated like just another child was obvious from the bitter look in his eyes as he slapped on his hat.

"Good night then, Miss Corbin. I hope you ladies remain safe while unattended."

It sounded oddly like a threat, but she figured she was just being paranoid by his wording. Nonetheless, she watched as he climbed his horse and headed off the property.

She hated that being alone on the estate *did* intimidate her. It wasn't as though the cabin had an alarm system or a phone to dial 911. She was basically a sitting duck to any danger that might come.

She knew she shouldn't have been thinking about that and frightening herself. Instead she went back to the stew.

The light drizzle became a steady downpour by the time she and Lotty sat down to eat, the thunder rolling closer over the thickening storm clouds.

"I don't like this," Lotty choked out. "It's getting too dark."

Tess fought back her own panic, reaching out to stroke Lotty's hair. "I don't like it either, but he'll be all right. Your father knows what he's doing. This isn't new for him."

Lotty set down her utensil. She was just as disinterested in eating as Tess was.

"Why don't we try to get some rest," Tess suggested softly. "We can just lay down on the couch and wait for him to get home."

Getting up, she put a hand on Lotty's back and steered her toward the living room. Laying down together, Tess wrapped her arms around the girl, drawing her close.

Lotty craned her neck, looking up at her with fear-filled eyes. "I'm scared," she whispered. "Real scared."

"I know," Tess crooned.

"I don't want to be alone tonight. You'll stay, won't you, Tess? You're not going to leave again, right?"

"I won't leave you, Lotty. I promise. I'm right here."

"You'll stay..."

"Of course, I will. Shh. Rest your eyes."

Lotty snuggled up against her.

Tess had no idea how long they'd been resting on that couch with the lightning flashing and thunder roaring until they'd fallen asleep.

She didn't wake until what felt like hours later to the sound of banging on the front door.

Tess opened her eyes to complete darkness. The rain sounded like it had let up some.

The knocking on the front door continued and Tess's heart hammered, hoping it was Heywood.

Removing herself gently from the child, she bolted upright and swung open the door. Only it wasn't Heywood.

Her heart faltered at the woman in the doorway.

Antoinette had the sort of physique that could withstand even the heaviest of torrential downpours. Despite being windblown and damp, the lady was a goddess.

But Tess wasn't about to let her know that. Instead, they simply stared at each other, both equally surprised by the other.

"Grace told me that you left," Antoinette finally said, her chin arched to look down on her though they were of similar height.

Tess leaned on the doorjamb. "I came back."

Antoinette sneered, exposing beautiful teeth beneath full scarlet lips. "Thought he'd have tired of you by now."

That again. Gabe had already made it clear how easy and corrupt the town thought she was.

"Apparently there's been some rumors spreading about me," Tess said tightly. "But I don't think I have to tell *you* that none of them are true."

Antoinette ignored her accusation and adjusted her shawl. "I am not one to gossip, but I do find it interesting how much further you're willing to destroy Heywood Paxton's reputation in Half Hallow." She tsked Tess, shaking her head. "Meanwhile poor Lotty is the one who will suffer from it."

Tess gritted her teeth. "I am not doing half as much to hurt him as you are."

Antoinette glared at her. "I'm sure by now you've heard the rumors about Heywood killing his wife," she finally blurted. "The whole town is sure of it. He killed her and disposed of the body."

Tess inhaled sharply. "You don't truly believe that."

"He'd given up everything for her, but the woman was a free spirit. Her mother's side was of Central American ancestry, it was in her blood to explore. It was only a matter of time until he would wake up and discover that she and the little girl had gone off to discover new places. He loved Lotty too much to allow it."

Tess furrowed a brow.

"What part of shooting down and disposing of a body do you suppose Heywood would have struggled with?" Antoinette purred. "Big strong man like him."

The words of Ms. Tuttle fumbled back into Tess's memories. *He was a hunter with a talent for a clean kill.*

She shook her head. It wasn't possible. "Heywood wouldn't do that."

"How then can you explain why Mr. Delacourt came after him?" Antoinette leaned forward; her expression serious. "Though the doc didn't have any business getting physical with Heywood, as Emeline's father he had good reason to do what he did."

Tess studied her, trying to fathom that remark.

Good reason? To beat a man within an inch of his life, shoot an arrow through his body, and then leave him for dead – there was good reason for that?

"So, you agree with Dr. Delacourt then?" Tess asked.

It was unreal. All this from the woman who claimed to still want him.

Then she understood. "You don't believe any of it," Tess murmured. "You have a claim to him and are just trying to scare me away."

Antoinette just shrugged. "What I think doesn't really matter, does it?"

A dark shadow suddenly highlighted her petite features and Tess jerked back just an instant before she recognized Heywood's broad form.

Antoinette must've seen it in her eyes and swung around.

By now the man was drenched straight down to the bone, his body dirty and tired, but his eyes were heated.

Tess was ecstatic that he was alive. She might have run out into the rain to greet him if it wasn't for the rigidity of his body.

He stepped onto the porch and eyed Antoinette.

She gave him one of her most dazzling smiles and threw her arms over his wet shoulders. "Thank God you're okay! I came to check on you as soon as I heard."

He sneered and pried her hands off his body. "Leave," he snarled.

Antoinette shook her head, flabbergasted. "What?"

"I heard what you said, and I want you off my property."

She furrowed a beautifully sculpted brow at him. "You can't be serious."

He stared at her.

After a moment she snarled. "Truly? After I came through this storm to check up on you, you're really going to turn me away? For what, this whore?"

"You can keep calling her that till you're blue in the face. Won't make it true."

"My brother will never let you get away with this."

"No, I'm sure he'll give me a good ass whooping. I still won't marry you."

She curled her lip. "You'll regret this, Heywood Paxton."

"I'm sure I won't," he mumbled coldly.

"You don't know who you're messing with."

"I think I do."

Hissing a long string of obscenities, she marched back out into the rain and mounted her horse.

Tess watched Heywood's back as he glared at her departure in the darkness.

When he finally turned around and walked into the house, his shirt was transparent, and his pants stuck to his thighs as though he'd swam his way home.

He was moving too fast to detect injuries.

"Are you okay?" she asked, following him to the living room where he found Lotty fast asleep.

He stopped and looked down at his daughter, his eyes softening.

"I'm fine," he whispered.

"What happened?"

"We put the pack down. Got hairy for a moment, but all ended up okay."

"Got hairy? Are you hurt?"

He looked back at her. "I told you I'm fine."

She sighed. "You already know I can handle wounds, now is not the time for playing the macho card."

He grunted at that. "I'm not playing any cards. But I *have* had a rough night and would like to tuck my daughter into bed now. Would that be okay, Miss Corbin?"

She gritted her teeth. Why was he back to being so formal? "I suppose I'll allow it," she whispered mockingly.

"I appreciate that," he murmured with tired wit, then scooped his daughter up from the couch and carried her out.

****

Heywood stared at the blank canvas and all the paints in front of him, his anger boiling to rage. He hadn't slept at all that night – and if anyone needed rest it was him.

Glaring at the sunrise, he again thought of what he'd walked in on last night. Antoinette's desperation to mark her territory had reached a new level of low, even for her. The things she had said to Tess were filthy, remembering it made it even difficult to breathe. With one quick left-handed motion he forced a large angry slash of red across the blank-white canvas.

He set down the paintbrush then and sighed tiredly. He didn't even know why he bothered dragging out this makeshift art studio.

Painting had always been a stress reliever for him in the past, but this was too much. No amount of painting would erase what these people thought of him… it wouldn't take away how ridiculous his feelings were toward Tess.

He gritted his teeth, not wanting that.

It was laughable… he couldn't have really been falling for her that hard. It was too soon, too dangerous.

Sinking back on his stool, Heywood kicked aside the easel and glanced at the cloudless cerulean sky. Faint noise on the property turned him around so that he was facing the mountains.

Something was seated between him and the highlands with more natural beauty than the landscape itself.

He shifted forward on the stool, gazing at where Tess reclined on the edge of one of his haystacks, air-drying her sopping curly hair while Lotty played with a critter in the grass. She was wrapped in a pale blue dress that she clearly hadn't bothered to layer underneath. He guessed that she'd bathed that morning and then dressed in a hurry to tend to Lotty.

When she adjusted her feet, the dress rolled up a little, exposing a better than perfect leg.

Grabbing the easel and a new canvas, he turned it and his stool to face her. Dipping the brush into the paint, he began to fervently outline her breathtaking shape.

He hadn't been this deeply engrossed in a painting since he sketched Emeline's tree at least three years ago. He never thought another woman would be his next bout of inspiration. The urge to capture Tess had hit him with alarming passion.

Glowing skin and a long neck like hers had to be the reason art utensils had even been invented. Conserving this kind of beauty was why prehistoric men first began outlining the human body on cave walls, the reason the Kodak had ever been pioneered and was still launching new depths every day. To not share physical proof of such magnificence seemed a crime.

Tess suddenly jerked into an upright position, eyeing the cabin behind her. Heywood froze, never so embarrassed in his life when she climbed down from the haystack and began a jog toward him on the porch.

Only she wasn't looking at him at all, and then he smelled it too. Something inside was burning.

He set down the canvas, deciding to finish the mountain backdrop another time. After hiding it against the house, he walked to the front door where Tess had run in and was now cursing and grumbling in the kitchen. He couldn't help but grin at that.

"Everything okay in there?" he called, barely able to hold it in.

"Yeah, I just ruined the bread," she muttered on her way outside. "Are you laughing?"

"No, ma'am! I wouldn't dare." Then he saw the black steaming loaf in her mitted hand and had to hold his breath like a dam ready to burst.

"You're going to give yourself a seizure," she hissed, slamming the bread down on the porch. It cracked and shattered at her feet like a piece of slate.

That did it for him, he was practically wiping back tears of laughter by the time he began to apologize.

Tess set her hands on her slim waist, giving him a look of contempt though he could see she was clearly biting the inside of her lip to keep from smiling, herself. Letting out a theatrical huff, she then paused when she noticed the makeshift art studio.

"I didn't know you still painted," she said, gazing at all the supplies.

That sobered him right up. Luckily, he'd set the painting of her out of sight.

With a pitiful shrug he admitted, "It's been a while since I've pulled it all out of storage."

"Hm," she said, picking up the canvas he'd knocked over with the angry red slash. She looked it over thoughtfully and humiliation coiled inside of him.

She set it down on the easel and he saw the corner of her mouth daintily arch upward. "Well, Mr. Paxton. Looks like you paint just as well as I bake."

"Woah, woah," he said to the teasing light in her eyes. "Take it easy."

"You can dish it out, but can't take it?"

"At least we don't have to stomach *my* shortcomings."

Tess's jaw dropped.

Was that too far?

She grinned widely with clenched teeth, and he was relieved to see the humor still in her eyes. "Well, you can eat your share off the floor."

She bent down and grabbed a fistful, rapidly tossing it at him.

"Ouch! It's like being stoned to death!" he teased, swinging away from her line of fire.

She crinkled her nose at his insult and threw more as he took cover behind the canvas.

"Put down your weapon and I'll put down mine," he said, bringing up a saturated red paintbrush.

Her handful of black rock-hard bread froze mid-air. "You wouldn't dare."

He took the challenge and ran with it, flicking the red paint at her, getting a splash of it on her cheek.

She gasped as though she'd been doused with a bucket of ice-cold water, then ran for the paint containers, nailing him in the chest with a big glob of green paint. Heywood ducked again behind the canvas. When he peeked out to return fire, she got him again in the forehead with a glob of blue.

He feigned a howl and wiped his face, this time clobbering her with a yellow splat across the side of her face and neck.

They both ran for cover, fully armed with paint containers and a desperate need to best the other.

Paint fired from both sides of the porch like a strange, but colorful war. When she bent down to retrieve more, he made a stealthy dash behind her, going in for the triumphant tackle before she could straighten. They both landed in a fit of laughter.

He arched up on his elbow, just barely making out her eyes underneath the paint globs.

"I hope this stuff isn't toxic," she said from beneath him.

He wiped the yellow paint away from her mouth so she could breathe without tasting it, but suddenly all he could think of was how much he wanted to kiss her. Maybe he would have if she didn't bring up her hand still full of purple paint and smash it over the top of his head.

She guffawed as it trickled down his face.

"Thanks for that," he snorted, wiping it out of his eyes with his shirt. He stood and pulled her onto her feet. They were both unrecognizable and loving it.

Tess walked over to the easel. "Now *that's* a painting."

He followed her eyes to the canvas which had once only bore one long angry slash of red. It was now a firework of dripping color.

He grinned and turned around to face her, saying what he wanted to fast before he changed his mind. "Can I take you somewhere?"

"Sure."

Her quick response was pleasantly surprising.

"I'll need to clean myself off though."

"I think we both do," he said with a snort. "I'll use the water pump and drop Lotty off with Grace while you bathe."

He walked away, knowing he shouldn't be doing this.

A better or wiser man would have just walked away. He was neither.

CHAPTER ELEVEN

Heywood white knuckled the oars, drifting the rowboat further away from the barge. It glided down the river, the sweet song of crickets and locusts forming from the banks.

Tess sat across from him in a pretty white dress, but he could still see the tendrils of paint lingering in pieces of her hair. He supposed the blue dress had to be discarded. He couldn't say he was sorry. He had needed a good laugh like that, and something deep down sensed that she did as well.

Tess watched the scenery for a few moments before opening the silk parasol and resting it on her shoulder to block out the sun.

Heywood studied her a moment. He just couldn't figure this person out.

"Miss Corbin…"

"We've already agreed that we should be on a first name basis by now. Your daughter and I already are."

He snorted with a smile. "You're right. Sorry." He flicked his eyes back on hers and hated that it made him feel like a red-faced, awkward Gabe. Shaking his head, he tried again. "Tess, I just want to make sure you're okay."

She pulled back, apparently surprised by this, though he wasn't sure why.

"I've already expressed these concerns to you, and I don't mean to be repetitive, but I really need you to tell me if you're in danger, or afraid of someone who might come looking for you."

She scoffed. "Are you worried about me or yourself?"

He was taken aback by her defensiveness. "Both, I suppose. But mostly you."

She tried to scoff again, but he stopped her by leaning forward, closer.

"I just want to understand."

That seemed to soften her. In response, she shot her eyes away from him, letting out a slow breath and shaking her head. "That wouldn't be possible," she finally said. "You wouldn't understand even if I told you *everything*."

"I'd like to think that I would. You already know a bit of my past, unfortunately. I've run away from a home and life too…"

"I'm not running."

He sighed and leaned back to row harder, tired of this same lie.

"Is that why you brought me to the middle of a river?" she asked. "To confront me in a place where I can't run away from your questions?"

Heywood was thrown off by that. "I didn't bring you here to confront you."

"Then why did you?"

Her anger was unexpected. But maybe she wasn't all that off. He clenched his jaw and relaxed the oars.

"You're right," he admitted sheepishly. "I suppose maybe it wasn't just about taking you somewhere nice. I suppose deep down I wanted a place where we could be alone. *Really* alone. After all, Mr. Delacourt's attack had been a direct result of him watching us fish at the lake. Who knows who could be following us here? At least out this far they won't hear anything."

Her body seemed to slacken. "I guess I know what you mean. My family has been on display since before I was born. I don't know any other life than the kind where people publicly criticize me. I've had strangers walk up to me and ask blatantly about my career, and love-life, and clothes. But nobody has ever once asked me if I was happy."

"Are you?"

She blinked, clearly not expecting him to actually ask. "Well, I should be, right?" She shook her head as though any doubts would be the most absurd thing. "I have everything I could ever want. My life has never left me wanting, it's…" She stopped short suddenly, clearly hearing her own bull crap.

Heywood studied her sympathetically. It was the first vulnerable moment he'd seen from her and he ached to touch or hold her.

Instead he took the oars and continued to row.

It had just been too damn long since he'd been in a situation like this. He hadn't even touched another woman since Emeline. Some nights he made himself crazy trying to remember he and his wife's final hug or kiss. When was that last time they had even made love? Had it been the night before she died, or maybe a week or two before? It couldn't have been a month, could it? That was something he figured he should have remembered.

Thinking now about something as simple as just holding this sweet lady's hand made him feel anxious and scared.

She blinked slowly and leaned back. "It must be harder for you," she said somberly.

He didn't understand.

"Trying to stay happy for Lotty while being so miserable."

"I never said I was miserable."

"Why do you put up with these narrow-minded townspeople? Are you really that scared of them?"

Caught off-guard, Heywood exhaled at the truth in her words, but immediately covered it with a hard scoff as he picked up his rowing pace. "I'm as afraid of them as I am of your cooking."

She squinted at him.

"You don't understand the history here."

"Then tell me."

He set down the oars once again and looked into her eyes. "I didn't kill Emeline, if that's what you're wondering. I heard what Antoinette told you."

Tess lowered the parasol and sat upright. "That, I already figured."

"What makes you so sure I'm telling the truth?"

"I can see it in your eyes every time you say or hear her name. You really loved her."

He blinked wildly, forcing his eyes away from her. Looking at the steady water that rocked the boat, he finally wilted. "I wasn't raised by parents who fell in love, I was raised by parents who worked well together and would benefit from their family's resources. I always knew they expected the same of me and Theo. We were never wealthy people, and my parents knew that it was only a matter of time until we lost everything. Instead they came up with a plan that when we were of age to be married, they'd bargain one of us to a better off family *with* the farm."

"I see," Tess mused. "In that case the farm would remain somewhat in the family while it received the financial help of a wealthier spouse."

Heywood nodded. "Theo fell in love though and married fast. Grace came from a respectable home who had no interest in the farm. She was the mayor's daughter, and he offered Theo a job in his office immediately, which soon led to town Sheriff. Suddenly I was all that was left in order to keep the farm going." He smeared the sweat from his brow with the back of his hand. "I never agreed to that marriage with Antoinette."

Tess leaned back thoughtfully. "She's still obsessed with you."

Heywood grunted. "I don't know, maybe I would have gone through with it if not for…" He stopped himself, not wanting to say Emeline's name again. "I never even thought it was possible. I was raised to understand obligation to your family and land. Emeline and I were just kids, we didn't even realize what love was when we fell into it." He smiled softly. "She was better than anybody I'd ever known… all I ever wanted was to make a life and family with her."

"So, when you married Emeline instead of Antoinette and broke your family's arrangement, they banished you?"

Heywood was surprised by that. "Yes, actually. That's exactly what happened. How did you know?"

Her eyes widened only briefly, then she shrugged. "I'm only guessing."

Heywood furrowed a brow and then continued. "We had no choice, but to leave. We were used to fighting against all odds but knew that if we were at least together we'd be alright." He shook his head. Damn. He hadn't talked about this for a long time. He didn't realize how hard this was going to be.

Tess's hand was suddenly on his knee, squeezing it with encouragement.

He looked up and saw the gentle reassurance in her eyes. "Tell me, Heywood. What happened?"

He stared at her for a long moment. It wasn't simple curiosity or hostile judgment like he usually saw in the people who used to ask. Her eyes seemed genuine, as though she truly just wanted to understand.

Taking in a deep breath, he closed his eyes once again. "My father had sent me a message only about two years after Lotty was born."

"How did he find you?"

Heywood snarled. "Emeline wanted the family to know about their granddaughter. We sent a message to both families within a month of her birth. Neither responded… until almost two years later when my parents got ill."

"Wow," Tess whispered, disgusted.

"Your own family is probably looking a lot better to you right about now."

She shook her head. "Go on."

"Theo was dead set on selling what was left of the land, so my father begged me to stop that and keep it in the family."

"Your brother didn't want to help rebuild?"

Heywood scoffed. "Theo's still trying desperately to get me to sell. He brings it up almost incessantly so that he can get half of the sale profit. He makes nothing off the business while I'm running it."

"Huh. I got the vibe that he was still wanting you to marry Antoinette."

"He does make it seem that way, doesn't he?"

"But if you married her and she now owned a part of the farm, wouldn't that counter his plan to sell and gain revenue?"

"Exactly. He doesn't want me to marry Antoinette. But he knows the anxiety that whole thing causes me. I think he's just trying to wear me down, make it seem like those are my only two options – to either keep to the original bargain and marry her, or to free myself of the agreement once and for all by selling the farm."

"That's pretty dirty."

"I guess I can't blame him for wanting a piece of the family business. It's not as though we were left with anything else after our parents died."

She shook her head. "So, you obviously came back to help with the farm like your father asked."

"Well it *was* technically still my responsibility. On our way back to Half Hallow, we pitched a tent. I remember that it was howling that woke me in the middle of the night. I knew Emeline was scared to death of wolves and instinctively went to hold her. But when I rolled over, she was gone."

He stopped and leaned forward. He didn't want to relive this.

Tess touched him once more, this time holding his shoulder, squeezing it. "You don't have to tell me the rest," she whispered. "I can imagine."

No. There was no way that she could. A person could never imagine the things that he saw. They weren't meant to. Every time he closed his eyes, he remembered the thick trail... he could still see the dirt beneath his feet wet with Emeline's blood, the air heavy with its scent. He could still feel the anguish over losing her, but the gratitude that Lotty was still alive.

"I was too late," he whispered. "I was too exhausted from traveling and must not have heard her when she stepped out of the tent. I should have woken up and watched to make sure she got back to us okay." He scraped a hand over his face. "She probably stepped out to relieve herself, and they took it as her marking her territory, or *theirs*. She got attacked while out there, and it's my fault for sleeping while she was dying." He dropped his head, humiliated to be breaking down like this, racked in guilt. "I'm sorry. I'm so sorry."

Tess scooted over and put her arms around him. "It's not your fault that the wolves came or that she died or that you were sleeping. Your wife wouldn't have expected you to know, and she wouldn't have wanted you to leave Lotty."

He looked up at her, and then shifted back, regaining himself with embarrassment.

She scooted back to her seat, but he wished she wasn't still watching him. He didn't want her to see him like this.

She held his gaze, regardless, leaving him no choice but to change the subject.

"Your turn, Miss... Tess," he corrected.

She seemed a bit rattled by his statement, and he liked that.

"Tell me one real thing about you."

When she didn't answer, he nodded at the sizeable diamond on her finger, and she closed her fist in response.

"Is that what's going to bring you that happiness you're hoping for?" he asked bluntly. "Or is it just a way of satisfying the herd that are watching and judging you?"

Her lip twitched, but she didn't answer.

"Do you love him?" He couldn't help himself. "Can you see a future with this man? Not just financial security, but can you see sharing a home, carrying his children..."

"I don't know," she blurted.

He shook his head. "Then don't marry him. At least not until you *do* know."

"You sound like your daughter. Someone who hasn't experienced the world yet enough to understand it. She always makes it sound so simple."

"It *is* simple."

She closed her eyes. "No, it's not." Letting out a deep breath, she whispered, "Don't judge me until you've seen my life."

He wilted at that. What she asked was similar to what he'd asked of the many who'd damned *him*.

"I'm sorry."

She grinned dejectedly at him. "So am I."

"Do you want to keep going? We're almost at the other end. I packed us a lunch."

"Sure," she said softly and reopened her parasol just as a light drizzle hit the boat.

He hadn't expected rain. Though last night was a torrential downpour, this morning had been cloudless and sunny. There was no way…

He looked up and his stomach sank at the thickening gray clouds overhead.

"You've got to be kidding me," he grunted, grabbing the oars.

"What's wrong?"

"Nothing," he said quickly. "I just suppose yesterday's storm wasn't a fluke after all, but rather a weather pattern I should have been expecting. I apologize. Taking you out here was senseless."

The boat creaked noisily with the breeze and Heywood leaned back on the oars to get it moving faster.

Tess must have felt the small pellets by now because she looked panicked. "Are we going to sink?"

"We're almost there," he grunted. "Just hold on for me."

She looked around a little anxiously and then dropped her parasol. The wind picked up and she gripped the sides of the small rowboat on both ends as they swayed in the breeze.

The drizzle was cold and growing thicker by the minute. He felt like such an idiot. "I'll get us off this river. We're almost there."

Then it began to pour. Dammit to hell, he had the worst luck imaginable! Colorado weather never *could* make up its mind.

Tess tried to open the parasol again, but it was only meant for blocking the sun, not the rain, and it crumbled from the heavy pellets. She tossed it into the river and began to laugh.

It was the last thing he expected. He stared at her as he propelled the boat, completely dumbfounded. Then he laughed too. He couldn't believe how contagious it was.

She shook her head at him, nearly hysterical, finally throwing up her arms in a ginormous shrug.

He doubled over at that. She was right, they'd already been drenched in paint this morning, what was a little monsoon in the afternoon?

They were just a beautiful mess, weren't they?

The raindrops sounded like shattered glass as the current grew stronger and swayed their small boat.

She grabbed onto him, but he could see they already made it to the shallows. Just another few feet to the surface.

Tess let out an audible gasp as the boat tilted into the river. Her shift of weight made it capsize, both of their bodies whirling and spinning into the water.

Heywood swiftly recovered his footing, then grabbed onto Tess to pull her up as well.

They barely had time to take a breath though before the water dragged them back under.

Again, Heywood struggled to get them both on their feet. It shouldn't have been this difficult. Then Heywood realized that it must have been the heavy dress that was weighing them down. He pulled at the buttons on back, shredding off the material, and kicking it away. The pretty white gown vanished swiftly into the dark water while Heywood dragged Tess onto dry land.

He knew this area well and pulled her to the small cave that he and Lotty used to picnic in on Summer afternoons.

"I'll be right back, I have to get the boat," he explained, making a run for the water where it had begun drifting in the small waves. He was able to catch it quickly and haul the thing out.

By the time he got back from hunting down the oars, however, he found Tess curled up in a ball and shivering intensely.

He immediately laid down on top of her, hoping his body heat would take the chill from her skin. It wasn't freezing outside, but she was wet and practically naked.

She snuggled close to him, taking in his natural warmth, and he swallowed hard at the sweet torture of her body against his.

The rain rumbled outside the mouth of the cave and they both watched it silently, waiting for its end.

Tess had rolled over onto her back beneath him, and he wondered if it was because he was crushing her hip. Shifting his weight, he said, "I was able to pull the boat to shore and will get us back as soon as this ends. I assure you; I had no idea this would happen."

She smirked at that as she shivered. "I didn't assume this was some dastardly plan to trap me." She looked around then. "Should I have?"

His heart hammered. "Of course not."

She smiled again and he realized she was teasing him. He grinned, letting out a relieved breath.

She bit down on her smile, suddenly touching his cheek. Her eyes seemed curious as she ran her fingers over the stubble on his jawline then back through his thick smooth hair.

He didn't expect that. He swallowed hard as he stared down at her, at this perfect woman whose heart was all he wanted in the most terrifying way. Her fingers tugged, urging his head down toward hers.

He closed his eyes and let go of everything.

Of Emeline.

Of his distrust.

Of his vulnerability.

For once, he didn't overthink things and instead allowed this amazing lady to pull him down into the honied warmth of her soft kiss.

Her full round lips trembled, moving with such chaste sweetness that it almost made him wonder if she'd never been kissed before.

With the most unexpected rumble of desire, he took control, cradling her cheek and opening his mouth to her sweetness. She tasted of everything he didn't know that he'd been lacking.

She moaned into his mouth, as his tongue stroked hers in a slow sensual dance. Her hands remained in his hair, pulling gently as he groaned above her.

He could barely contain the unruly feelings that raged through his body. The hand that he wasn't using to prop himself up now traveled greedily down the side of her ribcage to her waist and hip. He wanted her so badly though he knew that he'd be a bastard to try.

The thought of leaving this secret cave without making love to this woman was unbearable. But it wouldn't have been right, and he knew that he needed to get control of the situation no matter how long the rain trapped them there.

With great effort, he forced his mouth away from hers and removed his hand from her body, bringing it instead to her face.

He stroked her wet hair, trying desperately to quiet his too-loud breathing. She gazed up at him through impossibly long lashes, her eyes a sizzling dark green.

He knew that he must have been crushing her, but she only seemed to shiver more when he moved away.

He realized then what an idiot he was to allow the river to swallow her garment. He gazed down at the transparent underdress, riveted by her luminous skin and beautiful curves. He sat up quickly and undid his shirt. Pulling it off in a hurry, he draped it over her quivering wet body. It wasn't warm or dry, but it would cover her up.

"Thank you," she whispered, wrapping it around her exposed body. She shifted to cradle herself against him yet again. He lowered himself back down to hold her and keep her warm, forcing himself to think of anything other than the beautiful person quivering against him.

****

Tess stared out her loft window at Heywood and Gabe rounding up the cattle below. A tremor ran through her entire body as she thought back on yesterday's cave expedition.

Her girlish nervousness had been silly. It wasn't as though it were the first time that she'd seen Heywood shirtless, but it *had* been the first time she'd felt his skin against hers. She'd never before seen the way his muscles moved when he walked, or the way they flexed when he rowed the boat back across the river with Tess still swathed in his shirt.

He really was stunning.

She closed her eyes, reminding herself of how it felt to be held and kissed by that man. Her mouth dried as she thought of the way his stubbled beard had tickled her face. She'd never been so brazen to initiate something like that. She thought again of how he catapulted that frightened kiss into something deep and sensual, and her cheeks flushed red hot.

She folded her arms, gently tracing her side where his fingers had once touched her. She'd never wanted anybody like she did him. If he initiated, she knew she'd do it again. God, she hoped he'd initiate.

She walked away from the window, berating herself. They shouldn't have even kissed the first time. It made things too complicated.

Heywood was an incredible man. He'd been so open and real with her yesterday, not like anyone she'd ever known. But she had a reason for coming back, and this wasn't it.

Pinning her hair into a neat chignon, she made her way down the stairs in a hurry.

The men were on their way back to the barn when she got outside. She followed them over there, hating how weak in the knees she felt.

They both paused on their horses when they saw her.

There would be no use beating around the bush, or awkwardly stumbling over their hello's. She and Heywood were adults, after all. Clearing her throat, she blurted, "I was wondering if I could borrow a horse."

Heywood frowned thoughtfully, clearly taken aback by that. "Is everything okay?"

"I just need to get to town."

Heywood dismounted and walked toward her. "You're not leaving—"

"No," she interrupted. "I just have errands."

He leaned back to look her over. "Errands. In Half Hallow."

She pursed her lips. "It's so lovely out, a perfect day to get it all done."

"Not as lovely as you," Gabe murmured behind them. They both turned to eye him, as he readjusted his hat.

Tess forced a smile but saw that Heywood didn't.

"I could ride you up there," Gabe offered, still messing with his hat and itching his hairline, but Heywood waved him off and took Tess's arm, walking her gently away from the awkward teen.

"This isn't about yesterday," he whispered. "I didn't frighten you off, did I? Because if so, I apologize. I didn't mean for…"

"It has nothing to do with that. I just need to get to town and it's a long walk."

"I can hitch up the carriage."

"I need to do this alone."

Heywood furrowed a brow at that. She looked down at her fingers, trying desperately to avoid the heat of his stare.

"Okay," he said at last. "I've got a mare in the barn who's real gentle and easy to work with. She'll take care of you."

"Thank you."

Heywood cinched up the horse for her and then lifted her up onto it. She could see the amusement in his eyes when she straddled the thing between her legs. Propriety be damned, she wasn't about to die trying to ride side-saddle.

She nudged the mare gently, and they lurched forward toward the half-moon pond on the edge of the Paxton farm and beyond it. It felt like a great success to know her way around without proper street signs.

Tess knew that she shouldn't have been getting comfortable. She had a mission, and it was detrimental that she succeeded if she didn't want Lotty's death to be the only way out.

CHAPTER TWELVE

Tess walked into Dr. Delacourt's office with her game face on. She didn't want to be back there, didn't want to even look at the man. Ever since his brutal and unnecessary attack on Heywood, she'd ranked the good ol' doc somewhere close to a leech in terms of parasites she'd want to be close to.

He bustled down the stairs at the sound of her entering and seemed to feel the same. With a snarl, he said, "Come to fix my door?"

She walked in and stopped at his counter, looking him over sternly.

He stared back, the hate in his eyes dissolving with a slow blink. "I'm not about to apologize for what transpired. I'd rather you leave and not come back. But I am grateful to what you did for my granddaughter."

"She almost died."

He winced visibly at that.

"Her heart stopped, and she couldn't get air into her lungs."

"Please don't." He squeezed his eyes shut.

"Do you have any idea how I saved her? Even after pumping her heart, do you understand how I was able to fill her lungs to get her breathing again?"

"I heard you blew into her mouth. And I'm grateful for that forward thinking."

"I don't need you to be grateful, I need you to really take that in and consider how many people, children and adults alike, die every year from something like that."

He furrowed a bushy white brow. "I'm not sure I understand what you're implying."

"It's just something I want you to think about. If I hadn't been there, Lotty would have died."

"Yes. I understand the logic of that."

"But as a doctor, consider what you could create that would help others who need oxygen to continually fill their lungs when they are incapable of taking a breath on their own and don't have anyone to stay with them in order to physically do it."

He looked her over thoughtfully. "What are you getting at? You think I have the manpower and intelligence to build something like that?"

"I do. If you had the right drive, you definitely could."

The door suddenly swung open behind her and Tess ground her teeth at being disrupted. This was too important.

She turned around and did a double take at Gabe walking into the office.

He froze in the doorway, looking at her like a deer in headlights. "This was your errand?" he asked, looking from her to the doctor. "Are you sick?"

"No. Did you follow me, Gabe?"

He shook his head, wide-eyed.

"What are you doing here then?"

"Heywood sent me."

She heard the doctor snarl with contempt behind her, but then Gabe scratched his head irritably. She saw him do that before she left the farm, it seemed like he was in a bit of discomfort and pain.

"Lice?" she asked softly.

Dr. Delacourt nodded him over. "Come on, boy, let me have a look."

He combed through his hair and glanced at Tess, clearly agitated that she'd been right.

"I've got some kerosene right here. That'll rid your scalp of these unwanted guests."

Tess's jaw dropped. "You can't be serious. Is that really what you do?"

"It's effective."

"And incredibly dangerous."

He waved her off. "Come, boy."

She followed Gabe, and nearly grabbed the kerosene from the doctor's hands in panic. "Don't you have white vinegar? Soak his head in that and then comb it out for God's sakes."

"Quiet down, woman, and let me do my job."

Tess snapped her mouth shut. This was insane.

"If you disapprove, I suggest you leave."

Tess blinked at him, clearly seeing that her chance at convincing the doctor to move forward with the respirator wouldn't happen today.

Defeated, she walked out and took a deep breath as she leaned back on the building. She looked around solemnly. It was so interesting how much had changed here in the last hundred and twenty years. She gaped over her shoulder at the mercantile where she'd met Mr. Tuttle the other day, the grandfather of that sweet museum curator. It was unreal.

Antoinette made her way out of the store just then with that large man she'd once seen going at it with Heywood in the street. She still never found out what it had been about, but it was easy to guess Antoinette had something to do with it. He certainly didn't seem to be a lover of hers, but maybe a close friend or brother. They both paused when they saw her, and it made her feel anxious.

Turning away, she quickly began making her way back to the church property where she'd secured Heywood's mare. She'd been trying not to focus on anyone, but the street was crowded. From the corner of her eye, she thought she might have spotted Theo and Grace in one of the restaurant windows, and the distraction caused her to trip into one of the small fractures in the dirt road. She stumbled and caught herself, limping away from the damn pothole to the church property where she could fix her shoe.

Gabe came ambling by just then. "Are you okay?"

She was irritated, readjusting her shoe and checking her ankle. "Fine, I think."

"I can kiss it and make it better," Gabe said.

She rolled her eyes and finished putting on her shoe.

He leaned on the side of the church; eyes fixed on her. "Thank you for trying to help with the doctor," he finally said, voice thick with adoration.

"No problem," she murmured.

His eyes that had once been singularly focused, now flitted to the ground where he noticed one of the church's lanterns had fallen and rolled into the road. Being helpful, he scooped it up.

Tess hadn't noticed the lanterns earlier when she'd tied up the mare, and now realized that there had been an entire line of them lit to decorate the outside of the small building. The one he held must have lost its flame and fallen in the wind.

Gabe reinserted it on its hanger and then went to one that was already lit to pass over the flame. "I can join you back to the farm if you'd like."

"Careful," she said.

He lowered his head. "I didn't mean anything by it, just that we're heading in the same direction."

"No, careful with that open flame. Your hair is covered in–"

No sooner did she even think it that the fire caught to his scalp and Gabe dropped the lantern, bolting forward in a panic.

Tess shoved him onto the road and scooped dirt onto it, beating his hair until it was out. "Are you okay?"

"I'm okay!" he gasped, feeling his head. It smelled like burned hair, but that was better than burned flesh. "At least the lice are gone now, right?" he said with a quivering smile. Then he looked behind her. "Oh no!"

She swung around and saw that the lamp he had dropped was catching to the side of the church building. "Go get water," she told him fast, and began kicking dirt on it just as she had Gabe's hair.

She hurried to the front door and called to anyone inside. To her astonishment at least fifteen men and women began to flee with alarm. Pastor Micah ran out from the back, hurling a bucket of water over the last of the flames.

"Holy Mary Mother of Jesus!" he panted, staring at the small black mark on his church. "What was that?"

"Gabe had a head full of kerosene and it lit from one of your lanterns."

"Is he–"

"He's okay. It looks like the church is too, luckily."

"Thanks to you. I didn't even smell that," he gasped. "The way this wind is going, it could have spread fast and burned down the entire street."

"Probably."

"We were having our choir rehearsal." He held a hand over his chest and breathed slowly in and out. "I apologize, just a little winded. I'm glad you were here. They all could have died."

"Maybe those lanterns aren't such a good idea in this weather."

"I think you're right."

Gabe suddenly reappeared with a fresh bucket of water, but then froze to look over the church.

"It's already out," Tess told him, still a little shaken. "Come on, I'll walk you back to the doctor to get checked for burns."

There was no hiding her I-told-you-so face when Gabe explained to Dr. Delacourt what had occurred.

Heywood noticed the bandage on Gabe's head as soon as he and Tess made it back to the farm.

He didn't have time to ask before Gabe was gushing out the entire story. All the while Tess could feel the boy's eyes on her, worshipping her.

She would have expected to feel flattered at a time like this but didn't at all. She was beyond that. And being the object of such adoration struck her as disconcerting, even in this other world.

"Well, it sure sounds like Miss Corbin is a good person to have around in a crisis," Heywood said with a hand on the boy's shoulder and an inquisitive eye on Tess. "I'm glad you're okay, Gabe. You need to go home now and rest. No more work today, you can pick up again when you're feeling up to it."

"I'm fine, I assure you."

"*I'd* feel better if you rested though. Tomorrow's another story. We can talk then."

Gabe's eyes flicked at Tess, then back on Heywood. "Fine," he said somberly. It was the same defeated and angry look he'd given her when she sent him home during that storm. "I'll see you tomorrow then," he grumbled.

Tess folded her arms as she watched him withdraw from the property.

"Wow!" Heywood whispered. "*You* had a fun day, huh?"

"Fun isn't exactly the word I'd use to describe it."

"You've got Gabe floating in a blissful cloud. What the hell happened?"

Dread gathered in the pit of her stomach.

"What's the matter?"

She shook her head. "I just didn't want to give him any more reason to... you know, be infatuated with me."

Heywood snorted. "The kid has a crush. It's harmless."

"That night that you left us to hunt, he tried to kiss me. Well, no, he did kiss me."

Heywood blinked. "That sly little dog."

"No. It wasn't as innocent as that."

He chuckled softly and Tess nudged his shoulder to stop him before thinking through if she really should have been touching this man again.

Backing up and crossing her arms, she said angrily, "It's not something to take lightly. It was unwanted and inappropriate."

He shook his head. "You're right. It's just, I never thought a guy like him would have the courage to do something like that." He forced down his grin. "What happened afterwards?"

She shrugged. "I told him to never do it again and sent him home."

He nodded pensively. "Good. That was right." Tapping his chin though, she could see the small indent of his dimple and knew the man still found humor in it.

She gasped and shoved him again, this time with both hands square in the chest. He caught her at the wrists, still chuckling.

"I'm sorry," he said, then seemed to notice his hands on her wrists and sobered as he let them drop. "Sorry," he said again, this time in a more serious tone. "It's just that Gabe isn't like other kids. He's never had a father or has done well socially. That's why I gave him a shot here. Figured I could teach him a skill and give him a little independence and extra cash. I mean, I'm not exactly the most popular guy in town either."

"That's nice of you, but–"

"I've just learned to be patient with him. As far as I know, you're his first crush so I didn't really know what to expect, but I'll talk to him man-to-man tomorrow. Let him know what's acceptable and what's not."

"Thank you."

"Well, thank you too for tolerating the boy. And also for, you know, putting out the fire on his head."

She snorted. "Any time."

****

Heywood closed his eyes as he strummed the guitar, lowering his own singing voice so he could hear Tess's. It wasn't like the crystalline tune he'd usually heard from talented choruses, but rather there was something dark and solid in it with a touch of grit.

Lotty loved it too. She'd asked for a song before bed and was mesmerized as she watched Tess from under the covers.

It felt much too comfortable. Like a family.

The sun was a dazzling orange by the time they kissed Lotty goodnight.

Tempted beyond all common sense, he found himself asking Tess to join him on a nightly stroll down to the water. He shouldn't have done that.

She shouldn't have said yes.

He noticed that Tess seemed surprised when he brought her to Saturn. He supposed he should have been clearer on what a *stroll* meant. Nonetheless, she climbed up onto the saddle just as she had the mare earlier that day.

He mounted behind her, his thighs and arms cradling her slender body as the horse trotted through the wavelengths of orange and red above them.

It was a clear night; he was sure that the view would be spectacular for her. She'd already seen the lake, but never at sunset.

As they drew closer to the water, he heard Tess gasp. He wondered if he'd had that reaction the first time he saw it too. He'd grown up living beside it and couldn't even remember anymore. All he knew was that at dusk, the water had a way of looking as though it had been lit up by the floating embers of a sunken volcano. It was exquisite.

It was also secluded. He might have loved that most.

Only the water and sky – and now the two of them.

"It's beautiful," she whispered, gazing out in awe.

Heywood smiled, his eyes drinking her in as Saturn moved forward, into the shallow water.

Surprised, Tess leaned back with a yelp and unsteadily gripped Heywood's legs at her sides. With one hand on the reigns, he lowered the other to her waist, steadying her as Saturn took off in a fast-paced sprint.

Clearly, she hadn't been accustomed to horses. She leaned her back against his chest, clinging to the arm now wrapped around her middle.

The water soared beneath them, the wind whipping her hair wildly. Tess closed her eyes.

It was like flying on a Pegasus with nothing beneath them but a dark ocean. Tess smiled dreamily, then leaned fully into him, resting the back of her head into his shoulder.

He felt the hand that had been gripping his elbow slowly lower to meet his fingertips on her abdomen. She pressed her hand over his, intertwining and locking their fingers.

Heywood dipped his face into her blowing hair, letting the scent of her wash over him until his cheek was against hers.

They remained in that dreamlike embrace as Saturn flew across the bed of water, their hearts speeding, adrenaline running, and their bodies holding on together.

It was unearthly, something that felt like only a dream or fantasy could.

They were breathing heavy when Saturn slowed to a steady gentle trot. Heywood wondered if she could feel his heart racing against her spine.

Breathing deeply, Tess craned her neck to look at him, cheeks pink from the wind and eyes sparkling. Heywood instinctively wrapped his arms around her and met her mouth with his.

They kissed with the same building passion they had in the cave. She tasted just as sweet as he remembered.

He cradled her face, tongue exploring her mouth. He'd never been kissed back with such passion, and he reveled in the force she used.

He couldn't believe that she wanted him as much as he wanted her. It did delicious things to his mind and body.

She arched her mouth away suddenly but welcomed his kisses on her jawline and under her earlobe.

She hummed gently at that, tilting her head back, inviting it.

"What on earth are we doing?" she breathed out in a whisper.

"I have no idea," he said against her throat.

She shifted, making herself less inviting and he knew that it was because she wanted to talk about it.

He shook his head, not even sure where to begin. Was it seriously the right time to get real and analyze all of this? Her eyes said, yes, so he shrugged and said, "The truth?"

"That would be nice," she hummed.

"The truth is, I didn't have these intentions. I didn't hope for any of this at all when we first met. In fact, I did everything in my power to not let it happen. To never give myself too much to lose ever again. But the more I'm with you, the more I *want* to be. I haven't felt this way in so long. I guess I don't know what this really is, all I know is that I don't want it to end."

She only stared at him in the growing darkness and he chewed the inside of his cheek. He'd said too much, made himself too vulnerable.He cringed at what he'd just admitted to her.He'd never been good at this sort of thing.

She put her hand on his face, as if making sure he was real. She bit her lip indecisively, but then pulled him toward her.

"This doesn't make any sense," she breathed against his lips. "It's frightening for me too. But I don't even care anymore."

****

The water was black and still as a pool of oil by the time they steered the horse back home.

Heywood had tasted of honey and beer and everything else that Tess knew was too stupid and dangerous to be wanting.

She rested against his chest, feeling her heart flutter in a way it never had before. This was exactly how she thought falling in love should be... something that took no effort, that just sank a person and held them captive no matter how much they resisted. Being with him was like quicksand, it was almost suffocating in its immaculateness.

And yet it wasn't supposed to happen. She wasn't supposed to fall in love with *this* guy. Why did he have to be so wonderful?

She closed her eyes, cringing as she reminded herself of her life back at home. Killian was there waiting for her. And Heywood was dead.

Oh God, he was dead! He died so long ago.

And he was much too young. She needed to go back and figure out how it happened so she could change it for him.

The sky was filled with brilliant stars when they made it to the farm. There was just something spectacular about a sky with no pollution of city or even regular street and stop lights.

She cringed as she climbed off Saturn, knowing that time couldn't be wasted. It had to be now, tonight. For all she knew he would die tomorrow.

"Heywood," she whispered.

He stopped and looked at her. Then his eyes lit with understanding from her tone. "No. Tess, don't. Please don't leave again."

She wiped her brow, aching at his sweetness. Leaving him this time wasn't going to be easy. "It's only for a little bit. There's something I have to take care of."

"What is it?"

"I can't tell you."

"Why?"

"Because it's too crazy."

"I can understand crazy." He walked up on her, but she shifted back.

"Let me do this, Heywood. I have to go and take care of something important, but I'll come back."

"When?"

She shook her head.

He took her hands and held them to his mouth, kissing them. "I suppose I can't talk you out of this."

"No," she whispered.

He breathed heavily.

"I'll say bye to Little Lotty like I promised. But it's not final. I will come back as soon as I can."

He let go of her reluctantly and she dragged herself inside, waking the sweet girl out of her sleep. She hugged her deeply and made the same promises as she had to her father. Stealing another knife, she made it back outside and found that Heywood had already hitched up the mare.

"Is there any way I could come with you? Make sure you get there safely?"

Tess bit her lip and shook her head. She hated how much this hurt him.

He sighed deeply and pulled her into a hug. "I shouldn't care this much."

"I shouldn't either."

A small breath seeped out from behind his sad smile. "I'm just kind of worried that I'll never see you again."

"Believe me, you will."

He nodded. "I guess I have to," he murmured.

She mounted the horse, her heart breaking as she sped away.

She wasn't sure if she could even believe herself.

CHAPTER THIRTEEN

"TESS, WAKE UP!"

The shouting woke Tess with a terrified jerk, and she landed hard on her bedroom carpet.

She sat up and looked around groggily. She was back. Yes, she remembered now how she had gotten home late last night and climbed into bed.

"Where the hell have you been?" Mrs. Corbin hissed. "Killian told me he had you here at the house the other day. I was on my way back and you still took off!"

Tess rubbed her eyes, still trying to wake. "I had somewhere I needed to be."

"For three days without even a call or text?"

Tess sighed. "You're right, that was pretty crappy. I would have contacted you if I could."

"Well, consider these little trips over."

"I'm an adult, mother. I never promised to stay in Half Hallow every second of my summer visit."

"Answer your phone next time, I was terrified."

That surprised her. "You were? Of what?"

"What do you think? If Killian starts to consider you fickle and unmanageable, he'll move on."

Her stomach sank. "So, who you were *really* terrified for was yourself."

"For both of us."

Tess rolled her eyes and climbed back onto her feet, pulling on her robe. "Nice, mom. Would have been pleasant to wake up to a hug hello, and to hear that my mother was mostly just worried for her only daughter's safety, but this is fun too."

Mrs. Corbin followed her to the bathroom. "Is it so bad to want a secure future for the both of us? You know what I've been dealing with. I could lose this house – *your* childhood home. I can't understand why you seem to care so little about that."

"I do care."

"Not enough to help your family though. I've given you everything all your life and all that I ask for is *one* favor in return."

Tess sighed brokenly. "A marriage shouldn't be a favor."

"You'd rather I live out the rest of my days in humiliation and grief? My God, how can you be so disappointing, Tesla?"

Tess's heart ached at that comment. "You can keep pretending that I'm the bad guy here, but it won't make you feel any less guilt for what you're asking me to do." She turned around in the bathroom entrance.

"Where are you going?" Mrs. Corbin demanded.

"I have to get dressed, I have errands to do. We can talk more after I get back."

"Killian better be one of those *errands*. You owe him an apology."

Tess closed the door between them, but still heard her mother's voice over the separation.

"No matter what you say, deep down I know that you do care. I know that you *are* on my side and will do the right thing!"

Tess breathed tiredly. As much as she hated it, her mother was right about at least one thing. Killian *was* still her fiancé, and he deserved an explanation.

She was in love with another man, after all. She hadn't planned on that. Even if she never saw Heywood again, what happened with him shouldn't and wouldn't have happened if she really loved Killian.

When she finished dressing, she found her phone and plugged it into the charger. She felt sick waiting for it to power up enough to at least text Killian.

Tess – I'm back. Sorry for running off. We need to talk.

Then she ordered herself an uber.

The phone had a low, but decent charge by the time she made it to the museum. The smell was of old furniture and a hint of cinnamon. There was something inviting about that.

There were a few other people walking around when she made a beeline for Heywood's portrait.

"Miss Corbin, you're back," Ms. Tuttle said, shuffling through the small crowd.

Tess turned around and smiled at the plump woman moving toward her. It wasn't long ago she'd been standing with Ms. Tuttle's grandfather at the mercantile.

"I'm surprised you remember me," Tess said.

"This place doesn't bring in that many new faces. Is there something I can help you with?"

"Actually yes. I was hoping to learn more about Heywood Paxton." She turned to the portrait, but then did a doubletake. There was something different about the abstract painting beside it. "Where'd *this* come from?"

"You don't remember it? I thought I showed it to you last time."

"You did show me a painting, but it wasn't this one."

"I'm sorry?"

Tess furrowed a brow, studying it for a long moment. Gone were the chaotic heaps of angry slashes that she remembered. This was a canvas of thick colorful globs that appeared as though it had been splashed together in a paintball field.

As she spread her fingers along the painting, a small strange burning aroma came to mind. It reminded her of a bake sale gone terribly wrong. Then she remembered the burnt loaf of bread, and gasped.

The paint fight.

It was the same canvas from that morning. He saved it. Her heart wilted as she looked again at his image in the original portrait.

"You can really see what a passionate artist he was in this other piece," Ms. Tuttle said, calling her over.

Tess was still too lost in the depths of his ice blue eyes to look away.

"Miss Corbin."

"Sorry," Tess murmured, tearing her gaze away and glancing at the other painting. Her breath hitched when she saw it.

With the Colorado mountains as a backdrop, it was a painting of a wide-open field of hay bales, with a girl sitting upon one of them. Though a face wasn't exposed, Tess knew that it was her.

Heywood had replicated her golden locks in a way that made them appear more angelic and less tangled in the breeze. The thin blue dress opened just enough for a long bare leg to hang outside of it. He made her look like a goddess. It was awfully diplomatic of him. Or maybe that was truly how he saw her.

Tess's heart twisted as she took in the breathtaking image.

"Do you remember when he died?" she whispered gently, forcing her eyes back on Ms. Tuttle. "You told me last time that he disappeared without a trace, but is there any documentation of exactly when that was?"

Ms. Tuttle's face crinkled with concern. "I must have been mixing up stories. No, that's not what happened to Heywood Paxton."

Tess turned around to fully face the woman. So, it did change. Saving Lotty must have saved him.

"His death is actually quite infamous, especially around here. He was the first of many murders that originated in this town."

The hope she had felt withered immediately. "No, that's not right."

"I'm afraid so. It was a long time ago, during the summer of 1900."

That was now... or, then. That meant it was going to happen any day! And it made absolutely no sense at all.

"I am truly astonished that you haven't heard of the Olive Stem Killer. It's much too gruesome for me to speak about in detail, but I'm sure the information is out there for you."

Tess's phone chimed and she pulled it from her pocket in a daze.

"Thank you, Ms. Tuttle," she murmured, feeling dizzy. "I'm sorry for taking up your time."

Glancing down at her phone on the way outside, she found the incoming message.

Killian – I arranged a driver to pick you up at 7am tomorrow to take you to the airport. The ticket for your flight is in your inbox. No arguments, please!

Tess had to have expected that. Of course he'd want to talk face-to-face. She didn't know what she was going to do. Tell him the truth, she supposed, and see if he still wanted her. She wasn't sure what it would mean to her if he did. Wasn't sure if it mattered if he didn't.

Tess – OK

She got into her email and wasn't the least bit surprised that it was a one-way ticket. She'd have to book her flight back home herself.

The phone battery didn't have much life left, so she hurried to text Joel.

Tess – Want to meet up?

He answered much quicker than Killian had.

Joel – You're back?! We need to talk about what happened

Tess – lunch? I'm at the museum if you want to come get me.

Joel – Be there in a few.

By a few, he meant forty-five minutes. Tess climbed into his jeep, hopeful that she'd find Matthias in the backseat. Her heart sank when it was empty.

"Please tell me Matthias is with Skylah."

"There are those names again," he grumbled.

She sighed. "And there's you still being a dick. Maybe those two are the only reason you were once cool."

"What the hell are you talking about?"

"I'm still not over what happened last time, Judas."

He snorted. "Yeah, I'm not over it either. What *was* that? You were right there and just sorda… I don't know, disappeared. Killian thinks I'm nuts now."

"God forbid, Sir Master of the Universe Killian Seymour thinks low of you."

He rolled his eyes. "Just answer the question."

"I already told you. I traveled in time. I know it sounds crazy, but it's the truth. The tree is the portal."

"Yeah, yeah. Portal. Time travel. Really cute, Tess."

She took a heavy breath, not in the mood for this. "Hey, you're a cop, what do you know about the olive stem killings?"

He snorted. "Probably about as much as you do."

"I know nothing of it."

"That's like saying you don't know about Jack the Ripper."

"Fine, I'll just google it."

He sighed. "The Olive Stem Killer is basically a worldwide unsolved case. It dates all the way back from 1900 till the 1930's."

"Why the stupid name?"

"The psychopath always left an olive stem of course. That's how they even knew it was the same person."

She stared at him, completely dumbfounded. "It all happened here in Half Hallow?"

"No. It was actually pretty strange. Back in 1901 or so people in Half Hallow began receiving letters from an anonymous source that contained threats along with personal information that only the recipient and their close relations claimed to be aware of."

He waited for her to give him some form of recognition to this story then drooped when she didn't. "This asshole would order the recipient to either fix what they'd done wrong or to just come clean publicly about it and would threaten severe violence and penalties

If not.

The screwed-up part is that they all pretty much died anyhow one way or another. Just seemed a cruel way to publicly humiliate people before the kill."

She shook her head. "Half Hallow back then was just a small town. The kind where everyone knew each other."

"Unfortunately, it was much easier back then to commit these kinds of crimes. Some victims died from boobytrapped mail, others bludgeoned to death or houses burned down with their families inside. It was like some kind of small-town vigilante that never got caught."

"But you're saying it continued over a thirty-year span?"

"Just a few years later it happened again in San Luis, then Leadville. It happened all over Colorado with no exact science to the location or timing. Sometimes there'd be letters involved, other times a phone call, sometimes nothing. Always that damn olive stem though."

Her heart was racing. How the heck could she have caused *this*?

She racked her brain. "I heard it started before that though. 1900. Heywood Paxton was the first victim."

"As far as we know, he's the first on record, before it was known to be a serial killer. Was found bludgeoned to death in the mountains, left with an olive stem in his hands."

She swallowed back vomit. "You would think that murder would have had to have been personal then, right? A serial killer's first victim usually isn't random, is it?"

"There's not an exact science to it, but it's definitely likely that their first taste of murder would come from a crime of passion. Some DNA was left behind, a sock with blood, but it's never led to anything over the years. It's a real mystery, that's why I compared it to Jack the Ripper. Anyhow, why so curious about this suddenly?" He furrowed a brow and then threw his head back with a short cackle. "Oh right, because of the time travel. Did saving that little girl not only take away my alleged son, but also create a serial killer and dozens of deaths?"

She sucked in a startled breath. Yes, that's exactly what it could have been. Every life she saved, and every person impacted by it had potential to be the cause.

It made her physically ill.

She was still sick in fact the following morning. Riddled with guilt and fear, she somehow forced herself out of bed and managed to dress and catch her flight. Almost three hours later, a limo driver with her name on his banner brought her to Killian's Los Angeles home.

There was a key left for her in his usual hiding spot in the garden, and a handwritten note placed on the entryway table.

Baby doll, text me when you get in and make yourself at home. A dress is waiting for you on the bed and my personal makeup/hairstyle team will be there by two o'clock. The limo will arrive to pick you up at 6pm. Can't wait to see you.

She couldn't help but wonder for what.

She turned around and went straight for the staircase to find this mystery dress.

Wow! Vintage!

The thing was gold and gorgeous. She hadn't ever worn anything quite like it.

She held it to her body and stared at her reflection already afraid of wrinkling the thing.

Pulling up her phone,

Tess – Made it. Dress is beautiful. May I inquire as to the occasion?

She set the dress down and ventured downstairs to find food, but there wasn't much in the kitchen that didn't need preparing. The man barely lived there. She finally found a few fresh apples on the counter and rinsed one off as her phone chimed.

Killian –Already saw you on the security cam, looking sexy as always. To be honest, I wasn't sure you would make it.

She rolled her eyes, apple paused three inches shy of her mouth.

Tess – I told you I'd come. Already said we needed to talk. Where are we going in that fabulous ensemble? Thought we could talk alone.

She took a bite. The fruit felt good in her belly after so long of no breakfast or lunch. Some peanut butter smeared on top would have been perfect.

Killian – Work

She paused mid-bite as she read this.

That was never good.

Tess – Thought you were finished with all the interviews and advertisements for this new movie.

Killian – obviously not. The promotion has barely begun.

An anxious flush warmed her cheeks as she stood in the middle of the modern kitchen, realizing now why he'd dragged her there rather than flying out himself.

It wasn't to talk or reconcile like she'd hoped. This was Killian's movie junket, and he needed her there for arm candy, simple as that.

She was thoroughly restless by the time the prep team made it to the house and began their work on her.

She was already familiar with this level of histrionics due to all the other times she'd attended his junkets, award shows, and premiers. But she no longer wanted any part of that life.

She grimaced when she saw her reflection at the end of their masterwork. It wasn't her.

This was some Jessica Rabbit sort of unreal perfection. A golden slave Princess Leia, the curvy woman-child Tinkerbell, and all of the over-sexualized videogame and comic book characters rolled into one. It was all too dreamlike, because it wasn't real and never could be.

She was a Greek goddess in the flesh. But take off the makeup and dress and she'd just be her.

Her heart melted at that thought. Heywood always seemed to view her as a goddess even when she was far from it. Killian only ever sought after creating her into one. As beautiful as this was, she hated the fake version of herself, inside and out.

The limo arrived at six o'clock sharp. Her mouth dried when she climbed inside to a stunning Killian Seymour holding two champagne flutes.

She slid into the seat beside him and took the glass he offered.

"To us being in the same place at the same time... finally," he said as though it were a toast.

He clanked her glass and then she sipped.

"Something you want to say to me?" he asked, eyes heated. "Another bout of Fugue state you wish to explain?"

She gritted her teeth, but then forced a sweet smile. "Nice to see you too, Killian."

He clenched his lips into the smallest semblance of a smile. "We'll talk about it later."

"Yes, we will. But in the meantime, please do try to remember that I am not a child and have the right to come and go howsoever I decide."

Still wearing that clenched grin, his hand shot out and gripped her knee, tearing her leg toward him and nearly ripping the dress along with it. "I'm not in the mood for your smart mouth tonight, baby doll. I may not have control of who you've been opening your legs for, but I can at the very least keep your mouth shut."

She stared wide-eyed at him.

"Do we have an understanding?"

She blinked with astonishment.

He released his hold and took another sip of champagne as his hand found hers and held it firmly.

The limo finally pulled onto the property and someone waiting on the red-carpet yanked Killian's door open.

"Slide down, I want you right behind me," Killian ordered, just before exiting.

Tess did as she was told, climbing out behind him in a dress that wasn't meant for sliding.

Immediately the paparazzi and the bug-like zap of their cameras invaded. There were blinding flashes and screams from the crowd. Luckily, she knew how to handle the press and held herself impeccably. Killian, looking just as delicious and debonair as ever, pulled Tess close, posing quickly for the photos.

Inwardly she grimaced thinking of all the new pictures of her that would be posted all over the media. They'd deem them once again the perfect couple, having no idea what he'd just done to her in that limo.

She was still so shaken up over it. He'd always been somewhat possessive, but he'd never laid a hand on her like that or spoken such foul words.

A small part of her wondered if she was overreacting. It wasn't as though he hit or attacked her.

Killian took her hand and pulled her forward on the red carpet. She dreaded what came next. These mind-numbing affairs were always the same – people gathered, took photographs, and received great food, drinks, and keepsakes while awaiting the popular celebrity that would arrive to promote their project. Tess had always hated when that celebrity was Killian and he'd drag her along on the endless interviews.

This night, however, he led her straight to the refined dining area filled with not only members of the press, but a good amount of A-list celebrities she'd never met before.

Killian waltzed through the opening, Tess in one hand and an unlit cigarette in the other. He waved like it was *his* audience, always the master of his domain.

Tess held her breath and put on a brave smile as he dragged her through.

A voluptuous woman from one of the tables they passed pulled out a lighter, and Killian stopped and backtracked a step to light his cigarette.

Some spectators laughed. The gorgeous blonde lit it like it gave her an orgasm.

Tess chewed the inside of her cheek, feeling like an idiot. Was she just supposed to stand there while he publicly played around with other women? The answer was, yes. She knew that she had to smile, otherwise she'd be made a fool in front of the worst crowd imaginable.

She played the part well. Outwardly Tess was everything that the high-ranking press and the magnificent A-list celebrities expected of Asher Corbin's daughter and of Killian Seymour's fiancé. They didn't know the truth though – that she enjoyed showtunes over rock, that she wished she could try out dreadlocks without looking like an idiot, or that she'd take tacos over caviar and beer over fine wine in a heartbeat. They had no idea that every time she gave them a new Stepford smile, she was hiding resentment underneath.

She was grateful when they finally sat.

Their server was a pretty just-barely-over-eighteen-year-old who clearly hadn't been used to this sort of setting. Her eyes immediately found Killian's at the table and she visibly blushed.

"Hi, I'm Casey, I'll be taking care of you tonight."

"Casey," Killian said, leaning his elbows on the satin tablecloth, and chin upon the outside of his wrists. "Beautiful name. I used to know someone named Casey."

"Wouldn't mind you getting to know *me* too," she giggled, gazing at him from beneath long fake lashes.

He smirked at her and winked.

Tess's entire body tightened with that, but he put a hand on her knee before she could physically respond.

"We'll each start with a glass of Chateau Lafite Rothschild, if you have it."

"Of course, we do."

"And sparkling water."

"I will be right back with those."

When she left, his fingers began to roam up Tess's leg to the inside of her thigh. "Jealous, were you?"

Tess clenched her teeth, shifting, trying to pull herself away from him.

His hand clamped down on her thigh, stilling her as Casey returned with a coy smile, carrying their drinks at a ridiculous speed.

She leaned over just enough to reveal significant cleavage as she set them down and then stood back up, sweeping the salon highlighted hair from her cheek. "I'm sorry, Mr. Seymour, I know I'm not supposed to do this, but I just want you to know that you were amazing in your last film. Breathtaking. I can't wait to see this new one."

He beamed. "Thank you!"

She glanced over at Tess as though she just realized she was there. "You're a lucky woman."

Tess grinned phonily and reached for her wine in desperation.

"Did you have a chance to peruse the menu?"

Killian didn't need to. "We'll start with house salads and a Filet Mignon each."

Even Casey seemed stunned by his ridiculously smooth control. Tess hated it.

"And for your sides?" Casey asked looking briefly at Tess.

Her eyes flicked immediately back at Killian when he said, "Whatever potato and vegetable the chef has on special tonight." He handed her their menus and winked. "Thanks, doll."

She flushed again at him and took off in a hurry.

Killian watched the young beauty leave the table with her hips swaying. "See what I'm giving up for you?"

"That isn't funny," Tess hissed.

"Loosen up."

Tess sputtered a bit into her wine as Killian's fingers began again to travel up her leg. With her eyes darting in panic around the restaurant, she clenched her thighs together to stop him.

His jaw tensed with that, and she could tell he was a little pissed off. Quite frankly, so was she.

She tried the wine again, this time chugging.

"Easy," he whispered, also giving the A-list crowd a glance.

He was worried about them seeing her guzzle down a drink, but not what he was trying to do beneath the table? That didn't even make sense to her.

A few people stopped by the table to shake his hand, which luckily ended his little game below the silk tablecloth.

He was charming to the men and flirtatious with the women. She knew what he was trying to do. She'd somehow managed to make him jealous and insecure with her absence, so he'd make her feel the same. But Tess without any shred of doubt knew that she wasn't interested in living like this.

She sipped on her wine and shook hands with those who acknowledged her until the food finally arrived and they were left alone to eat.

"I saw that you bought yourself a ticket back home for tomorrow," he said softly as he picked at his salad.

"How would you possibly know that?"

"The private investigator I had hired the first time you went missing."

"You never cut him loose?"

"I'm glad I didn't. You won't be taking that flight. I'll need you here for the duration of the junket."

She shook her head. "I don't think so."

Killian set down the fork and put his arm around her shoulder with a wide imitation of a smile plastered across his face. Pulling her into a kiss, he then rested his cheek against hers to whisper in a very formal, meticulous voice, "Don't make the mistake of thinking you're in control."

The breath froze in her throat. She wasn't in control of what – her own life? When did that happen?

Casey returned to swap out their salad bowls for the steaks. Again, she flushed when she looked at him.

Killian seemed to enjoy that. "Your face is absolutely stunning when you blush like that."

She put both hands over her cheeks. "I'm sorry. I always get a bit red-faced when I'm nervous."

"Well no need to be nervous. And no need to apologize either. I've actually read that women who easily blush are usually the best lovers."

This made her face nearly scarlet. She offered a small flirtatious smile. "I suppose there could be ways of testing out that theory."

"I suppose so."

Tess's jaw dropped at the blatant seduction going on right in front of her. She couldn't blame the kid, she was starstruck and inexperienced. Killian should have known better though. If his hope was to see his fiancé possessive of him, it backfired. She wanted out. Now.

Mrs. Corbin would have to understand. There was no hope for this relationship no matter how much it benefited her mother. She didn't know why she didn't see it from the very beginning. Killian Seymour would never be a husband or partner, he'd be her lord and master and she deserved better.

Tess waited for the waitress to leave before pulling the napkin off her lap and setting it on the table. She began to stand to walk out, but Killian grabbed her wrist and pulled her back into her seat.

"Don't ever get up from a table like that again," he said.

Other women might have enjoyed such macho possessiveness from this gorgeous specimen, but not her.

"This isn't going to work," she said quietly, leaning close to him. "You need a woman who will follow you adoringly, and it's not me."

"Eat your food."

"Did you hear me?"

"We'll discuss it later."

"No, I think a public setting is probably a safer place to give you this back." She tried to remove her ring, but he clenched his fingers around hers, a look of warning in his eyes.

Maybe he was right. This wasn't the appropriate setting of spectators for such a bold move.

"Eat."

She finally did, forcing herself to withstand the two-hour dinner due to Killian with his, *Sure, Casey, we'd love more wine and dessert.*

But as soon as it was finished, she had an uber waiting outside for her. Killian had no idea she'd made that arrangement when she excused herself to the ladies' room. When he saw it, a shadow passed over his face like a cloud crossing the sun. He didn't say anything when she hurriedly climbed inside.

She felt sick the entire drive to the hotel. There was still a chance that the investigator would track her tonight and the last thing she needed was Killian showing up at her suite or literally tearing her from the aircraft.

Her fear made it impossible to sleep that night as she watched the clock waiting for morning.

She didn't mind that sneaking out meant leaving behind the overnight bag she'd taken to Killian's house, or that she'd have to travel in this skintight expensive dress. All that mattered was that she got home.

Laying in the dark hotel suite, she flicked the heavy diamond around her knuckle. She'd have to figure out a way to successfully return his ring as well as the dress.

She knew that she would have her chance soon enough. Even if he didn't chase after her and drag her back to his manor, she was still certain that this wasn't the last she had seen of Killian Seymour.

After how he treated her tonight, that thought made her shiver.

CHAPTER FOURTEEN

Heywood had awoken earlier than usual. He must have slept awkwardly on his shoulder because it ached with every use.

It was probably caused by stress. His body had reacted the same sort of way when he first returned to Half Hallow with Lotty on his hip.

Saying goodbye to Tess Corbin had upset him more than he figured it should have. He didn't want to care about her as much as he did, but it was more than just attraction. Finding her was like finding another piece of himself and he liked who he was when with her.

Shoving his pitchfork into the pile of straw, he cringed again at the soreness in his arm and took a break to rotate the knot out of it.

"Need help with that?" a soft voice murmured from the barn entryway.

He twisted around and froze at Tess standing in the open doorway.

She came back! Part of him didn't truly believe that she would.

The blood drained from his face as he gaped at her, still wearing the same dress she'd left in, but her hair now long and curly down her shoulders. The sun behind her made it blaze exactly how an angel's ought to. But the thing that took most of his notice was her naked ring finger. No more diamond... no more promise of engagement.

She stepped into the barn. "I meant to offer help with your shoulder, not the manure."

"I figured," he snickered, loving her teasing grin. "I wasn't sure I'd see you again."

"I told you I would come back. I had to."

He didn't know what she meant by that last part, but then she cupped his face and stared at him with the same depth she had that night on the horse. Again, it was as though she were trying to memorize him.

He didn't know if it was too audacious to scoop her up into his arms, but his joy at seeing her again was too strong to *not* hold her.

She drew her mouth down to his. He never tasted anything so divine.

She pulled back suddenly, their shared breathing heavy and uneven. "I thought you hurt your shoulder," she panted, shifting her weight in his arms.

"I'll be alright," he whispered, then kissed her again, long, hard, and passionately. He could feel his own breath mounting as her hands twisted in his hair, anchoring herself to him.

He never thought he'd experience anything like this again, especially not in the middle of the mucky barn.

The whole world faded when he was with her though. Tess took his breath away.

The barn door suddenly opened, and Heywood broke away, immediately lowering her back onto her feet.

"Tess!" Lotty shouted from the doorway.

He raised an eyebrow at Tess who was still shaking out her skirts when Lotty came running into her arms.

"You're back!" Lotty squealed, then looked around curiously. "What were you two doing in here?"

Her innocent, yet forward questioning, made Tess's eyes widen with embarrassment.

"Miss Corbin was offering to help out," he said without missing a beat. It was at least somewhat true. "Come on, let's get breakfast."

"This is so perfect!" Lotty carried on, on their way to the house. "You're back just in time for the Independence Day Picnic!"

Oh crud. "Is that today?"

Lotty gave him an incredulous look. "Yes, pa! I reminded you last night."

"Well, I apologize. I had a lot on my mind."

"You said we could go. You promised."

"I did, didn't I?"

Tess gave a small shrug. "I think that sounds like fun. I remember you telling me about it. You should definitely go."

"All of us though, right?" Lotty said with pleading eyes.

Tess bit down on an undecisive smile. "Sure," she finally gave in. "I'll need to change first."

"It's not for another couple of hours," he said, never surprised at his daughter's uncanny ability to wear people down in her favor.

By the time they made it to the annual picnic, it was already packed. Delicious food spread all around them, but the real star of the event were the games. Lotty was already giddy and ready to make a run for it before he'd even had a chance to stop the wagon.

"Easy there," he ordered. "Let's not get ourselves runover due to mere excitement."

At a side glance, he noticed his daughter theatrically rolling her eyes and making Tess grin.

Once inside the grounds Lotty ran ahead to find her friends. It surprised Heywood how much more relaxed he felt compared to how he usually was at these sorts of gatherings. He barely noticed anyone or anything else as he walked beside Tess, hand in hand, wearing a silly foolish grin. It reminded him of when he'd come to these things as a child, back when he considered it the most perfect day. It almost seemed as though this could be shaping out to be the same.

"Tess Corbin, as I live and breathe!" a friendly voice called. They both turned around to Grace who was rushing over.

Tess seemed genuinely happy to see her, hurrying forward and inviting her into a friendly hug. "Everything's been so crazy, Grace, but I've been wanting to see you again."

"Me too. We should go shopping together. I can imagine you need more dresses. Maybe a swimsuit? It's getting so hot."

Tess seemed to take a liking to that.

Theo moseyed over behind her and began chatting casually with Heywood about some of the goings on in town, but Heywood had lost track of that the instant he noticed Antoinette across the way. She and Pastor Micah had been talking under one of the trees. The way the pastor looked at her was like how he had also looked at Tess when he'd come by that one afternoon for lunch. It made Heywood wonder if the pastor had lost interest in Tess and moved on. It seemed too good to hope for that Antoinette could have had any chance of moving on as well.

Callum Tuttle with his wife and a few others had joined their circle of conversation and laughs, but Heywood had zero interest in small talk. It was all only another distraction from the one person he wanted to be spending these moments with.

He didn't realize how much time had passed until Lotty came prancing over.

"I'm beating almost everyone at every game!" she sang, totally in her element. "Tess, I've got to show you this one where there's a fishing rod, and a pretend lake…" She pulled Tess as she spoke, who just shrugged at Heywood and the group as they disappeared into the array of people.

The others dispersed soon after to get food, leaving Heywood to search for the girls.

"Don't run off so soon," a voice suddenly purred, grabbing his elbow.

He turned around, and his stomach churned when he found Antoinette on his arm.

"I'm surprise to see you here. Join me for lunch?"

Her proclaimed shock was a bald-faced lie. There was no doubt she'd already spotted him and had been biding her time to catch him alone. "We ate before arriving, but thank you for the invite," he said politely, trying to pull his arm free. She stuck to him though like a leach.

"I suppose Lotty is running around here somewhere."

He nodded courteously. "Playing games, eating sweets, of course. She's been looking forward to it for months."

"The way you spoil that child." There was a touch of judgmental superiority in Antoinette's comment that he didn't care for.

Heywood glared briefly at the woman, catching a flash of resentment in her features just before she altered her expression to one of coy flirtation.

If he didn't know any better, he'd say Antoinette was nearly envious of his attention to his daughter. What an absurd idea.

"I think it's clear what this young lady has been lacking, Mr. Paxton. Fathers are often just too soft on their daughters. She needs a strong woman to step in occasionally, unless you want her out of control as she ages."

He swallowed his anger. "I can't help but wonder why this would concern you, Miss Cavaliere. You seemed rather comfortable with Micah Gibson not so long ago."

She smirked at that. "Were you feeling a bit covetous, Mr. Paxton?"

"On the contrary. I was relieved that maybe he's taken you off my hands."

She snarled and ripped away from his arm. Flinging her hand forward so fast, he wondered if he'd *heard* the sharp crack against his face before he felt it. He couldn't believe she slapped him like that, so hard and loud and in front of everybody, including the children.

He hadn't any patience for that and grabbed her arm tightly.

"Ouch!" she hissed. "Heywood!"

He pulled her quickly through the crowd, ducking her inside a narrow gap between two buildings. Once they'd been given privacy, he let go of her arm, giving her a small shove toward the wall as he did so.

"Ouch!" she yelped again. "What do you think you're—"

"Let's avoid any more confusion. Let me make this as simple as possible for you," he growled quietly. "There is nothing between us. Nothing now and nothing ever."

"Heywood, honestly…"

"I want you to understand this and move on without crying to your brother."

She smiled up at him coldly. "This is about that woman, isn't it? I saw you walk in together. It's disgusting what you're doing with her. And I cannot believe the audacity to bring her here around decent folks to celebrate our country."

"You're implying *you're* one of these decent folks, Miss Cavaliere?"

She went to hit him again, but he caught her wrist. "No," he sneered. "No more of that."

Antoinette screwed up her mouth and spat pathetically at him. Most of it ran down her chin in a frothy dribble, but she did manage to get him a little.

He wiped it off near his eye. "And you call yourself a lady."

"Get away from me, Heywood Paxton. You disgust me."

"That makes two of us," he sneered, backing away to let her pass.

Antoinette looked angry enough to kill as she took a step toward him. She shoved him hard in the chest, then shoved him again, screaming, waiting for a reaction that he wouldn't give her.

"Miss Cavaliere," a voice said softly, blocking out the sun in their small alleyway.

They both looked over at Pastor Micah who'd joined them with a look of distress.

Antoinette lowered her hands from Heywood and backed away.

"I apologize if we disrupted the celebration," Heywood said softly. "We only meant to have a private conversation."

Keeping a firm reign on his emotions, Micah replied, "A conversation that has clearly gotten out of hand. I think it would be best if we finish this another time, together, where I can facilitate."

Putting a hand on Antoinette's back, he nudged her toward the picnic grounds, then turned around to face Heywood once they were alone. Though the pastor was only a few years older than him, it still made him feel like a schoolboy about to get reprimanded by the teacher.

"What's going on?" Micah asked gently. "I know you and Miss Cavaliere have had your issues, but I can't ignore that you put your hands on her."

"I was only keeping her back. I wouldn't have hit her." It made him ill to even have to explain that. Of all the people in this town, Micah was one of the few who had never believed the rumors about Emeline. He knew that Heywood hadn't a violent nature. "She came at me and I just wanted to explain…"

"I'll make sure that you get your chance to speak your piece when I can be there to keep it civil."

Heywood sighed with defeat. "I appreciate that."

"There's something else I feel I should be open with you about, while I have you alone."

Uh oh.

"Miss Tess Corbin."

His heartrate spiked. "What Antoinette says about her isn't true."

"The Lord did not lead me to this church to judge others, but to speak truth and love to them. I only feel that if Miss Corbin plans to stay then she really ought to find her own place. It isn't appropriate to share a home and then flaunt the nature of that relationship at gatherings such as these."

"It isn't like that at all. We sleep in separate parts of the house."

"Nonetheless, it makes people uncomfortable."

Heywood's anger drained. "I understand."

"But I do hope that we can arrange that private meeting between you and Miss Cavaliere and that you and Miss Corbin do join us for Sunday services again."

"Not sure if we'd be welcome."

"Our Lord turns away no one who comes to sit at his feet and worship."

"No, but your flock might."

"You let me handle my flock."

Heywood forced a nod.

"You do understand what I'm saying about today though, right?"

Heywood did. It wasn't right for them to be there, holding hands and being happy, not while still living together unwed. They'd have to leave and start figuring out their living arrangements fast.

"Sure. No problem."

****

Tess watched the townspeople anxiously as Lotty ran from one game to the next, a ball of energy and bliss. She wished she could enjoy this time with her because she didn't know how much longer they'd have together. But truth was, Heywood was her only priority, and he was going to die unless she figured out who would kill him.

Lotty wasn't the only one who's life she saved, but Gabe's as well and the entire town due to the flames. Literally anyone on the streets that day could have died if she hadn't stopped the fire. And it wasn't just them either, but anybody else that had been affected by their survival.

This kill wasn't random though. This person had to have had a reason to make Heywood their first.

It made her stomach hurt and her chest pound to even think of it. She anxiously reminded herself that she would fix it, that this would not be his fate.

She spotted Heywood in the crowd just then, and her breath hitched. His eyes met hers and he immediately began toward them. His jaw was clenched, and she could tell he was upset about something.

He forced a smile when he met up to them. "Looks like it's time to leave," he said softly.

"No," Lotty argued. "We haven't been here that long. Please, just a little longer? I haven't even ridden the pony yet."

"You've got horses at home."

"But not ponies."

"I'm sorry Little Lotty."

Tess stared at him, seeing it all in his sympathetic and yet angered glance, that it wasn't by choice. Something had happened. They weren't welcome, at least not together.

"It's me, isn't it?" she whispered.

"Of course not."

But she could see in the slight shake of his head that it was exactly what she'd been suspicious of. It was why he took her out into the privacy of that lake those days ago.

This was a different time when people showing physical affection was unacceptable. She feared this earlier when Lotty had first mentioned the picnic and she feared it even more now. People didn't like seeing them together. For some odd reason, it hurt them in a way that she couldn't quite understand. It should have just been about her and Heywood, not the rest of the town. But she had to respect the era she'd arrived in and not let Heywood's reputation slip even further.

It was clear as anything how guilty he felt for having to take Lotty away from her fun, especially since he wouldn't even know how to explain it to her.

"You two stay," she offered. "I'll go."

"No, that's not necessary."

"Come on, she hasn't even ridden the ponies yet. I'll find Grace, she wanted to take me shopping anyway."

He seemed a bit relieved. She'd never been this attuned to a man's thoughts before and wondered if he could read her just as easily.

"You owe me a new dress anyway for the blue one you destroyed," she added, making him laugh.

She loved the sound of it and the way his eyes would crinkle just as much as she loved that shadow of a dimple that formed underneath the stubble on his cheek.

"I did not forget. Just tell them to put whatever you purchase on my credit."

"I planned to."

He squinted agreeably at her, rather enjoying this, and she was happy to have lightened the sullen mood.

"Meet me back at the house right after though," she said firmly. "Don't go into the mountains for any reason."

"Why would I?"

"Just don't. Promise me."

He nodded, clearly confused as ever, though a bit intrigued. "Okay, I promise."

She felt better leaving him, knowing that the murder in the mountains wouldn't be today, then set out to find Grace.

She'd hurried through the crowds, ducking under the tents of food, then past where the carriages and horses were waiting. Grace was nowhere in sight. The only person who seemed to be out this far was a brawny man seated on one of the fences. She inwardly moaned realizing he was Antoinette's mystery man.

She turned back in the direction she'd originally come from but could hear him climbing off the post and sensed his hefty footfalls behind her.

"What's your rush?" he asked, but she ignored him, hurrying back toward the crowd.

"You'll never look as good with him as my sister does," he said, catching up and falling in step with her.

So, he *was* Antoinette's brother. She looked him over. He smelled just as dirty as he looked. "What does that matter to you?"

"The happiness of my sister? Means quite a bit."

"She wouldn't be happy with him. There will always be something more she'll want."

"Maybe. But this is what she deserves." He stepped in front of her, forcing her to a quick stop. "She grew up in this town, you're the newcomer. It's only appropriate that you're the one to remove yourself."

She glanced up at the big man looming over her. "Get out of my way."

Instead he moved closer. "If you're so set on wanting to stay, I could offer to make an honest woman of ya."

She snarled. "Thanks for the proposal, but no thank you." She tried again to get around him and this time he did step aside.

She was grateful and relieved, and kept walking fast until she found Grace.

The store she took her to was fairly big. There were plenty of lovely dresses of all designs lining the walls, but also a section of materials and sewing supplies. She wondered if Grace had ever made any of her own.

Tess scoped out a few dresses hanging beside the ones Grace was looking at.

"Can I talk to you about something?" she asked quietly.

Grace seemed a bit caught off guard but nodded quickly. "Of course! You and I are friends. Anything."

"I'm just a little worried about Heywood. There's been some threats against him."

"What kind of threats?"

"I'd rather not say at this time."

"If it's serious then you or he should talk to Theodore about it."

"As of now the threats are rather vague, but I wanted to ask if you knew of anyone who might have a grievance against him."

Grace snorted a little under her breath. "Too many to count."

"You're right, I guess for those who believe he could have killed Emeline. Antoinette's brother seems to hold a lot of anger toward him as well."

"Axel just wants what he feels his sister was promised. Antoinette still seems to be very much infatuated with Heywood, after all. It doesn't mean that Axel would truly hurt Heywood."

"People said that about the doctor too and look what happened."

"Yes, that's true. I honestly couldn't see anyone being a real risk to his *life* though."

"What if it's not about vengeance then? What if it's someone who just wants something from him."

Grace shook her head, thinking that over as she skimmed her fingers over a few more dresses. "Maybe if he had something worth taking. All Heywood has got to his name is that land." She then noticed a pretty periwinkle dress and waved Tess over. "This one would look nice on you!"

Tess thought how the color almost matched Heywood's eyes. Buying another blue one just seemed like fate. It was perfect but would be worthless if she lost him.

Picturing that scenario made her ache. She couldn't imagine his life ending like that... of never seeing him again and having to accept that she'd been the cause of it.

There was no denying that something had changed the moment she met Heywood. Not just the ripples through time that changed their worlds, but something in *her* as well.

What if the tree wasn't just a coincidence, what if their blood reacted in that surreal way because they were always meant to find each other?

She didn't know.

All she was sure of was that wherever he was, that was where she wanted to be.

CHAPTER FIFTEEN

"Remember to hold the stone with your thumb and middle finger," Heywood told Lotty, curling her index finger along the edge of the flat triangular stone.

Tess had spent a great deal of time helping them collect at least a dozen small thin rocks, and now sat off on the grass while Heywood taught Lotty how to skip them. There was a specific technique to it that she'd never mastered, herself. Heywood had gotten as high as six bounces off the water and Lotty was determined for just one.

He'd offered to teach Tess as well, but she thought it better to sit this one out and give them alone time. Watching them together was more fun for her anyway.

Lotty growled as another stone flopped. "I'll never get it."

"Sure, you will."

"I just stink at this," she pouted, crossing her arms.

Heywood nudged her chin. "This is what the whole learning process is. When you learned to read, it took a little time didn't it? And now you're a pro!"

"Reading was easy."

"Soon this will be too." Heywood grabbed another. "When I was first learning, I kept thinking I was bad at it too. But really I was just learning all the different ways *not* to skip a rock."

She giggled.

He threw the small stone with a quick downward force. They watched it bounce across the still water. "I only needed to find *one* way that worked though."

Lotty grinned. "Okay. Give me another."

Tess watched until they ran out of stones. Lotty didn't get any to bounce like she wanted but was promised another day of it as Heywood gathered their things.

"Are you two hungry?" Tess asked, scooching off the grass. "I could make us some lunch."

"Can't today," Heywood murmured. "I've got to hurry and get cleaned up for that meeting today with Pastor Micah and Antoinette."

"Oh, I forgot about that."

She chewed her lip, bothered by the small bit of jealousy that sparked from his spending any time at all with that woman. It was silly to feel that way since the meeting was merely set to cut things off, but Tess just hated her. After all the things Antoinette put him through, she didn't deserve this much attention from him, nor to rob Tess and Heywood of their small precious time together.

Lunch for two worked just as well though as she and Lotty waited around for Heywood's return.

They both seemed to hear boots against the wooden porch at the same time and scurried to the door. Only it wasn't Heywood standing on the other side.

All blood drained from her face when she opened the door to Antoinette's brother.

"What are you doing here?" she asked timidly. "Axel, it is, right?"

He grinned a broad smile of uneven teeth and tipped his hat. "Nice to know you've been asking round about me, little lady."

She sneered at his cockiness. "Grace mentioned it briefly in passing. What can I do for you?"

"You can get me Heywood Paxton. Tell him that he and I need to chat."

"Chat," she repeated suspiciously.

"I heard what happened between him and my sister at the picnic yesterday, so it looks like I'll need to set him straight. Won't hurt him *too* bad."

Tess glanced down at Lotty, who'd been hiding behind her skirt, then back into his dark eyes. "I'll leave that between you two, but I'd rather you not threaten things in front of his daughter."

Axel flicked up his eyebrows and leaned back on his heel. "Then I suggest you send his daughter inside."

Tess snarled at him. "Lotty, go on in for a minute."

"Is Pa going to be alright?" she whispered in a shaky voice.

"Of course, he is," she said, eyeing the large greaseball in front of them.

He just huffed a condescending gurgle as she left.

"Mr. Cavaliere, I wish I could help, but unfortunately your savage beatdown will have to wait another day. Mr. Paxton isn't home."

"Hiding, is he? Saw me coming? Maybe I should check for myself."

Tess flung her arm out to block the door as he began toward it.

He responded with a leering gaze. "You really think you could stop me if I wanted in?"

A deep terror shuddered through Tess's body. She forced it down with a cold and controlled glare. "I already told you he's not home. And you should know this since he's with your sister."

Clearly, the man was not expecting that. He leaned on his heel again, thinking that over, then smiled. "Boy came to his senses, huh? Finished up with you just like I told him to." He gave her a crooked smile. "My offer still stands, by the way. Never been married and I reckon it's about time."

Tess grunted with disgust. "Get on out of here, Axel."

"Nah, I already told you I wanted *in*."

"That's not funny."

"Not trying to be. Your time with that little maggot is through. Can only go up from here."

"Marrying you would be a step *down*, believe me." She backed into the house, but he grabbed onto her arm and yanked her back out onto the porch before she could close the door between them.

"Don't disrespect me. Playing coy is one thing, but don't you dare disrespect me."

His words startled her. How was it that a person could demand respect from one they demoralized? She'd never have guessed a dirty dimwitted brute like this could have the same perverse outlook on women as her sophisticated ex-fiancé back at home.

The sound of a whinnying horse caught them both by surprise, and she was both relieved and worried to see Heywood arriving onto the property.

He dismounted in a hurry when he saw them and walked swiftly up the porch. He gave Axel a cold stare as he forced himself between them.

Axel grinned wickedly and flicked her arm free. There would be fingermarks left behind, but she didn't want to draw attention by rubbing it.

"You seem disappointed to find us like this, Paxton. No need for that. You had your time, but the lady belongs to me now."

"She belongs to nobody, especially not the likes of you. Get the hell off my property."

"Just thought I'd show her what it's like to be with a real man."

The tension thickened, and Heywood's muscles steeled, ready for whatever might come. Axel cocked the fist at his side, grinning, wanting this fight to happen.

Tess gently took Heywood's arm.

"It's not worth it," she murmured, giving him a tug. "Not with Lotty inside."

Axel snickered mockingly, but Heywood ignored that and gave her a swift nod, careful not to take his eyes off the brute.

"Let's go," he said softly, and Tess felt relief when they walked backwards into the house.

She hurried to close and lock the door behind them and Lotty immediately sprinted forward, throwing herself into his arms.

He kissed her head. "Everything's fine, Little Lotty."

Tess gave them privacy, drawing to the window to watch until Axel was gone.

****

Tess sat alone in the barn, watching the sun dip lower like a sinking wound in the sky. She'd never felt this frightened and unsure in her life. Heywood had grown to mean so much to her in such a short amount of time. It wasn't supposed to happen this way.

Heywood was right when he told her how terrifying it was to have so much to lose. Loving him was the most beautiful and awful experience, because she knew she didn't belong there.

Whoever said that it was better to have loved and lost than to have never loved at all clearly had never lived it. This was a pain she'd never felt before in her life – the pain of loving someone that she knew she couldn't have.

"Lotty's finally asleep," Heywood said unexpectedly in the dark. It made her jump. "Sorry. I thought you heard me come in."

Tess smiled despite her surprise and awkwardness. "I guess I'm still just a little jumpy."

Heywood's eyes darkened as he stared up into the loft where she sat. "What happened before I got home? Lotty was so freaked out, I didn't even want to ask you about it in front of her. But that bastard... he didn't... he didn't hurt you, did he?"

Tess wilted at the absolute fear and anger in his eyes. "No. He did nothing more than express his need to beat you to an inch of your life."

"No wonder Lotty was scared."

"Oh, and also to marry me."

He snorted with disgust. "Marry?"

"It wasn't a very romantic proposal."

He shook his head, giving a weak smile at her sarcasm as he climbed up onto the rickety loft beside her. He set a blanket over her shoulders while she looked out the barn window at the orange setting sun. Taking her arm, he inspected where Axel had grabbed her. His face wrinkled with pain at the red and bruising fingermarks left on it.

"I shouldn't have left you and Little Lotty alone. I wasn't thinking."

"Why do you call her that sometimes? Little Lotty."

"It's from the poem." He sat down beside her, massaging the part of her arm that had been hurt. "*A Child's First Sorrow* by Andreas Munch was one of Emeline's favorites."

"I thought Lotty was just short for Charlotte."

"She was named after Emeline's favorite grandmother, but Emeline loved the little girl in the poem and began calling Charlotte that soon after she was born. I don't know, it just sort of stuck." He pulled up his knee, resting his forearm on top of it as he looked back out the window. "Little Lotte thought of everything and nothing. Like a butterfly she flew about in the gold sun..." His voice drifted as he quoted the old poem from another lifetime.

Tess thought she'd heard it before. Something written in the 1850's.

"It's beautiful," she whispered. "You should create some music for it, something you and Lotty can sing in memory of her mom."

He looked at her, eyes becoming gray against the darkening sky. There seemed to be so much he wanted to say, but instead he only shook his head saying nothing.

"What is it?" she finally asked.

"Nothing. I'm just thinking things that I shouldn't be."

"About me?"

He looked over, staring at her in a way that tightened all the muscles in her belly and took her breath away. It was the kind of look that made her feel as though she would catch on fire.

He didn't have to say it, she already understood how hard he'd been trying to control his feelings.

"It's okay," she murmured. "I'm thinking things about you that I shouldn't be either."

Heywood smiled at her and it was better than anybody else's smile in the world because it wasn't just something that curled his lips like most people. It encompassed his entire face and lit up his vivid blue eyes. His smile was the most sincere and most alluring smile that Tess had ever seen in her life.

He leaned over and put his hand against her cheek as though he was touching the most delicate china. He kissed her on her forehead, nose, then lips. She opened her mouth to him, craving that sweet moment when their tongues could meet.

He stroked her throat with his fingertips, and she moaned into his mouth, pouring all her angst and fear into this kiss. She could sense that he was doing the same, and knotted her fingers into his hair, binding herself to him.

Emotion filled her body, a wonderful warmth that almost made her heart ache because she knew that in a thousand years, she'd never find anyone else like him. No matter how many different lifetimes she ever saw, or how many other versions of this world that she visited, she'd only ever be searching for him.

It was as though she was sinking, falling head over heels, and she clung to him as they dropped back against the wooden floor. His hand went to her leg, pulling it up so that it nearly wrapped around his hip.

He broke off the kiss, and she knew she was breathing too loud. His eyes were luminous with desire in the early moonlight. It scared her as much as it excited her.

It felt like everything in the world rested on what would happen next.

She'd never loved anyone like she loved him. She never *wanted* anyone to this capacity. She had been told by many how lucky she was to be with Killian, but none of it had ever been as real as this.

She could see in his eyes how much she must have meant to him. But he hadn't been with anyone other than Emeline. Falling in love was just as foreign to him as it was for her.

"You nervous?" she asked, gently stroking his cheek.

He smiled and turned his face to kiss her fingers, cherishing her. Then his mouth was on hers again and she knew they reached the point of no return.

She never thought this would happen with him, especially not here in his barn. The place didn't matter though, only the person did. And she'd choose him on a barn floor over the most lavish penthouse suite in the world. If this was never meant to be and she lost him at the end of it all, at least they could have had this one night.

****

Heywood wasn't sure what roused him but was grateful to awaken wrapped in Tess's body. He scooted down and rested his cheek against her chest, holding onto her and feeling her heartbeat.

He never felt such blissful contentment. Even the air around them seemed to hum. Part of him had wished he'd let his guard down with Tess a long time ago, but also knew that it wouldn't have been right until now. He didn't even care that it happened on the old rickety loft, not when his body was still warm with desire for her.

She stirred against him, opening her eyes to the sunrise where hours earlier they had watched it set. She cradled him sleepily, her fingers in his hair. "I never knew it could be like this," she whispered.

"Me neither." He kissed her softly. "I love you. I'm not going to let myself be afraid to say it. Even if there's still some things you're not ready to tell me. I love you."

Her face crinkled a little at that. "I love you too. And maybe…" He kissed her again, absorbing anything more she was going to say. This wasn't the time to pressure her into talking about her life outside of Half Hallow. He wanted only to savor this time together.

He thought he could have stayed in that moment forever, but then he heard movement outside the barn and rolled over fast to listen.

It must've been Gabe. He cursed under his breath and Tess sat up immediately.

He didn't mean to scare her. "It's just Gabe," he explained. "I forgot he was working this morning."

Her knees drew instinctively to her chest under the blanket. "He can't find us like this."

"Stay here," he murmured, pulling on his trousers and climbing down the ladder.

The barn door opened before he could make it to the bottom and Gabe gasped with surprise at the sight of him.

"I thought the barn was empty," he wheezed, holding his chest. "What were you doing up there?"

Heywood forced a grin. "I'm sorry for startling you. I didn't realize I'd fallen asleep in here. It's gotta be the first time you beat me to work."

He expected Gabe to laugh it off, but instead he stared up into the loft. "Somebody else with you up there, Mr. Paxton?" Then his face shattered. Heywood had never seen a heart crush to the capacity that Gabe's did when he spotted Tess. There really hadn't been much hope of hiding her on that small loft.

Gritting his teeth, Heywood shook his head. He didn't regret a single moment of last night but was damned sorry that Gabe had to walk in on the aftermath.

"You didn't!" Gabe murmured, swallowing hard. "Mr. Paxton... you and Miss Corbin... you couldn't have..."

Heywood reached out and took his shoulder paternally. "It's okay, Gabe. Everything's fine."

"No," he grunted, shaking his hand off.

He'd never done that before. Heywood froze.

"Gabe."

"No!" This time he yelled it, making Heywood jerk. "You violated her!"

Heywood inwardly cringed. He could only imagine what Tess had felt in that moment. He forced a gentle hand on Gabe's chest, wanting desperately to calm and quiet him, but Gabe only shuffled back as though his touch was disgusting.

"You knew I loved her," he hissed, lips curled, eyes dark and furrowed. "You knew it and still you... what the hell kind of a man would do that? Who the hell are you?"

Heywood sighed. "Gabe, please try to understand..."

Gabe shook his head and backed up further, snarling with revulsion. "What they've been saying about you two is true after all. I didn't want to believe it." Looking up into the loft at Tess, he visibly shuddered then ran out of the barn.

Heywood followed after him, but the kid was gone by the time he made it outside.

That kind of reaction was the last thing he expected. Tess emerged from the barn behind him and Heywood shook his head, still watching the swirl of dust from Gabe's horse.

"He's going to tell everyone," he murmured.

"Does it even matter anymore?"

He turned around to look her over. He supposed she was right. It didn't mean much if Gabe spread to the entire world what the town had already believed to be true.

But something about the way she said it… it was too dark and empty. Tess squeezed her eyes shut and took a breath.

It made Heywood's heart sink. Did Gabe make her feel ashamed for what happened between them? Did she regret it now?

His chest tightened. "What's wrong?"

She shook her head. "I can't do it anymore. It was okay before, but not now. I didn't plan on this; I need you to understand that. I didn't expect to fall in love, I never thought I'd find *you*."

She wasn't making any kind of sense. It frightened him.

Taking her face in his hands, he looked into her gorgeous green eyes that now seemed almost gray. "Okay, you're right. Maybe we shouldn't have let our emotions get the better of us last night, but it happened, and it was amazing. Please don't overthink it now. Everything's still so fresh."

"It isn't that, Heywood."

"Then what?"

"You asked me to open up to you. To tell you the whole truth… this is it."

He swallowed hard. "Okay. I'm ready."

She shook her head, pretty full lips curling as she finally whispered, "I'm not from here, Heywood. I'm from the year 2020."

His heart felt as though it had stopped, as a terrible ache filled him. "2020?" he repeated, letting go of her and stepping back.

"Yes. You were right. I do remember my past. But you were wrong too, because I wasn't running away, this was all an accident. Though maybe subconsciously I *was* trying to escape that life, because this is everything I never knew I wanted."

"What are you saying?"

"I was climbing a two-hundred-year-old tree with a knot in it. It was in my backyard and hit my head, waking up here." She instinctively grabbed onto him, as though she knew he'd walk away. "I know that this seems ridiculous, but I need you to trust me."

Heywood wilted.

"Something about Emeline's tree brought me to you." She stopped to take a breath. "None of the *why's* or *how's* even matter anymore because I've seen the future and all that matters now is that I protect you."

He jerked at that. "Protect me?"

"Yes, you're going to die unless I stop it."

That was enough for him. He gently took his arm out of her hand. "Stop it, Tess. Just please stop."

"Together we can figure this out."

"Tess…"

"If we can find who the Olive Stem Killer is, then we can—"

"I said *stop!*"

She visibly froze. He didn't mean to yell at her, but this was ridiculous. It was the worst story she could have possibly come up with.

"Heywood," she gasped, taking a step toward him.

"No," he groaned, moving back.

If he let her touch him, if he let himself feel for her again… it would kill him. Why did she have to do this? Tess was the only other woman he'd ever cared about. He never should have allowed himself to be so vulnerable with her. Never should have given her the power to hurt him like this.

"I know it sounds crazy," she muttered softly.

"Yeah it does," he growled back. "Only one of two things is happening right now. Either you actually believe this story, which makes you insane. Or else you're *pretending* to because you want out and are too pathetic to be upfront about it. Which of these two is it? I'd like to know."

She flushed red, her entire body wilting. There was a part of him that wanted to be glad that maybe he caused her the same pain she was causing him. He wasn't though.

There were tears in her eyes, but he couldn't tell if it was from anger or sadness.

"I'm sorry if this upsets you," she finally grumbled. "I do hear myself and know it sounds unbelievable, but it's the truth. Every time I came back here, I changed something. And now you're going to die in the mountains under the hands of a serial killer, unless we stop it. If you can't believe me then I'll take care of it myself."

"I think you should go." His voice cracked. "You can take the mare and the clothes; I can even give you some money if you need it. But I want you gone." He heard her sharp intake of breath but forced emotion out of his voice. "I don't know why you're doing this... but I can't have it around Lotty. I can't let you hurt her."

Or me.

"I would never hurt her," she whispered. "You know that. And deep down you know that what I'm telling you is true."

He cringed. He'd been so ready to love this person, to *trust* her. She was either delusional or cared that little for him. "Just go."

Tess choked back a surge of tears. "You don't really mean that."

He didn't want to say anything else, to risk any biting words that might damage her anymore, but if this was the story that she was sticking with then she had to leave. It was his own fault for allowing himself to hope for something good. He shouldn't have let his guard down where it concerned Lotty. This would break her heart.

Heywood looked down, no longer uttering a word. His silence left her with a small cry of despair as she turned back to the barn.

He closed his eyes, heading toward the house. A moment later he heard the mare's hooves on the ground and knew that Tess had left.

He wished he didn't care. Instead a cold and unbearable loneliness possessed him. It was the greatest sense of emptiness that he'd ever felt since Emeline.

CHAPTER SIXTEEN

Tess had never known a worse loss in her life than that moment in which Heywood sent her away.

She hated to admit it, but the truth was that she had barely known her father when he passed. Meanwhile leaving Killian had been a relief. In truth, there wasn't a single relationship that ended in her entire twenty-six years that had made her feel as bad as this.

She'd been spending a great deal of time on her balcony ever since she got home, staring out into the rolling Colorado Mountains and the pretty trees scattered throughout. She didn't mean to become a hermit but couldn't tear herself away from the property. She couldn't stop obsessing over her phone where she'd been flipping through every article there was on the Olive Stem Killer and Heywood Paxton.

Mrs. Corbin came outside, sipping her coffee. She studied Tess with the same confusion and contempt that she had ever since she'd returned.

"Time to pull yourself back together," she finally blurted. "Whatever it is you're holding onto, whoever you were sneaking around with – let it go."

Tess stared up at her mother. There was no way to explain any of this to a woman like Mrs. Corbin. It was a long shot to still be seeking out a serial killer from over a hundred years ago, but if she gave up and did nothing then the man that she loved most in the world would die a horrible death.

Then it all would have been for nothing. It would almost be as though none of it even happened, and he was just gone. She wasn't honestly sure if she could go on in a world like that.

She thought of Heywood, of the warmth in his eyes and the way his hands had touched her, and it made her heart sink to her stomach. The way he made her feel as though she was something great, something beyond all of this...

"Whoever it is, he isn't worth it," Mrs. Corbin muttered, taking another sip from her mug.

"You can't say that," Tess hissed. "You have no idea what he means to me."

Mrs. Corbin didn't seem the least bit surprised by Tess's confession; that she had been right all along about there being another man.

"That doesn't matter," she said, turning her nose up at it. "Your future with Killian Seymour is more important. It *has* to be more important."

Tess shook her head and shot up her naked left hand.

Her mother's eyes widened. "Where's his ring?"

"In my nightstand, waiting safely until I can return it."

"Bite your tongue."

"I already told him. It's over. I don't love him."

She snarled. "I can't believe you're willing to throw this away. And for what? Some mystery man who isn't even around? Who is he?"

"It doesn't matter. I found my place in the world and it's not with Killian."

Her place wasn't with anyone, if not Heywood. Waking up in the barn with him had been the most perfect moment of her life. It was the single first time where she truly felt that she belonged to someone and someone else belonged to her. It was the first time that she ever sensed that she was meant to be with a person, that there was a best friend for her in this life that could make her happy.

The carnal part of them that had enjoyed each other so much was nothing compared to the passion and love and ridiculous emotion that was all so new to her. She couldn't even imagine giving herself like that to anybody else ever again. Just the thought of holding or kissing another man made her heart weak and heavy.

Her phone buzzed on the railing and her mom arched a perfectly sculpted eyebrow. "I wonder who that could be."

Dread laced through her as she checked the name, but it wasn't Killian. "It's Joel," she said, getting up and walking into her bedroom.

"Hey," she answered softly. "This is kind of a surprise, you usually just text."

"This was too much to put into a text," Joel answered. "Are you sitting down?"

"No, but I can."

"I would."

"You're scaring me."

"Okay, so remember how I told you that a sock stained with blood was found at the murder scene of the Olive Stem Killer?"

"Of course."

"You remember what we talked about a while back, about how those genealogy databases work?"

"Oh yeah, the DNA testing that you said was a complete violation of privacy."

"Exactly. Violation of privacy, but a total game changer for detectives. DNA samples are coded into numbers that a computer can read, then those numbers get compared against public genealogy databases. The system is so advanced that the individual doesn't even need to be in a genealogy database themselves, the DNA can be tracked and matched through blood relatives."

"You found something," she exclaimed, too worked up to keep her voice down.

"Not me, but I have access to local investigations, and I saw that the team involved had used DNA recovered from the crime scene to find this person's relatives dated all the way back to the early 1800s."

"You're kidding!"

"I told you, this has been one of those infamously unsolved cases that everyone wants answers to. Ends up, they used this to create maybe twenty different family trees that contained thousands of relatives all the way down to present day. I was looking it over today and one of the forks led to your name."

"*My* name?" That didn't make any sense.

"I told you these genealogy sites save your DNA. When you and Killian sent it in, it connected you to one of the branches on one of the family trees."

"Of a murderer from 1900?"

"Of whoever's DNA was left behind."

"But no possible name of who that person is?"

"If this was a more recent crime, then yeah, they could look through potential perpetrators and gather their DNA to test, but being so long ago..."

"Right, I understand."

"Okay, I just needed to let you know that as soon as I found it. Something to think about. I gotta get back to work now."

"Thank you."

She hung up the phone, feeling more confused than ever. Heywood hadn't died yet in the realm she returned to, so that meant that she couldn't have been there at the crime scene. But could she have already left something behind from one of her previous visits that the killer or Heywood had on them during the attack? That would have been a good possibility if it hadn't been a *bloody sock*.

Was there even a chance that she really was just simply related to the murderer?

Her heart raced thinking that over. Where was this DNA found? At Heywood's crime scene, or was it one of the other murders that happened within the thirty-year span? What if that irresponsible night with Heywood had led to a pregnancy and her child...

She shook her head. That wouldn't have made sense for a thousand different reasons; the main one being that the first murder was to happen any day now. Even if some alleged child committed the later murders, who started it?

She couldn't even think straight and was driving herself mad.

Hurrying down the stairs, she found her mother in the kitchen, refilling her mug.

Mrs. Corbin was startled by Tess barging in.

"Tesla! You should know better than to jump at a person."

"Have you ever done yours and dad's family trees?"

"What a strange question."

"You know what I'm talking about, right? One of those genealogy kits?"

"No, I haven't. But I thought you and Killian had it done."

"We did, but I never got the paperwork from it."

"Well, I'm sure he did as he was the one paying for the thing. Why don't you ask him?"

That didn't seem a smart idea.

"You need to arrange to return the ring anyhow, don't you?" Mrs. Corbin added in her usual snarky tone.

****

Heywood tugged on the brink of his hat, shading his eyes from the blinding sun as he rolled onto the sheriff's property.

Grace must've seen him from the kitchen window because she was on the porch before he and Lotty even climbed off the wagon.

"Hey stranger," she called, veiling her eyes with her hands. "Come on in, I just made cookies."

Lotty wouldn't say no to that and hurried in ahead of him.

Grace held the door open, noticing the crate in Heywood's hands. "What's all this?"

"Just some stuff I thought you'd want back." He carried it into the kitchen and set it on the table while she poured them each a glass of freshly squeezed juice.

"How have you been holding up, Heywood? Anything you need?"

"Can't think of a thing," he said, taking the glass. "Thanks."

"Here ya go," she said, giving Lotty a cup of juice and a cookie. "Our new foal was born a few weeks ago. She's out back if you want to see her."

Lotty would have normally jumped at that, but she just shrugged and walked off. Heywood swallowed down the pang of guilt at how down she'd been since Tess's parting.

Grace went to the crate as soon as she was gone, and Heywood sipped as she rifled through her belongings. Her eyes seemed to lose its vibrancy as she drew out a gown and dangled it between them.

Heywood's mouth went dry as he stared at the fern colored dress with the stitched embroidery and a belt made of leather. It had been the first thing he'd ever seen Tess in. He could still remember how he thought the color brought out the green in her eyes.

Grace draped the gown over the back of a chair. Her face looked ill when she eyed him.

Don't say it. He didn't need her pity. "Just take them," he grunted. "They belong to you."

"It must be hard for you to let go of though."

"They're just dresses."

"I wasn't talking about the dresses."

He furrowed a brow at her. "Tess made her choice to leave. There's nothing I can do about that." He set the glass back onto the table. "Thanks for the drink."

"Hold on, this isn't mine," she called, and he paused to look over at the one-piece eyelet lace bodice she was dangling between them.

"You sure?"

"Well, it is beautiful. In fact, I've never seen anything made quite like it. But do I honestly seem the type of girl to wear something like this?"

"It's undergarments, how would I know?"

"Heywood," she said reprovingly. "These are not undergarments. I don't know what they are."

He scowled, suddenly remembering back to when Tess had shown up to his and Lotty's campfire wearing it.

"This isn't my negligee either," she said, handing him the torn piece he'd first found Tess in.

He closed his eyes, not wanting anymore reminders. "You might as well keep them. The owner of these things isn't coming back for them."

Grace furrowed a brow. "Are you sure about that?"

He curled a lip cynically at her. "I figured you guys would be happy. Finally, the one interfering with my obligation to Antoinette is gone. Maybe you win and I'll sell the land after all." He turned for the door.

"Heywood, stop."

He did as she asked but didn't turn around to look at her.

"I'm *not* glad she left. Tess was a good friend to me."

Heywood nodded bitterly. "Sorry for your loss."

Grace walked swiftly over, stopping in front of him so he had no choice but to look at her. "I know you've been doing your best for Lotty and putting on a brave face for the town. But I don't think anyone would think less of you if you were to confess that you miss her."

He forced a polite smile.

"I'm here if you ever want to talk."

"Thanks," he murmured, but couldn't help wondering if Grace was asking him to open up to her because she really cared, or if she'd been like most others who were just curious.

The sound of heavy boots on the porch had Grace spinning around. "Theodore, you're back early," she called out the door. "You look upset, is everything okay?"

"Just some trouble in town." He sighed as he walked into the house, then came to a quick and startled halt when he saw Heywood. A small puff of smoke seeped from between his lips and he immediately plucked out the cigar.

"Hey, Kid! Glad you're here, we could really use your help."

"Maybe another time," Heywood said, trying to get around him. "I was actually just leaving."

"Oh, come on," he said, blocking the doorway. "Don't be like that, I really need you now."

Heywood ducked under his arm to get past. "Some other time," he said, then rounded to the back to find Lotty.

He could hear Theo following him. "You sure?"

"Quite sure."

Theo shoved the cigar into the side of the house until its tip was just ash. "Some wolves were spotted pretty close to town. If anyone can get them, it's you."

Heywood stopped and turned around. "How many?"

****

The hunting party moved quickly up the mountain's narrow slope. They'd already broken up into pairs, each duo at least fifty feet from the next.

Theo reigned in his horse and began to dig for his canteen. After engulfing a mouthful, he went to toss it over, but Heywood shook his head at the offer, wiping his face with his sleeve instead.

"Find any tracks yet?"

Theo shook his head. "Not a thing. We may be out here a while." He tucked the canteen back away and picked up his trot. "You seem distracted."

"I'm not."

"Is this about Tess? It's a shame she left."

"Well, you can't really blame her. I told her to go."

"You did?"

"I don't want to talk about it."

"Hold on," he tugged the reigns and then reached out to grab Heywood's arm to stop him as well. "What's going on? You two couldn't keep your hands off each other." He leaned back thoughtfully and then nodded with understanding. "I knew it. I knew it!"

"You knew what?"

"She always seemed a little too guarded. Grace could never get any real information out of the girl."

"What are you talking about?"

"That she obviously had some big dark secret to hide! The way she just appeared out of nowhere, and then would disappear just to show up again."

"What are you suggesting?" he said mockingly. "That she was some sort of spy?"

"Well, maybe not anything that dramatic. But I always did wonder if she was secretly married or on the run from some crime spree. Wouldn't surprise me one little bit. As a sheriff I see some of the worst things. Even in this small town there are a lot of people with a lot of grievances they choose to run from rather than fix."

"Theo, listen to me."

"What?"

"She isn't on some crime spree. She thinks she's traveling through dimensions."

Theo scowled.

"That's right. She told me some insane story about how Emeline's tree brought her traveling from the year 2020 to 1900 to save my life."

Theo's shoulders quaked with amusement. "Oh man!"

"It's not funny. It was appalling."

"No, you're right, not funny at all." He burst out laughing until he snorted.

"I'm sorry I told you," Heywood grunted, picking up his pace.

"Oh, come on, I'm sorry," Theo called, racing to catch up. "Well, you can't say she didn't try her darndest with that one. Gave it a good effort to be believable."

"What do you mean?"

"Isn't that the year she originally told Dr. Delacourt?"

"So?"

"And then she'd leave your horses behind in the forest, never taking them very far or hanging onto them for her return."

"Mhmm."

"And the outfits."

Heywood thought again of Grace's comment over the fashion she'd never seen before. He thought of the uniqueness of Tess's shaded blonde hair unlike anyone else's. And even just the things she knew that were otherworldly, like that soap she made to wash her and Lotty's hair, and how to stitch him up, and that strange thing she did to save Lotty's life after she stopped breathing.

Oh God! She wasn't lying, was she? As absurd as it was, it might have actually been true.

But it was too late. She was gone now, and there was no way to find her.

Unless...

Heywood searched for his hunting knife.

Theo looked at the weapon but said nothing until Heywood began to back the horse off the trail. "What are you doing?"

"I don't know why I didn't see it before. She was right, it's the tree!"

Theo shook his head. "Don't do this!" But Heywood had already given Saturn's side a firm kick and they were sprinting down the mountain and into the trees below.

****

Tess's heart beat violently as she listened to her mother walk Killian into the house. She stood up when they joined her inside the sitting room.

"Thanks for coming," she murmured, twisting her fingers nervously.

"Where's my ring?"

She didn't know why it surprised her that that was all he had to say.

Mrs. Corbin ducked out and Tess nodded toward the piano where she had left both the velvet ring box and the extravagant dress that he'd gotten her for the junket.

He walked over to them and opened the box for examination. Slipping it into his pocket he turned around to look at her. His expression showed nothing more than simple disinterest.

She shrugged a little. "Did you bring the file?"

Killian leaned back against the piano, folding his arms across his chest.

His intense stare sent a shiver up her spine. She just wanted this to be over. "I'm sorry for how it ended."

He huffed with amusement, but she could see the anger in his eyes and looked down to avoid them.

"Nothing ended," he grumbled. "You ran away like the little twat you are."

She cringed at the insult. "I just went back home..."

"Abandoning me when I needed you. Making me look like a fool in front of my peers. And then I get a message saying you need something from *me*?"

She let out a tired breath. For a second no one said a thing.

"So, this file," he finally grumbled. "It's important to you."

"Yes," she squawked. "It is. I really need it if you have it."

"I do." His expression changed from one of dark amusement to one of scorn. "Why should I give you something you need when you haven't given me what *I* need?"

She was baffled by that. She thought all he needed back was the ring. She shook her head. "What is it you still need?"

"I need a wife who isn't a cheating skank."

She closed her eyes again, wincing.

"I suppose you can't give me that."

She exhaled slowly and shook her head, just taking whatever he dished out. She had no defense and wouldn't start arguing. Her silence only seemed to fuel his rage.

He began toward her and she automatically shifted back. He kept walking until she hit the wall, and even then he leaned forward, too close. She had to crane her neck to meet his eyes.

She regretted when she did. They were darker than ever, staring deep down inside of her with the foulest disgust a person could ever wear. "What makes you think I'll let you get away with this?"

She sucked in a sharp breath.

He seemed to enjoy that reaction as much as he did his ability to evoke it. "Have I ever been the sort of man to have the wool pulled over my eyes? Have I ever walked away from a problem without finishing it?"

"There's nothing to finish. There is no man around for you to find and take down," she sputtered hoarsely.

"Sure, there is."

"You can't control me anymore, Killian."

"I can't?"

She looked away from him, repulsed that she'd ever considered sharing a life with someone like this.

He slipped his fingers under her chin, trying to force her head back, but she smacked it away.

"Don't touch me. You don't get to touch me anymore."

"Is that right?" he growled, clutching her arm.

Mrs. Corbin must have been listening in because she forced the door open suddenly.

"Everything alright in here?" she asked coldly.

Killian shifted back, his face the picture of impatience and agitation.

"Everything's fine," he grumbled, but gave Tess a wink even as he said it. "We'll be in touch."

He went to the piano and gathered up the dress she left for him. She scurried forward on his way out the door.

"The file?"

He shook his head. "I don't think so, Tess."

"Come on, Killian. It's just a piece of paper."

"But it's important to you, isn't it?" He grinned darkly and walked out.

She stood in the middle of the room, completely stunned. Killian wouldn't give it to her unless he got what he wanted in return. But what he wanted was an obedient wife. What he wanted was to take Heywood down and destroy her for causing him this public humiliation.

Mrs. Corbin was suddenly in front of her, putting her hands on either side of Tess's face and drawing her out of her trance.

"Are you okay?"

"I don't know."

"I saw what happened. I never thought he'd put a hand on you like that. Had I known; I never would have encouraged you to stay with him. Oh honey, you deserve so much better." She pulled Tess into a very uncharacteristic hug and held her until Tess was ready to walk away.

That night Tess sat by the tree, watching the stars. She didn't know where to go from here. Heywood didn't even want her help, he no longer wanted her at all. So why couldn't she just walk away?

Clouds drifted over the moon, and darkness swallowed her. She closed her eyes, knowing she had to move on. With a shaking breath, she put a hand on the tree trunk, grateful for the gift it had given her even if it hadn't ended how she wanted.

Her fingers brushed over a strange groove in the bark that didn't feel natural or right. Taking out her phone, she flashed a light on it and her heart spiked at the carving that had never been there before.

It wasn't the usual thing you'd find carved into a tree like a person's name, or a date, or the initials of lovers. It was just three words cut deeply into the bark.

I Believe You

She smiled widely. It was a message from Heywood. Somehow, he'd figured out how to reach her and she didn't even know what to feel. Relief that the man she loved believed her and loved her back. Despair that she still didn't know how to save him. And always that question of what kind of future they had even if she could.

She still had no answers. Her emotions were running wild and she needed to put them on hold and analyze what to do next. Pulling up her phone, she made a rash decision to call Joel.

"I need your help," she blurted when he answered on the third ring. "Killian wouldn't give me my DNA results and I already called the company who did them. They said they can't hand them over due to the privacy he had set up on his account. Is there anything you can do?"

Joel groaned tiredly. "I can't just subpoena them. I would need a legit court order or valid search warrant. Your best bet if you really want this is to play nice with Killian."

"I already tried that."

"Maybe I can talk to him."

"Would you? That would mean a lot to me if you could convince him."

"I know. I don't understand why, but I know."

****

Heywood reared Saturn again to Emeline's tree. He'd been coming every day while Lotty visited Theo's new foal. He knew it was irresponsible, considering Gabe hadn't shown up for work since the incident and he had no help on the farm. But he needed to reach her, he needed to make sure the words were carved deep enough to last another century.

As he crouched down to begin his work on the bark, he thought he heard the soft sound of footsteps. That wasn't uncommon on a mountain full of animals, but his horse's spooked reaction was.

He immediately spun around and just barely saw a shovel striking out toward his head... then he saw nothing.

CHAPTER SEVENTEEN

It was mid-morning by the time Tess came out of her bedroom. Mrs. Corbin had been just about to knock, and now handed her the large manila envelope.

"I was just bringing this to you," she said. "I found it tucked under the doormat on my way out."

"Thanks." Tess took it and looked it over. Her name was printed with a sharpie on top, but no address. "This was hand delivered, you didn't see anyone?"

Mrs. Corbin shook her head. "For all I know it's been there for hours."

She tore it open and pulled out a stack of papers.

"Oh my God." It was the DNA and Genealogy Reports. A small post-it sat on the top in handwriting she knew too well.

Joel filled me in a little more last night on what's been going on. Pretty eye-opening stuff. I'll give you what you want from me since I've already taken what I wanted from you.

– Killian

She didn't understand his cryptic message but tore through the papers anyhow. Looking through the family tree, she skimmed until one of the last names caught her attention. It matched one of the people she had come face-to-face with from 1900.

The world spun for a moment. She closed her eyes, trying to breathe. This was the one she must have been distantly related to in some form or another, the one who was meant to die but would now eventually take part in a series of murders.

"Tess," called her mom. From the sound of it, she'd been calling her name for a while. "Is everything okay?"

"Do you believe in fate?" she asked, looking into her mother's eyes. "Do you think we are all connected on some level, and meant to find certain people?"

"I don't know. I suppose I always believed your future is what you make of it. Good or bad."

Tess nodded ponderously. "Did you mean what you said before? That I deserve better?"

"Yes." There was no hesitation in her answer, no indecisiveness in her tone like Tess would normally expect.

Of course, her mother might not have answered her so easily if she knew what it was her daughter was going to do.

Now wasn't the time to discuss that.

All Tess knew at that moment was that she had a fleeting shot at saving Heywood and had to take that chance.

She gave her mother a kiss, which Mrs. Corbin reacted to with surprise, then raced to the kitchen. She grabbed one of the knives and headed toward the yard.

I'm coming, Heywood.

She could hear her own loud and frantic footfalls in the wet morning grass as she raced down the property and turned down the beaten path to her treehouse.

She stopped short when she made it.

What she found made her knees threaten to buckle.

The tree was gone.

****

Heywood woke up with a headache.

For a few jumbled seconds, he had no idea what had happened or where he was. As the wooziness wore off, everything that had occurred beforehand came shockingly back to him.

He immediately sat upright, all his defenses kicking in.

He didn't get far, something physically held him down. He struggled against the rope, blinking furiously to get his focus back.

"Who did this?" he shouted. "Who's out there?"

A hazy figure drew out of the shadows. "Welcome back, Mr. Paxton."

He cringed at the muffled silhouette. He couldn't see her but knew the voice well. With a snarl, he said, "Good afternoon, Miss Cavaliere. Where'd you learn to hit like that?"

"Shut up."

He tried his arms again. It was no use. How'd she learn to *tie* like that?

"Upset about something, dear?" he mumbled cynically.

Her open hand cracked against his face much harder than she'd hit him at the picnic.

Blinking angrily, he regained his focus, finally seeing her clearly.

"Don't say another word!" she hissed.

He blinked slowly at her. "Whatever you say."

"I gave up everything for you. My father promised me a future and you tore it away. Do you understand how good I could have been for you? I would have been a good wife, I'd have saved your reputation, and even put money into the farm."

He grunted, searching beneath him for the knife he'd used to carve the inscription. He knew that he wouldn't have much luck with finding it though when he realized how far he was from the tree. He let out an angry breath. "There's more to marriage than that, isn't there Antoinette? Don't you want a husband who loves you?"

"You would have eventually. In the meantime, I could have loved enough for the both of us. Don't get up!"

He kept shuffling, both testing the ropes and searching the twigs for anything sharp. "You wouldn't have been satisfied with that. You want a man to worship the ground you walk on, to cherish you. Why would you even consider settling for something less?"

She shook her head angrily. "Because you and I belonged together, Heywood. But you ruined that. And I told you not to get up!"

"Relax, I'm not coming near you." He flicked his eyes to the shovel laying on the ground a few feet away. "What's your plan then?"

"My plan is to keep you on the ground." She kicked her foot square into his chest, toppling him over. He fell back hard against a tree.

"For how long?" he grunted.

She curled a lip at him, and he saw something in her eyes that made him understand. She was there to end him. Surely, she couldn't have been acting on her own. She would have needed help knocking him out, tying him up, and there was no way she'd ever killed before.

He nodded slowly, taking this in. "You're not alone." This wasn't a question, just an observation. "Who's with you, Antoinette? Your brother?"

She sneered. "Axel isn't a killer."

"But you are?"

She huffed daintily and shook her head.

He winced at that and searched wildly around the area.

Between the trees, a form slowly appeared. He squinted, trying to make sense of it. Who was this person who had hit him hard enough to knock him unconscious, who tied these ropes for her? He couldn't even imagine the kind of human being who would side with this lunatic.

Then he saw him come out of the shadows and it was nothing he could have prepared himself for. This was someone he trusted and cared about. It couldn't be real.

****

Tess stared at her demolished treehouse.

The beautiful trunk she'd climbed since she was six, the knot that gave her an opening to another world... it all lay dead beside its stump where Heywood's last inscription was still visible.

She couldn't think. She couldn't even breathe. What happened... why...

She hunched over, forcing a deep breath. *Hate* filled her veins, making her shake.

This was what Killian had meant when he said he'd already taken what he wanted from her.

She shivered when she felt him walking up behind her.

"Why?" she wheezed. There was nothing else she could force out.

"Joel told me about your so-called portal."

She hated how composed his voice sounded. It was as though what he'd done meant nothing to him.

"He seems to believe that *you* believe it to be real," he went on.

She closed her eyes, trying desperately to keep her breath steady. So, he just wanted to hurt her. He knew it was insane, but nonetheless found what she loved and set out to destroy it.

This couldn't just be *it*. It couldn't be over. Something deep down began to ache. It was a horrible physical pain that she'd never felt before.

Curling her lip, she forced herself to stand upright, to face him. "You unbelievable bastard," she hissed.

He scowled at that, then covered hastily with a broad smile. "I'm so sorry to have ruined your dreams, baby doll. Consider it an intervention." He pulled a cigarette from his pocket and lit it, breathing in the nicotine slowly. "We'll get you help, Tess."

She snarled at him, hating his wonderfully talented way of portraying *ease*. She knew what he was doing… that he was manipulating her. He'd done it so well from the moment they met.

He began to walk casually forward, forcing her to instinctively step back.

"We'll make sure to handle the press with care when we explain the reason for you being involuntarily committed to a psychiatric institution."

Her stomach dropped. She blinked away tears. Hell no, she would *not* cry from anger. That would only make her seem weak, and she was *not* weak!

Steeling herself, she glared at him. "You did all this to save face because I wouldn't marry you? You couldn't just let me walk away, you'd rather have me committed?"

He had no reaction to her question. It was infuriating. Instead he just grinned that beautiful sexy smile that half the world was already in love with.

"You're pathetic," she growled.

"I already told you," he went on smoothly. "I did this to *help*."

"Interventions are supposed to be a gathering of loved ones. This isn't an intervention. This is you against me. This is a threat."

He scoffed at that, and she moved back quicker.

The man wasn't right.

Only just recently she'd seen him truly angry and possessive, and she hated it. She couldn't imagine now dealing with this new level of rage.

She was certain that he'd hurt her if she didn't get back to her house quick. She imagined herself hurling ass through the yard and locking herself behind a closed door. Calling the police… getting a restraining order… being away from him.

"You're right, this isn't an intervention. This is just me putting an end to it," he said, coming closer. "You know, through my years in this business I've seen so many lives end. Shattered careers and livelihoods and even families torn apart. Too many, in fact. Over time I've begun to recognize the dread and anxiety in a person's eyes as it all starts unraveling, just before their life as they knew it is over." He grinned darkly. "I see it in yours."

She gripped the kitchen knife in the pocket behind her back.

"It's time you learn, baby doll, that one way or another I always come out on top."

He shuffled toward her and she pulled up the knife, holding it between them, stopping him.

He froze, but it didn't seem with fear.

"I'm impressed," he said, taking a step forward.

Tess turned the blade in her hand, ready for combat. "That's close enough," she hissed.

"Is it?" He was still smiling coolly as he took another step. Then another. "About here feels right."

He was playing with her. Making it some kind of game.

"Do you really think your family name can protect you?" he asked darkly. "Do you truly believe that *knife* can?"

Her heart shattered. Making a rash decision, she spun around and took off rapidly toward the house.

He caught up fast and grabbed her hair, yanking her backwards. She swung the knife, desperate to start hacking at him.

****

Heywood stared into the eyes of what he thought to be a friend.

This wasn't the Micah Gibson he'd known all these years. This wasn't the pastor who organized family events and encouraged him to join Sunday services when he didn't feel he belonged. This had to be someone else.

"Antoinette came to *you* for help?" he asked shakenly. "And this is how you plan to do it? What happened to God's law of mercy and love?"

Micah shook his head. "You can't honestly believe that I'm the first to kill in the name of God?"

"So, this is a religious war?"

"Oh, Heywood," he sighed, squatting down in front of him. "Do you have any idea how exhausting it is to watch the sins of those around me? To give guidance and not have them met? To watch the world crumble and feel helpless against it?"

"You're sick."

"No, I'm just tired. Tired and ready to dispose of the waste. I've met other likeminded men-of-the-cloth in Colorado who want to clean their towns as well. Maybe this here with you can become the start of something."

Heywood sniffed. He never should have been as blind as Micah's flock. Church people were easy to fool because they were just better folks all around. They wanted to believe in the good in people. A man like Heywood who only saw the bad shouldn't have been convinced as easily as the others that this man was moral simply because he stood behind a pulpit.

"I'm finished hearing of everyone's transgressions, I'm ready now to see redemption."

Fine. "I repent, Micah! I do, I repent of all my transgressions. Show mercy to me, an admitted sinner."

"That's good to hear. Maybe now you will find peace." He pulled what looked like an olive stem from his pocket and tossed it at him. Heywood remembered very little scripture but did know that it symbolized something from the beginning, in Genesis.

Micah stood back up and took the shovel. "Antoinette, you've done a fine job keeping careful watch over his movements for me, but now it's time for you to leave."

She nodded as she backed away.

"Go in peace, sister."

"You as well," she murmured, spinning and running off.

Micah watched her disappear down the trail.

"You're not letting me go, are you?" Heywood murmured, still fighting with his ropes.

"I'm afraid not. You know just as well as I that the only wage of sin is death."

****

Killian sprang at Tess, grabbing the knife from her fist.

She froze when he got hold of it, but he didn't strike her. Instead he held it up at her, waving it between them as though he were a child having just stolen a little girl's toy.

"See this? Huh? You see it?" he tormented. "Are you kidding me, Tess?"

"Calm down," she yelled, holding up her hands in defense.

"You wanted to try to stab me?" He slipped the knife into his back pocket, but his fist came up unexpectedly, punching her square in the face.

She fell backwards onto the grass. The pain exploded like fire from inside her cheekbone.

She felt herself being lifted by the collar of her shirt and blinked up at where he loomed over her. She only saw his hand an instant before it began slapping her over and over.

"You really want to threaten *me*? I can make your life a living hell. I can murder you long before you die."

He let go of her and stood up, fishing inside his pocket until he found a satin handkerchief and flicked it down at her.

"Clean yourself off," he instructed coldly. "And let's be done with this foolishness."

She felt the wetness of blood on her face but didn't touch the cloth he'd offered. He seemed to enjoy this assertion of dominance too much, maybe even the drawing of blood.

He knelt beside her and grabbed the handkerchief, roughly wiping her face himself. "Be a good girl and go willingly to the psychiatric hospital. It would benefit all of us, especially you. You need this."

During her entire relationship with this man, she never thought that he'd turn on her like this but was now certain that he would torture her until she complied.

It wasn't going to work.

When he grabbed onto her face, she turned and locked her teeth down hard on his hand. She would have torn off his thumb if she could. He managed to rip his hand free and then stared wide-eyed at the puncture she'd given him.

Shaking violently, he swung back his arm and hit her harder than he had yet. Her mouth sagged open as she struck the ground again, stars flashing behind her eyes.

The world felt as if it were rocking back and forth. Then she realized she was moving. He was dragging her by her ankle back toward the tree. He must have felt too out in the open here.

"Let me go," she bellowed, trying to kick him with the other foot.

"I will, baby doll," he huffed, pulling her further. "I will."

They had just barely made it to the treehouse when he suddenly stopped cold and searched around them.

It seemed too much to hope for that he had possibly heard someone approaching. Someone who'd seen what he'd done or heard the commotion.

Killian grabbed onto her, yanking her behind the rubble of her treehouse. Crouched nearly on top of her, he had the knife at her throat and his mouth at her temple.

"Steady," he whispered to her as he peeked out at someone walking down the yard.

"What the hell happened here?" Joel's voice asked from the other side of the debris. "Tess? You out here? Killian? We got a call from one of the neighbors about a disturbance, and I said I'd check it out. Is everyone okay? You guys out here?"

Killian sighed heavily. "Don't try anything," he hissed, putting the knife instead to her spine. "If you do, you'll lose."

Pulling her up to stand in front of him, she found Joel walking down the path in full uniform.

He quite obviously hadn't expected them to spring up from the wreckage and did a doubletake at what she must have looked like after Killian's beating. Joel faced them slowly, taking in the scene, a hand lowering to his side where she knew he kept his gun.

"Hey Joel," Killian said in his usual, suave tone. "Doggonit, we *were* making a lot of noise, and for that I apologize. After what you told me, I thought it only appropriate to take down the tree. I suppose Tess came to stop me and got in the way by mistake. Had a bad fall from the debris of the treehouse coming down."

Joel scowled, eyes flicking around the vicinity, studying them. He was a police officer and her friend, she had to imagine that he had an idea of what he'd walked up on.

Joel rested his eyes back on Killian. "You do know that it is illegal to cut down a tree that is not on your property."

Killian gave him that dazzling smile again, and Tess prayed he wouldn't be seduced by the actor's connections and charm again.

"I suppose I just wanted to help," Killian said sweetly. "You know what this was doing to her. I'm more than willing to pay Mrs. Corbin, or the town, double – even triple, the cost of the tree."

"Uh-huh," Joel said, frowning thoughtfully, inching cautiously closer. "Are you okay, Tess?"

Her heartbeat heightened. He didn't believe him. For once he was looking past Killian's influences and focusing on her.

The tip of the knife dug into her back and she winced.

"No broken bones or teeth," Killian said. "I was just checking her for that. Just a little scratched up. A few Band-Aids and Neosporin, and she'll be good as new."

"Okay, that's good," Joel said slowly. "Tess why don't you come over here. Let me look you over myself."

"I don't think so," Killian said, still holding her.

Joel shook his head, fingers closing around the butt of the gun at his side. "Come on, Killian. Let's just walk away from this mess and get ourselves situated."

Tess knew that Joel was offering Killian a way out of this, but felt the knife pressing too deeply into her back and was sure that Killian was panicking.

Her instinct of fight or flight kicked in and she instinctively thrust her heel into Killian's kneecap, making a run for it.

In the corner of her eye, she saw Joel's gun coming up from its holster, but then she felt Killian's hand catching onto her ankle. She was instantly airborne, tumbling over, and falling hard. She saw the tree stump directly below her, she felt the neck-breaking hit as her skull landed at the corner of it.

Then she saw and felt nothing.

****

This was how Tess had imagined it must have felt like to be born – only in reverse.

She landed with a hard thud that pumped her heart in an unusual way and drew an unnatural breath from her lungs. A brilliant light played behind her eyes, and then a flicker of darkness.

She gasped hard, regaining herself.

Her mind reluctantly twisted back to the stump she'd fallen onto and she panicked suddenly, knowing Killian would still come after her.

How had she survived that fall? She had felt the bones break in her neck, but it didn't hurt anymore.

There was someone in her peripheral and she focused on that – on Antoinette running away, down the path.

Her mind scrambled to make sense of that.

Seeing Antoinette meant that she was somehow knocked back to where Heywood was.

There still might have been a chance to save him!

But Cavaliere was not the name she'd found on her Ancestry. It was Gibson – she'd been related to someone connected to Micah Gibson's lineage. Maybe she was a descendant of a cousin of his or a sibling. All that mattered was the name in her bloodline. He was the one connected to the Olive Stem Killer, who should have died in Gabe's fire.

Resisting the urge to just lay there, she forced herself up onto her knees.

She saw the pastor standing just around the tree and knew that Heywood had to be close as well.

She cursed herself for having not figured it out as soon as Joel told her about the olive stem. She knew it from the story of Noah, when God rid the world of evil with the flood. It was the olive leaf that showed the end of the worldwide cleanse.

This lunatic had brought it upon himself to play God, leaving the branch with each sacrifice to symbolize his purification. No wonder he demanded confessions before his sacrifice.

Meanwhile as a pastor who took it upon himself to care for his congregation, Micah would have known more than anyone else about the people in his town.

Peeking out from around the tree, she saw that Micah had his back to her and Heywood was in front of him, tied up on the ground and bleeding from the head. Micah had a shovel in his hand. That must have been what he planned to bludgeon him with.

Tess rarely used the word *evil,* as it had been cheapened over the years, much like the word *love.* But there was no way around it. The closer she got to Micah Gibson, the stronger she felt it pressing down on her, this hateful and wicked spirit inside of him. How had she missed it before?

She was still crawling on her knees and found herself suddenly face-to-face with Heywood's message in the tree trunk. He had made it large and deep enough to surpass over one hundred years to reach her. She touched it, realizing that this must have been what drew him to this secluded spot, and what lured Antoinette and Micah to follow.

The bark looked freshly whittled, in fact. Heywood had probably been in the process when he'd been attacked. That meant there was a knife somewhere. Micah didn't seem to have it. Did Heywood? If so, he'd have already cut himself free. She began to scramble quietly through the leaves, feeling and searching.

"To everything there is a season," Micah began to rattle off, quoting scripture. "A time to every purpose under the heaven."

"You don't have to do this," Heywood hissed. "We can just both walk away from this."

"A time to be born and a time to die."

"Antoinette will always be a loose end. You'd have to kill her eventually too. Where does it end? Who else has to get hurt?"

"A time to plant, and a time to pluck up that which is planted." Micah lifted his shovel, holding it like a batter waiting for the pitch. "A time to kill, and a time to heal."

Tess searched frantically and gasped when her fingers struck something hard in the foliage. Gripping the handle of Heywood's knife, she tiptoed in a hurry down the last six feet of trees toward the pastor's back.

"A time to break down, and a time to build up," he went on. "A time to weep, and a time to laugh."

"We are all sinners, even you," Heywood shouted. "To rid the world of waste you'd have to kill all of us."

Tess moved forward carefully.

"A time to mourn, and a time to dance," Micah finished.

Just as every nerve-ending in her body focused on the knife, the target, and the danger in front of her, Micah suddenly spun around and smashed her with the shovel.

She dropped hard.

"Amen."

CHAPTER EIGHTEEN

Tess landed violently on her hip. He had whacked her left side with the shovel as though it were a paddle and she were a racquetball soaring at him.

The knife had fallen from her grip and she immediately scrambled toward it, but Micah stomped his foot on her hand and took it himself.

She stared up into the blackness of his pupils.

"I know what you are," she finally hissed. "Everything you hope to do in this world will end before you even get started."

He twisted his foot forcefully into her hand and she grimaced.

"By saving you from that fire, I kept you alive," she growled. "So, I have no guilt over being the one who ends you too!"

He furrowed a brow at that and opened his mouth but only took a deep breath.

She waited for him to say something, anything.

"For to me to live is Christ, and to die is gain."

He was quoting scripture again as he looked over the knife.

"If I am to live in the flesh, that means fruitful labor for me. Yet which I shall choose I cannot tell. I am hard pressed between the two."

She tried to pry her hand out from under his foot, but he only pressed it down harder. She attacked his ankle with her nails, even going at it with her teeth like she'd done to Killian's thumb.

"My desire is to depart and be with Christ, for that is far better." He cocked the knife overhead as he said, "Amen".

Tess waited for him to finish it all with one dramatic *Psycho* quality stab.

Then she heard Heywood shouting.

With his hands still bound behind his body he ran at them, dropping down fast to chop Micah at the knees.

With the knife already on its way to strike Tess, it caught into Heywood's thigh instead.

Despite the pain, he gave it all he had, sending Micah into a somersault and slamming him flat-backed on the ground.

The air audibly whooshed out of Micah, but he was scrambling dizzily back onto his feet almost as fast as Tess was. He was distracted searching wildly for the shovel but being familiar with a few modern-day self-defense courses, Tess ran up on him and drove a knee into his crotch.

Micah slacked at the full impact, and Tess rushed at Heywood, ungracefully stripping his thigh of the knife.

Micah had gained back his footing and Tess swung the knife. He blocked it with one arm, upper cutting with the other, which caught Tess in the throat.

An inhuman sound gurgled out of her, like a waterbed ripping open as she choked and fell onto her back.

Assuming she was done for, Micah found the shovel and groped it on his way toward Heywood. He was still lying wounded on the ground and now scrambled back on his elbows.

With a rush of unfiltered hatred, Tess forced herself upright and pounced. Having learned from her mistake, this time she didn't try to slash with the knife. She stabbed it hard between his shoulder blades, then began drilling it over and over until it got stuck.

A howl filled the silent mountain as Micah dropped.

Tess waited until he was still before falling in front of Heywood.

They were silent for a long breathless moment.

"I guess this means that you got my message," he finally grunted, hoisting up to sit against a tree.

Tess breathed out a small breath of laughter and leaned into him. She just wanted to hold him and be grateful that he was okay, but her mind was spiraling through her entire life. She could still feel her death in the twenty-first century and couldn't stop her violent tremble.

Heywood nuzzled her. "Breathe," he instructed gently. "Take a breath."

Why wasn't he holding her?

Then she remembered the rope. "You're still tied up."

"I'll live."

Heavy tears welled in her eyes. He would, wouldn't he? She finally did something right.

Looking back at Micah, she found him bloodied and face-down with the knife caught a few inches into his spine. His shirt was the same color as her hands.

She'd never taken a life before. Seeing what she'd done made her taste bile. She forced herself onto wobbly feet and moved toward the corpse.

"Don't think about it," Heywood urged softly. "You had no choice."

She put her hands around the knife handle and a foot on Micah's shoulder, then yanked the blade forcefully from his back.

With trembling hands, she wiped the blood off on some moss and then walked back to Heywood. It angered her how unsteady she was. She'd been training to be a doctor for goodness sakes! She knew how to handle a scalpel and had seen her fair share of blood. But she'd never been the cause of it. She'd never held a murder weapon and intentionally felt a life slip away.

"Stop thinking about it," Heywood whispered again.

"I can't."

"Just focus on right now. You and me... and the prospect of marrying a slightly battered dairy farmer."

She looked up at him with wide eyes.

He just shrugged.

"I think I'd like that very much," she said with a weak smile.

Reaching behind him, she sawed off the ropes.

His hands sprung immediately forward, cradling her against his body.

****

Eight Months Later

Heywood watched the slightest bit of sunrise slip through the bedroom curtains and fall over his wife's face. It still seemed too good to be true. What could he have ever possibly done right in his life to deserve someone as good and sweet as Tess?

He sat down on the edge of the bed beside her, thinking back to their wedding day, when Lotty and he had made Tess their family.

Truth be told, no one would ever take the place of Lotty's mother, because Emeline was a great mom. But there was one person in this world who could take part in a new family, who could love Lotty and himself like only a true mother and wife could.

When his daughter held her new mother for the first time, the only mom she ever knew... when he had kissed his bride and fastened their marriage... when the three of them danced at their celebration, it had sealed their fates. They were always meant to find each other. Two strangers from different worlds... worlds far more different than anyone could ever comprehend.

Upon reflection, Heywood willfully admitted that it basically took traveling between even dimensions in order for someone to wake the unlovable fool that he was from the depths of his own misery.

It was a miracle. Simple as that.

Though Micah had been undoubtedly evil, Heywood knew without a shadow of doubt that God was not. He had undeservedly brought them together. Heywood would forever be grateful for that.

Watching her sleep, he glanced at the journal that lay open and unfinished on her stomach. He thought of the entries that Tess had begun writing since that first night they'd returned from Micah's attempted murder in the mountains – that same night that Antoinette had been arrested for the crime that had sent the town into an uproar. They may have lost some of their innocence and some of their people, but they gained wisdom and truth, as well as an amazing new doctor with knowledge they'd never have obtained without her.

Glancing curiously at the open page, he shamefully read her newest letter:

March 7, 1901
Dear Cora Corbin
Mom
As I've written in this journal before, and pray to God you will find, I am still good.

I know it's been a while since my last entry and that's only because I've been so busy. I think I'm getting closer to formulating the full structure of Dr. Delacourt's forced respirator. Should I succeed, tell Matthias hi for me.

Meanwhile, Lotty has been growing at an immaculate rate. Her seventh birthday was last weekend and I cannot even fathom that I missed her first six. I had never believed that cliché "love them like your own" until I met her.

It's still so strange to believe that I once thought I could be happy with anything less than Heywood. A lot of me still holds dear to who I used to be when I was with you. And I can't pretend that I am not still haunted by what had to happen in order to get me here. But I'm grateful for it. I'm grateful that I wasn't forced to live the rest of my life never feeling again what I feel when I'm with him.

Heywood and I ended up giving Lotty the greatest birthday gift we ever could – she's going to be a big sister. Mom, your grandbaby is on the way. I don't know what that means for our family tree. Maybe in your time (what used to be mine) I never existed at all. But that doesn't seem to make sense. I feel the more plausible outcome is that our superstar, Killian, is in prison for my murder and you are mourning this.

Please, don't.

Follow these journal entries and find peace in my happiness. Search for your family line at the appropriate time, because they ARE out there. I will continue to pass on the information in this journal so that one day you can find your great-great-great grandchildren.

But until then please be content and even happy, knowing that I am well.

Love Always,
Your daughter
Tess (Corbin) Paxton

Heywood closed the journal and set it on her nightstand.

He always knew that she regretted the way she had to leave her world, but she'd told him so many times that she would never regret what it brought her to. Reading that made him certain it was true.

As more light skulked into the bedroom, Tess stirred.

Heywood stroked her hair as her eyes fluttered open.

She squinted at the sunshine and then smiled up at him, hiding her face instantly under the blankets.

"I told you to quit watching me sleep!" she teased. "It's creepy."

He pulled down the blanket. "Just wanted to make sure you were still here."

She laughed and touched his face, fingers trailing over the rough stubble of his jawline.

"I'm not going anywhere," she said pulling his face down, her lips brushing his.

He kissed her back, then leaned his forehead against her abdomen, kissing where their child was growing.

She stroked his hair softly. "I don't know how we'll ever explain any of this to our children. None of it makes sense, does it?"

He looked up at her and grinned softly. "That's okay. We've got years to figure it out." Climbing forward, he kissed her lovingly. "Years and years."

Cassandra Jamison is an author of Romantic/Suspense novels.

Though originally from Long Island, NY she spent a good part her adult years in Colorado before moving to a small town in Pennsylvania. With the support of her husband and two small children, she is both a full-time writer and an even fuller-time stay-at-home mom.

For more information or to contact Cassandra, visit her at **www.CassandraJamison.com**

If you enjoyed Ripples Through Time, please leave a quick review and follow her on:

Facebook
https://www.facebook.com/authorCassandraJamison

Goodreads
https://www.goodreads.com/author/show/16118099.Cassandra_
Jamison

Amazon
https://amzn.to/2ZcBL5C

Instagram
https://www.instagram.com/author.cassandra.jamison/

Also check out her other books at
https://cassandrajamison.com/my-books
&
https://amzn.to/2ZcBL5C

NOT HER BABY

What if the only person in the world that could save your best friend's life was a baby conceived in a laboratory dish for you to carry? What if you were still in high school? Someone lurking on the sidelines, ready to destroy this so-called abomination, can only add to the complication.

LOVELY SCARS

Snooping on your boyfriend's phone is never a good idea. Collins can't help herself after he unexpectedly commits suicide, but what she finds makes her grateful that he is dead.

THE GIRL BEFORE

An orphaned teenager is taken into the foster home of an older couple, but discovers through deadly mind games that they may be trying to do more than just replace their deceased daughter.

FAVOR OF THE KING

It's no secret that the king is a womanizer and a tyrant, but Emma never expected the price of his help for her dying mother to be her.

UNDER THE STAIRS

The final book her husband wrote before he was murdered suddenly turns up and as Emery reads through it, she finds that the events and characters are too familiar to her own life and may be a warning that her and her son's lives are now in danger as well.